THE HEIGHT OF DARKNESS

JESS RENAE SHERER

ISBN (ebook): 979-8-9885842-0-9

ISBN (print): 979-8-9885842-1-6

Cover design: Leah Hale

Photographers: Velizar Ivanov and Jack Redgate

Editor: Kristy Phillips

To my soulmate, Andrew, and my soul friend, Angie.
Thank you for loving me through all my darkness, and always staying with me until the light is restored.

CHAPTER ONE
JENNA

Cold cheeks. Before my eyes are open, that's all I'm aware of. Next I register the light through my eyelids, then the soft warmth of the bundle up against my chest. I open my eyes, and there's Everett, his long black lashes against pink cheeks. I inch forward and put my lips against his soft skin, which is cold, like mine.

We have to get out of here.

The feeling settles over me like a blanket, originating from nowhere and everywhere at once.

I roll over and touch Travis's shoulder. His blue eyes pop open, wander for a moment, and finally rest on me. I watch as it registers that we're sleeping in the family room, to be near the fireplace, with our babies bundled close.

"Fire," I whisper.

Everett whimpers.

As Travis backs out of the covers, I roll back toward my baby, whose pink lips are puckering as I untie my nightgown. I pull him to me, and he closes in on his target.

"Good morning, bubby." I rub his head, the fine, downy

hair like silk beneath my fingers. His eyes close, and he swallows, his tiny lips a machine.

The popping of the fire as it comes back to life is enough to wake Jacob. His mouth opens before his eyes.

"Is the power still out?" he asks.

He's up on his knees, looking around, surveying.

"Yes, baby, it's still out," I answer.

"Daddy, can I help?" He scrambles out of the blankets, but his foot gets caught in a tangle of sheets, and he falls forward. He lands in a heap, already giggling.

"I need help with this one here. Hurry, it's too heavy!" Travis grasps one side of a thick log, groaning with effort.

I watch as my boys tend the fire, as if this were a normal February morning, as if I could savor the sight of father teaching son. But the light coming through the tall windows of the family room seems too bright, the round arm of the love seat has an edge that's too sharp, and the toys shoved in the corner in haste are a reminder that we aren't having a slumber party. We're in a strange, altered dimension, where our routine is suspended, and our eyes strain under natural light and unaccustomed darkness.

Packing turns into a mad dash as soon as we crank the radio and hear fuzz.

All those cans and boxes of food, bought on impulse because they were on sale, are like discovered gold. Who knew I had seventeen cans of beans, peas, and corn? There's oatmeal and cereal, chips and crackers, tuna, rice, and soup. Two boxes of blueberry muffin mix, three boxes of corn bread, and plenty of oil for more. I wonder how many eggs we have in the fridge. There are six boxes of pasta but only two jars of sauce. We have more crackers than soup, more cereal than milk, and only two loaves of bread. My pantry is now empty.

"Good job grabbing all this ice at the store, babe," Travis says as he transfers our frozen food to a cooler.

Everett, in his jumper a few feet away, slaps at a toy, making it light up and dance. He lets out that deep baby laugh and swats it again.

"How much meat did we have in there?" I ask.

"Plenty."

For a week or two? Three at most? I look at my other tote, the one dedicated to jars of baby food and toddler snacks. It's only half full.

Jacob struts into the kitchen with his cowboy hat perched sideways on his head and his silver toy gun in his hand. "I'm ready to help!"

Surely this won't be more than a few days.

"Mama! I said I'm ready to help!" Jacob shouts.

I feel like screaming, but I close my eyes and take a deep breath.

"Here, bud. Help me load up this cooler," Travis says, and he hands Jacob a box of organic corn dogs.

Raiding the medicine cabinet, grabbing pills and syrups and Band-Aids, I drop them in a box. I fill a canvas bag with the candles and flashlights that are stashed around the house in case of storms. There's a tote dedicated to toys and books and another just for arts-and-crafts supplies. I wonder if I'm grabbing too much, but I don't want to regret leaving something behind.

"Why aren't these in the car?" I ask Travis as I point to the totes.

"They're unnecessary."

"But ..."

Travis continues loading as Everett slaps my chest and squeals, spilling a line of drool.

"Mommy!" Jacob calls from the top of the porch stairs. "I need help!"

"Be right there, baby."

I wait a few seconds, counting them.

"Honey?" I say to Travis.

He stops. "What?"

"Can we please bring those totes too? Just in case?"

"Seriously, honey?"

I look down at my feet.

He sighs. Loudly. "They'd have to go on the roof."

"Isn't that what we got the roof cargo thingy for?"

He rolls his eyes but goes to the garage, comes back with the ladder.

"Thank you," I whisper, brushing his lips with mine.

"You'll pay me back later," he says, grinning.

"Mommy, where's my binky?" Jacob asks from the back seat of the car.

We have to get out of here. The feeling is growing stronger, demanding action.

I twist around as best I can to look at him. The excitement of our adventure has turned into fear. His face is tense, and he's on the verge of tears.

I panic. I haven't seen his blanket. I have no idea where it is. Beauty, our Labrador, begins whimpering behind me and rests her head on the edge of Everett's car seat, watching Jacob. She can't stand to hear either of my sons cry. My head is throbbing. Have I eaten anything?

"Mommy will find it, baby, I promise."

I move the stack of pillows from my lap to the driver seat, extricate my feet, climb out, and go around the car to where Travis is coming down the ladder.

"Have you seen his binky?"

Travis's forehead creases. He stares at the ground.

"Fudge!" I run up the back stairs and into the house; scan the floor, room by room. I finally catch a glimpse of the worn blue blanket thrown under the vanity stool.

My heart starts pounding as soon as we back out of the driveway. No one is outside on our street. No children playing, bundled up and hoping for snow. No lights in the windows. As we come around the corner, a woman is standing in the middle of the street with her long, straight hair flying wildly in the wind and her arms outstretched. She has three coats on, as far as I can tell, and she's shouting, her face contorted with intensity.

"I'm not stopping," Travis says in a hushed tone, his eyes darting to the rearview mirror and landing on Jacob, who's silent and watching.

"We have to," I say.

The woman puts both hands on the hood of our Cherokee, her arms spread, as if in an embrace. She looks through the windshield at Travis, and then her gaze settles on me. She moves around the car and is at my window. I hold my breath as I push the down button, and cold air assaults my face.

"Please help us," she says.

Her eyes look from me to Travis, then back to me.

"My boys are in the car, but I don't have much gas left. It's too cold in the house. I don't have any firewood. I gathered some sticks from the yard yesterday, but it's hard with the boys. They're so young. I can't leave them alone ..."

She looks at Jacob, who's leaning as far forward as his booster straps will allow, and then to the car seat next to him, which is facing backward.

"We just moved in a month ago. I can't reach my husband." Her eyes fill with tears, and mine begin prickling.

"He's in Colorado on business. I ... I have no family here." Her voice breaks as she looks back at her car. "Please."

"How much gas do you have?" Travis asks the woman as tears are streaming down her red face.

"I don't know." She runs to her car in her driveway, gets in the front seat, says something to the children, and then is back, breathless.

"A little over a quarter tank."

I look at Travis. We can't leave her here. What will they do? I envision her lugging two small children around, begging door to door in the cold. I see them in my mind's eye. The children begin coughing. They develop fevers. They cry that they're hungry, and she has nothing to feed them.

"Travis."

He looks again at Jacob's face in the mirror and takes a deep breath, his hands tightening on the steering wheel.

"We're headed to a cabin in the Blue Ridge Mountains," he says. "It has a generator, a propane tank, and well water. It's going to be cramped if my entire family shows up, which I think they will. But you and your children are welcome there. You can follow us up in your car. You should have just enough gas. It's about an hour drive."

"Thank you! Thank you ... I ... thank you."

"It's okay," I say. "Do you have anything packed?"

"No."

I look at Travis. "I'll help her get a few things together."

"Shut off your engine for now, and be back out here in ten minutes. I'm serious. Ten minutes," Travis tells her.

I jump out and follow the woman to her car. She shuts it off and reassures her boys she'll be back in a few minutes. Crammed between their two car seats, they're buried beneath a mound of blankets, with faces tense like Jacob's.

As we go in through her garage, I ask how old they are.

"Mikey is five, and Caden is three and a half. Two years apart, more or less," she says.

"Our son Jacob is almost five, and Everett is seven months and two weeks."

She stops and turns to me. Her blue eyes once again fill with tears.

"Thank you for stopping. Thank you for helping us." She shakes her head, as if she's willing away the scenarios she imagined before we stopped.

I squirm at the display of her emotionality. "It's okay, really. What do you have that we might need? How much food do you have?"

Now she's the one to squirm.

"Not much. We just moved in."

We find a cooler in the garage that's dusty with cobwebs and bring it to the kitchen. In her refrigerator, I find a jug of orange juice, two liters of Coke, an assortment of Lunchables and condiments. I wonder if she knows just how much sodium is in one Lunchable.

"I had to throw the milk and meat away. They soured. But I think the Lunchables might still be okay to eat," she says, wringing her hands. Her nose is running, but she doesn't seem to notice.

"I think we should avoid them, just to be safe."

I suck in my breath as I pull open the freezer. There's a melted tub of double-chocolate ice cream leaking down the bottom shelves, and four bottles of liquor. I'm about to close the door when she stops me.

"Times like these call for a cocktail or two, am I right?"

She takes two bottles of vodka from the freezer and puts them in the cooler. I look at her forehead instead of meeting her eyes, note the three wrinkles there as I say, "Why don't you pack some clothing and toiletries, a few of the boys' favorite things, while I pack the food?"

She nods and disappears down the hallway. I drag the nearly empty cooler across the floor to the pantry. Her meager food supply includes a pack of ramen noodles, several boxes of sugary cereal, crackers, and a half dozen cans of SpaghettiOs. I toss it all in the cooler and rummage through a few more cupboards. They're fully stocked. I look around for moving boxes but see none.

I check the time on my Fitbit, stamping my foot distractedly. Stacks of plastic to-go containers fill the sink, unrinsed and crusty. The trash can is so full I'm not sure the bag can be tied. I check my watch again and walk through the dining room toward the hallway. The table is littered with Cheerios. There's a sippy cup on its side, and a wineglass. A week's worth of mail spills from the center of the table.

I pass a child's room on the right. Above the single bed,

"Mikey" is spelled out in dark-blue calligraphy. A large duffel bag is already packed and waiting in the doorway. I continue down the hall to the next bedroom, on the left. A large suitcase sits open atop a king-size bed. I hesitate at entering a stranger's bedroom. But then again, we are inviting her into our family home. I can hear her around the corner, tossing things in a bag. I clear my throat and enter.

"We really need to go."

She comes out of the master bath, a small travel bag in her hands. She tosses it on the bed's mountain of clothing and zips the suitcase. She looks angry. Her face is red and mottled.

"I'm ready," she says.

I go back to the pantry, grab the cooler, and carefully maneuver down the garage stairs. Travis is waiting at her car and loads her things into the trunk. I look at the time. We took fifteen minutes.

"I'm going to check the house one more time. I'll be really fast," she says, then turns and runs before we can argue.

I open the back door of her car and lean over to see her sons.

"Hi. I'm Jenna." I smile, but only the older one smiles back, tentatively. Then he looks down at his feet. His hair is dark brown, almost black, and he has a large bruise on the right side of his chin. "What are your names?"

"I'm Mikey," he says, and then dips his head to the left to indicate his younger brother. "That's Caden."

"Very nice to meet you both. I'm going to buckle y'all in while we wait for your mommy, okay?"

I reach for the younger boy, but he flinches and pulls away.

His brother puts his hand on his arm and says, "It's okay, Caden. She's nice."

Caden lets me lift him then, carefully, into his booster seat. As I strap him in, Mikey climbs into his own seat and buckles himself.

"Look at you! What a big boy!"

Mikey's face flushes red.

I pull the blankets over them, tucking them around their seats. I can feel Mikey studying me. I smile at Caden before turning to meet Mikey's dark-brown eyes. He opens his mouth, closes it, looks toward the garage door, then back to me. Taking a deep breath, he gives me a tight-lipped smile, then nods.

"Do you want to know where we're going?"

His smile loosens, and he nods several times.

"We're going to a cabin in the mountains. It's warm and has good water to drink. And guess what?"

The boys look at each other.

"I have a little boy too. He's almost your age, Mikey. So, don't worry, okay?"

I nod and squeeze Mikey's knee gently.

"Yes, ma'am," he says.

I close the door and get back in our Cherokee, where Travis is tapping the steering wheel with his fingers, his knee bopping up and down much faster than normal.

"Are they coming with us?" Jacob asks.

"Yes, sweetie."

"Who are they?"

"They're our neighbors."

"And strangers?"

"Well, not really strangers anymore."

The woman comes out of the garage carrying a black leather bag.

"Finally," Travis says as he shifts into drive.

My stomach starts flipping as we approach the end of the neighborhood. So far, we haven't seen any other people—no one else in the street, no cars passing by. Travis stops and looks at me.

"How long till we get there?" Jacob asks.

"About an hour, bud," Travis says as he eases on the gas.

The main road is empty. We pass the grocery store, and I stare, looking for signs of looters. I can't see the front windows of the store, but the parking lot is littered with trash and odds and ends. I see a smashed box of cereal and a solitary can rolling across the pavement. There's not a single soul wandering out there and only one car, right in the middle of all that concrete. The gas station is covered with boards.

We turn onto the highway, heading north, joining the few cars also loaded down like ours. I check the side mirror. Our neighbor, in her silver Lexus, is right on our tail.

I realize I don't even know her name.

CHAPTER TWO
JENNA

When we arrive, the sun is setting; the mountains behind the cabin are cast in blue and gray shadows while the horizon beyond is streaked with orange and pink. I sense Travis's relief at the sight of his mother—at first just her legs—as the garage door rises.

She runs to him and hugs him as soon as he steps from the car.

"Thank God you're safe!" she says.

"We are, Mom, we are." He kisses the top of her head as she reluctantly releases him. "Have you heard from Chris?"

"No, we haven't," she says. Then, spotting the silver Lexus, she asks him, "Who's that?"

"A neighbor who had nowhere else to go."

Kathryn's nose crinkles as she eyes the car over Travis's shoulder.

"She has two children," he says.

"I can see that."

"We didn't know what else to do."

The woman gets out of her car as Jacob begins demanding attention. "Nana! Nana! I'm back here!"

Travis opens Jacob's door and unbuckles him. Everett's whimpers turn into screaming, and I untangle myself from the pillows and bags to get out and open the back door. Beauty jumps out and runs straight to a nearby bush. I can see introductions being made on the other side of the car but can't hear them. Everett's face is bright red; he's wet, hungry, and angry.

I bypass the crowd and go straight for the cabin and the sanctity of Kathryn's bedroom. By the time Everett is drinking happily away, my mother-in-law has found us in her rocking chair and sits on the end of her bed.

"Well, I've heard Kelly's story," she says. "But how did y'all manage to pick her up?"

"She was in the middle of the road, screaming hysterically. So, her name is Kelly?"

"Yes, Kelly. And there's something about her I don't like."

"I'm sorry for bringing a stranger into your home."

Kathryn sighs. "It's what a Christian should do. What Jesus would do. And I'm sure this won't last too long, despite how scary they're making it sound."

When I finish breastfeeding and emerge from the bedroom, Kelly and Kathryn are standing in the kitchen, where Kelly is apologizing for not bringing more food. Coolers are lined up, lids open.

"Oh, that's alright, my dear. What kind of Christians would we be if we let neighbors go needin' in times like these?" Kathryn says. "Besides, you just moved in, right?

Haven't had time to stock the pantry, I'm sure. Moving is so much work! You're lucky my daughter-in-law Jenna was the one to find you. She has the biggest heart of anyone I know. She'd let every stray cat and dog into her house if my son didn't stop her!" Kathryn chortles at her own joke. Then, with her hand paused midair on its way to the refrigerator shelf, she adds, "Not to say y'all are strays! Oh dear, I didn't mean that!"

I can't see Kelly's face, since her back is to me, but she says, "No, of course not."

"Besides, we'll only be here a couple days," my mother-in-law says. "Surely, they'll have the power back up by then. Based on how much Jenna packed, apparently, she thinks this outage will last much longer. Maybe she was hoping for a weeklong vacation." Again, she chuckles to herself.

Spotting me, Kathryn says, "There he is now! That baby fed and happy?" She closes the refrigerator door and heads toward me. "Let me see my baby boy!"

I want to correct her and firmly assert that he's mine and not hers. But I let it pass, as I always do, and hand her Everett.

Jacob comes running over, looking up at her and saying, "I showed him how to roll over, Nana."

Kelly stays in the kitchen but turns to watch us, one hand on the counter, the other on her hip. She must have brushed her hair on the drive; it falls around her shoulders in a beautiful blond sheen. I put my hand up to my own messy brown hair. I have no idea what it looks like. I hadn't even thought to look in the mirror. I spent the car ride playing I spy and Bingo with Jacob to keep him occupied.

Kelly's boys, sitting on the overstuffed red couch, look around the room silently.

As Kathryn makes cooing noises at the baby, Jacob's jealousy expands by the second.

"Nana! Did you hear me? I'm gonna teach him to crawl!"

"Aren't you a good big brother!" Kathryn says, kissing the crown of Jacob's head.

"Jacob, why don't you give our new friends, Mikey and Caden, a tour of Nana and Papa's cabin?" I suggest.

"That's a great idea," Kathryn says. "Show them around, Jacob, while we decide where everyone is going to sleep."

Jacob runs over to Mikey and Caden, who sit very still, hands clutched between them.

"C'mon," Jacob coaxes, and I smile. They stand up slowly and walk around the pile of totes and suitcases.

"I was thinking you and Travis could take your usual bedroom upstairs, and Kelly and her boys could take the upstairs room with the bunk beds," Kathryn says to me as she turns toward the kitchen, but Kelly has moved to the center double doors to the back deck, looking at the view. My mother-in-law says to the woman's back, "You think your boys can handle bunk beds? Or have enough room if they share the lower bed?"

Kelly turns and smiles at Kathryn. "We can make it work. I'm just so grateful y'all are letting us stay in your beautiful home. Such a gorgeous view."

"It is. God created a majestic world for us, didn't He?"

Kelly nods. "Glorious. Truly. Do you mind if I check out the deck?"

"Not at all," Kathryn answers, then turns back to me. "Then, when Lauren comes, they can have the other bedroom on the main floor, with the crib, and Chris and

Amanda can take the downstairs bedroom, and his brood can just camp out in the playroom down there."

"Sounds like a good plan," I say, then grab my first load of bags to bring upstairs. By the time I get to the landing, Kelly is out on the deck, leaning against the railing and smoking a cigarette.

We eat a hurried dinner of deli sandwiches, with frozen chicken nuggets for the boys. After dinner, Kelly wipes Mikey's and Caden's faces roughly with a paper towel and orders them upstairs to change for bed. She goes out to the deck to smoke, while the boys stall, looking uncertain. Mikey takes Caden's hand and leads him upstairs. A few minutes later, Mikey is at the loft railing, softly calling, "Mommy? Mommy?"

Beauty runs in tight circles, stopping to look up at him and whimper. With Everett on my hip, I walk to the center of the great room so he can see me. "What is it, bud? Mommy went outside for a minute."

He peers down at me with big, dark eyes and shakes his head, his dark-brown locks falling into his eyes. He pushes them away with a chubby little-boy hand and looks like he might cry.

"Can I help?" I ask.

"I can't find"—*hiccup*—"pajamas."

"I'll come help you find them, sweetie."

Just as I reach the top of the stairs, Kelly comes back inside. She looks up and sees Mikey standing at the railing.

"Mikey!" Her voice rings out against the high ceilings as she strides across the great room on her long, thin legs. She has me by at least four inches. "I thought I told you to get in your pajamas!"

Mikey whirls around to face me, gives me a timid smile, and runs back into their room. I meet Kelly on the middle landing on the way down. Up close, she looks tired, with dark circles under her eyes.

She nods curtly, her lips in a thin line, and says, "Sorry about that."

"Don't worry about it. He couldn't find his pj's. He's nervous. New place, new faces."

"I should have thought about that and brought them up." She crosses her arms and shrugs. "My nerves are pretty shot from the last few days of worry."

"I can't imagine being without my husband in a time like this," I offer, without adding, *and relying on the kindness of strangers.*

"I don't know what we would have done if you didn't stop." Her face softens, and she looks down at her feet. I get the feeling she's not accustomed to saying thank you.

"I know it's cliché, and not everyone is a believer, but I really try to live by it: What would Jesus do?"

Everett, who has been playing with my curls, winding and unwinding them around his little finger, happily shrieks and gives my hair a hearty tug. I kiss his forehead, saying, "That's right, bubby, What would Jesus do?"

She opens her mouth and closes it, her lips taut again. She uncrosses her arms and puts a hand on the railing. "I guess I should thank God a Christian drove by." She nods again, and I move aside so she can continue up the stairs.

~

When we tell Jacob he gets to sleep with Nana and Papa in their big king-size bed, he squeals and runs straight for Nathan, who catches him midair in his jump. I excuse myself to unpack the boys' clothes and run their bath.

As I suds up Jacob's hair, reminding him for the third time that this is a quick bath with no time for playing, Travis comes to the bathroom doorway and says, "You really didn't have to bathe them tonight, Jenna."

"But they were so dirty. We haven't had hot water in three days."

He sighs and comes over, kneeling next to me on the floor. He picks up a cloth and starts washing Everett, who beams up at his daddy with a smile.

"Why couldn't we take a bath in Nana's tub?" Jacob asks for the fourth time. "It's so much bigger and funner!"

"More fun. *Funner* isn't a word," I say.

"Sure it is. Daddy is funner!" Travis says, winking at him. I bump him with my shoulder, and he gives me that infuriating smile, saying, "You're so easy."

I squint and glare at him, which only makes him laugh harder.

Once the boys are settled in bed, my father-in-law, Nathan, pulls out his small AM/FM radio. It gives us only glimpses of information, the broadcaster's voice skipping in and out between the fuzz.

"Emergency shelters are opening in the next ... we've been assured they'll in ... New York City ... Philadelphia ... Chicago ... Houston ... Atlanta ... all that can be done is being done ... the best place to be ... if you have enough food ... sewer systems are overloaded and water treatment facilities are down ... generator fuel ... officials working ... army and first responders continue to assist ... one who is responsible ... we have sacrificed before ... pull together as a great ..."

I don't realize I'm biting my cuticles until Travis pulls my hand away from my mouth. He intertwines his fingers with mine. I look down at my hand and the half-circles of blood framing my fingertips.

Nathan turns off the radio. He doesn't look at us, but he stares at the fire as he says, "We don't get very good reception up here in the mountains."

I sway when I finally close my eyes and have to put my hand against the tiled wall to steady myself. The hot water is a dream after three days of extra layers of clothing, sleeping four to a bed, and getting a chill any time I left the family room.

When I dry and dress, my legs are weak and wobbly, and my mind feels strangely similar. Yet when I get into bed, I can't sleep, even though my cheeks are finally warm. I'm uncomfortably aware of Kelly's presence, and though I know my level of apprehension is ridiculous, it's there just the same.

I roll toward Travis and strain to see his profile, but it's too dark. All I see is black. It's enveloping me as if it has force, as if it's a presence that can physically bear down on my body. My chest is tight.

Breathe, Jenna, Breathe. In, out. In, out.

But I can't think about my breathing. It's making my chest feel tighter. My throat is closing. My stomach won't inflate, it won't deflate. My pulse is quickening, and my upper lip is sweating. I clench my hands and unclench them. They're shaking. Think of something else, anything else.

I can't wake up Travis. He hates it when I get like this. It makes him feel incapable. Useless.

Everett giggles in his sleep. It rings through the room like church bells, light and airy. My chest expands, and I can breathe again. My eyes fill with tears. *Thank You, God. Thank You. My family is safe. Thank You for keeping us safe. Please, please, please keep us safe.*

I will away the thoughts of all the tragedies that could befall us. I lay my hands flat on the bed; I will not clench them. I will trust in Jesus to keep my family safe.

Please, God, keep us safe and healthy. Hear my prayer. Keep my loved ones safe and healthy.

How long until this is over? How much will we be tested?

Please, God, give me strength. Please let me have strength and courage and grace. Please keep us in Your light and love.

I've asked for too much. We're so much better off than so many others.

I'm a sinner. I don't deserve Your grace. But I thank you, thank you (please keep us safe) for everything You've given me. My cup runneth over.

I whisper three Hail Marys, even though I'm technically Baptist now, and then say, "Amen, in Jesus's name I pray."

Then I mark my chest with the sign of the cross.

CHAPTER THREE

JENNA

The light wakes me as it fills the room. Travis softly snores beside me. I inch toward him, rest my cheek against the soft skin of his back. He knows he's my rock, but he doesn't know my world would crumble without him. I put my hand around his waist carefully, even though he could sleep through a fire alarm. I listen for sounds of others. Hearing none, I relax against my husband.

I still remember the first moment I saw him. I was working at the ice cream parlor on Main Street, since I was too shy to wait tables. The limited dialogue of, "What would you like?" and "That'll be $4.50," suited me much better. He walked up to the window with two little boys in tow, his wavy sand-colored hair mostly hidden under a baseball cap. I would find out later they were his nephews. I was entranced with how sweet he was with the boys, tousling their hair and listening to them with sincere concentration. He didn't say much when he ordered their ice cream, but there was something in his smile and his eyes—the color of a brilliant blue October sky—that made my heart skip and my hands shake.

I didn't think he'd noticed me, but before he left, he asked for my name. That's all he asked. He came again, every week for a month, until finally, he asked me out on a date.

Years later, when I asked him what took so long, he said, "I had to make sure you were the one."

I hear rustling and roll over just as Everett starts cooing. He kicks his chunky legs and grabs fistfuls of air.

"Good morning, sweet bubby." I bring him into our bed, and, just as he's latched on, I hear movement across the hall, then crying and the distinct sound of a slap. I hear Kelly's shrill voice but can't make out her words. The crying stops. Footsteps sound in the hallway, and the bathroom door closes. The bathroom shares my wall, and I can hear Kelly again, that harsh, piercing tone.

"You're five years old! What's wrong with you?"

Muffled sounds, then a thud. A whimper.

My body tenses, and Everett stops sucking.

"Shh, baby boy, it's okay." I rub his head, gentle strokes from front to back. It never fails to soothe him, my sensitive boy. So different from Jacob.

In my head, I hear my mother's voice: *Such a cry baby! Always so serious!* And I see her disdain—how she would lift her chin and look at me sideways, like she could never figure out how she got stuck with me.

Everett squinches as he pulls away from me, pumping angrily at my breast with his fist.

I can't think of her. Think instead of this beautiful boy in my arms.

I hum and rub, focusing on the light still filling the room. Together, our bodies begin to relax. He puckers and finds my nipple as a voice calls out, "Mikey?" Then again, with more urgency. "Mikey?"

"Caden, hush," comes a commanding snarl.

"I'm scared. Where's Mikey?"

Everett fails to latch on and cries outright.

Travis stirs and sleepily comments, his eyes not even open. "Maybe it's time to wean ..."

Exasperated, I sit up straight, pull Everett against me, and bounce him.

"Shh, bubby, shh."

I promised myself I'd breastfeed until he was a year old. I barely made six months with Jacob. With Everett, I promised not to fail again.

Everett's crying dulls to a faint whimpering. Travis begins softly snoring again when more commotion comes from the hallway. I slip on my bathrobe and creep to the door, continuing to bounce the baby with one arm. I hear hushed voices but can't make out what they're saying.

I crack the door just as Caden comes out of their room. His face is wet with tears. He clutches a colorful stuffed parrot with one arm and is sucking his thumb.

I step out into the hallway and kneel down. "Good morning."

I hear rustling sounds coming from the bedroom behind him. He sniffles but doesn't wipe the snot on his upper lip.

"What's the matter, bud?"

He looks back at their room and the half-closed door, then back at me and shakes his head. A pile of sheets lands near their bedroom door just as Everett reaches out and grabs hold of the parrot's bright yellow beak.

Caden giggles. "You want bird?" he says, though he still clutches the toy tightly.

The door to my right creaks open. Mikey peeks his head

out, exposing his bare shoulder. His face, too, is wet from crying.

"Mikey, baby, I'm sorry I'm taking so long," Kelly says as she comes out of the bedroom with a pile of soiled pajamas. She drops them at the top of the stairs. Looking at me, she says, "I'm so, so sorry. He wet the bed. He never does this at home. I don't know what's got into him."

"It's okay. They're still learning, right? Plus, he's in a new place, surrounded by new people."

And how long has he been potty-trained if Caden is still in a diaper at three and a half? But I smile brightly and stand to let her pass. She's not as pretty without her makeup as she was yesterday. Her eyes are puffy and bloodshot.

"Is it okay if I give Mikey a quick bath?" she asks as she reaches the bathroom door.

"Of course. There are towels under the sink."

"Thanks. Caden, come here."

He nods and toddles toward her.

"Might as well bathe them both, right?" she says with a tight smile, putting her hand on Caden's back and pushing him into the bathroom.

I pick up the pile of dirty linens and pj's, then carry them downstairs to the mudroom off the kitchen. The washer and dryer are the one-unit stackable kind, since the cabin is a vacation home. What will happen when Chris, Amanda, and their three children show up? And Lauren and her family? How will this tiny machine wash clothing and bedding for seventeen people? *Don't be silly,* I tell myself. *I'll be home in a couple of days. A week at most.*

Once the sheets are washing, I go out to the deck to finish feeding Everett, grabbing a thick quilt off the couch as I pass. Pulling one of the tall Adirondack chairs closer to the railing, I wrap the blanket around us both and unbutton my nightgown. Everett latches on the moment I get him into position.

After a few moments, he closes his eyes, savoring his breakfast. I turn to the view, the lake so calm it looks like a mirror, reflecting the peaks and color-streaked sky. I wonder where my mother is, and my brother. I feel the usual twang of guilt. I haven't seen my mother since Travis banished her from my life. I shake my head, willing away that memory. I whisper aloud the Lord's Prayer, even though they would laugh at me for doing so. The Bible says we should pray for nonbelievers, enemies, and those who have wronged us. I don't know how many prayers I've said for them both, but they don't seem to be working. The feelings remain unchanged, heavy, and jagged.

I sing softly as I burp Everett, trying to quiet the tremor in my heart that things will get darker before the light is restored.

To distract myself from my own thoughts, I decide to make a big breakfast. I've brought enough food to feed a small army, after all. I strap Everett in his bouncy chair in the kitchen, making a mental note that I need to create a safe space out of everyone's way so he can get in his floor and tummy time.

I start with the homemade biscuits, since they'll take the longest. I roll out the dough exactly how Kathryn has taught me. I remember the day she entrusted me with the secret Covington family recipe—in that moment, I realized I was fully accepted. As I'm cutting the dough in circles, I hear a door open upstairs.

"Shh! Straight to the room!" Kelly snaps, even though I haven't heard a peep from the boys.

I wonder whether Jacob is awake. I place the cut circles of dough on the cookie sheet and figure that he should be by now. Maybe he's snuggling and talking with Nana and Papa. The thought spreads warmly through my belly. I'm so grateful my sons have at least one set of wonderful grandparents.

Once the biscuits are in the oven, I start the bacon. While the first batch sizzles on the stove, I crack sixteen eggs and beat them.

The blackout started while I was shopping. After initially being startled by the grocery store going dark and calming Jacob's fright, I was debating what to do with my cart when I realized I had cash. I made my way to the front of the store, aided by bright-white lights from the emergency generator, to see if they'd close the store or ring people up the old-fashioned way.

The manager stood near the cashiers, his arms waving a bit frantically, as he loudly addressed the confused shoppers.

"We can run approximately four to six hours of transactions on generator power. It will take more time, but we can ring you up, folks, no problem. Please be patient with our cashiers. I'm sure the power will come back shortly."

He glanced around at his employees. "Keep bagging. Ring up barcodes. Your scanners won't work right now."

His employees looked dubious.

"Type in the barcodes. The numbers beneath the lines."

The white-haired cashier near him said, "No big deal,

folks. We'll figure it out!" Then he smiled and nodded at his customer, squinted at the cereal box label in his hand, and typed one number at a time.

Because of the circumstances, Jacob held my hand, standing uncannily still. The manager had moved to a young cashier, who pushed her glasses up on her nose as he showed her something on the register. I moved closer so I could hear.

"The generators are powering the registers, but the automatic scanner won't work. You'll have to type in the barcodes." He repeated the directions with patience, pointing at the label.

Several people abandoned their baskets in the middle of the store and walked out to the bright parking lot. Didn't they care about the extra work they were creating for the employees who were undoubtedly going to have a hectic, stressful day?

Travis had held a home poker game the night before, Saturday, and won big. After Kroger, I was headed to the ATM to deposit cash. I looked at my basket. I was almost finished with my shopping. I looked at Everett, cozy in his plush shopping cart cover. He was only halfway through his Cheerios necklace. I'd seen the idea on Pinterest, and every time I needed to shop, I clipped one to his bib so he had something to nibble on while we shopped. It worked so well I almost forgot how difficult it had been with Jacob, who would toss his pacifier or toy or both to the ground twenty times before I could get through produce.

I imagined Travis at his buddy's house, both men yelling at the TV as soon as the Falcons game turned to a black screen. I wondered how long he'd wait out the outage before coming home.

I didn't want to admit it, but I'd come to resent Sunday

football. Why couldn't he stay home to watch the games? Why did he always have to go to Mason's house to watch it and drink beer with his best friend? Couldn't Mason come to our house every once in a while? I'd changed my shopping day to Sundays during football season, after church, so I had a distraction from the unwanted desire to scream at my husband. As their little routine took hold, I'd initially cooked extravagant Sunday-night dinners. But I learned that a full day of beer drinking didn't create a healthy appetite for Travis, so I switched tactics. I shopped and baked instead. I'd take a picture of whatever scrumptious new dessert I'd created and text it to him, motivating him to come home to us. I've never seen a sweet tooth like my husband's.

I pulled Jacob along with me, trying to maneuver the cart with one hand. "Come on, buddy. Let's finish our shopping, go home, and bake!"

I put his hand on the cold metal side of the cart. He looked up at me with his father's bright-blue eyes, searching my face.

"Everything is fine, baby. We're going to finish our shopping and go home."

Where was I? What do I still need to get? The dairy aisle. I'd been headed to the dairy aisle.

"Will the lights be off at home?" Jacob asked.

"I don't know, buddy. Probably, though."

A deep crease formed between his eyebrows.

"It'll be okay. We'll light some candles."

He trotted along beside me, and as we neared the dairy aisle, he said, "Candles are little. I'm scared of the dark."

"We'll use our new flashlight set we got for our camping trip! Those are really bright!"

I grabbed a gallon of milk, and as I was putting it into the cart, the emergency lights flickered.

Jacob's arms shot up. "Hold me, Mommy."

His eyes were filling with tears.

I grabbed him and held him close. "Shh, sweet boy, it's okay." I rubbed Jacob's back. He was sweating.

I grabbed another gallon of milk. If it went to waste, it was only a few dollars. I continued down the aisle, one hand under Jacob's bottom, the other straining to push the heavy cart. Everett started whimpering. He has a knack for knowing when I'm upset, but when Jacob is upset, he quickly goes from calm to hysterical. I forgot exactly what I needed, so I just grabbed two, three, and even four of our normal staples. Butter, eggs, cheese, yogurt. I circled back to the meat aisle, grabbed more bacon, beef, and chicken.

I could already hear Travis's criticism in my mind as I grabbed extras.

"Why?" he'd ask, his arms crossed against his chest.

"Just in case," I'd answer.

"In case of what?" he'd question, unable to understand.

There's no way to explain how sudden disaster is to someone who's never known it.

I wondered how much gas we had for the generator.

Another circle, back to the frozen aisle. While loading three bags of ice, I was asking myself if I should stock up on canned goods. Just in case.

Everett's whimpering turned to crying as Jacob buried his face in my shoulder.

Time to go.

~

I place a thin layer of Saran Wrap over the bowl of eggs and place it in the fridge. They'll be the last thing I cook. Using tongs, I pick the second round of bacon from the pan and put the pieces on their layer of paper towel. I peel another slice of raw, pink bacon. It sizzles and pops as I place it in the pan. The rich maple smell fills the kitchen. Tiny dots of hot grease hit my chest as I hear another door open upstairs.

I hear Kelly's voice, but I can't make out what she's saying. The door closes again. I look down at my bathrobe. I hadn't thought to change after feeding Everett.

I picture Kelly eyeing my sagging, milk-heavy breasts. I quickly peel the last few pieces of bacon, take a glance at Everett—happily fingering a bright, blinking toy—and scamper across the kitchen and family room in my slippers. Once in our room, I slip on my bra and rummage through my suitcase for my sweatpants. Throwing a sweatshirt over my head, I consider brushing my hair but decide against it. What would Kathryn think if she came out and saw Everett unattended near a stove sputtering hot bacon grease? Resigned, I smooth my hair with my hands as I hurry back to the kitchen.

~

"Jacob, do you smell that feast?" Kathryn says as she emerges from her bedroom.

He runs across the family room to me.

"Be careful, baby, the oven is hot," I say as I'm pulling out a cookie sheet.

"Did you make Nana's biscuits?" Jacob asks.

Kathryn, in blue jeans and a pretty peach sweater, nods

approvingly as she smooths a wayward blond strand in her chin-length bob.

"I did." I set them on the hot plates on the counter. Jacob stands inches away, face tilted up to smell them, an adorable concentration wrinkle between his brows.

"Mm, Mommy, they smell so good!"

"I hope they turned out as good as Nana's." I pull the second tray from the oven.

"Of course they did," she says. Then she goes to the stove, where I've turned the sausage gravy to a simmer.

She's taught me how to cook all of this. My mother showed me how to use the microwave.

"All I have to do is the eggs," I say as I move toward the fridge.

"Why don't you go get freshened up? Jacob and I will set the table." She leans over Everett, making soft sounds. He gurgles and slaps his thighs.

My cheeks burn as I retreat upstairs.

Travis says, "Hey, baby. Is that bacon I smell?"

I'm looking in the mirror above the dresser, applying mascara. My hair was a frizzy mess, so I plaited it in a French braid.

"Yes, darling, it is." I wiggle my hips so that my ample butt shakes back and forth. It's the one part of my body I know he adores, without a doubt, no matter its size. He's sitting up in bed as I turn around, his fuzzy chest appearing from underneath the sheets. I rub my hand across his matte of hair as I lean in for a kiss. "I'm about to start the eggs, so hurry up."

"Everyone else up?"

"Your mom and Jacob are. Kelly and her boys were up early." I start whispering. "Mikey wet the bed." I remind myself to put the sheets in the dryer. "She bathed them, and they haven't come out of their room since."

"We should probably knock on their door and let them know breakfast is ready, in case they went back to sleep."

I'm about to ask him if he'll do it when I picture her standing in the kitchen yesterday, hand on hip, gorgeous blond hair falling around her shoulders.

"Okay, I'll do it," I say as I lean in for one more kiss.

We're all sitting down for breakfast. A round table has the disadvantage of making it possible to see everyone's faces at once. I prefer rectangular tables, where I can avoid the gaze of all but a few. Thankfully, Kathryn places Travis next to me. His solid presence comforts me, quiets the noise in my mind. Kathryn subtly orchestrates assigned seats for every family meal. She sits between Travis and Nathan, always. She only relinquishes her spot if a grandchild asks.

But Jacob has been seated next to Mikey and is excited to have a new friend. Nathan, oblivious, sits between Kathryn and Kelly, approaching breakfast with the same manner he applies to every task: deliberate, conscientious, and silent. I often wonder if he hears anything at all, or if he hears every word and is too busy keeping a catalog to comment.

"Do you live here full-time?" Kelly asks.

"No, this is our weekend getaway. I haven't retired yet." Kathryn takes a bite of biscuit. "Mm, Jenna, you made them perfectly."

My chin goes toward my chest instinctively, but I stop midway and look up instead. "It's your recipe."

"This is quite the five-star breakfast," Kelly says. I've noticed she's moving her eggs around instead of eating them. "What do you do?" she asks Kathryn.

Travis is shoveling his food into his mouth, his plate half empty. A small bubble of satisfaction rises in my chest. God, I love feeding him.

"I'm a nurse," Kathryn says. "In a small family practice, part-time."

"Before she semiretired, she was the head nurse," Travis says. "ER."

Kathryn swats his shoulder, smiling.

Everett bangs on his tray. What's left of his eggs and biscuit is smeared in a gooey, slimy layer across the white plastic. I break off an edge of my biscuit and put it in front of him.

"Daddy, can we go fishing?" Jacob asks. "With our new friends?" Then he sticks nearly half a biscuit in his mouth. He looks from Travis to Mikey to Caden. "Pweez?"

Mikey giggles. Jacob chews vigorously. "Pweez?" he tries again, but there's still too much biscuit in his mouth.

Travis laughs, fork midway in the air. "Sure, bud. Later this afternoon we'll go fishing. Y'all will have to dig for some worms, though."

Jacob nods, his little chin bobbing. He chews frantically, hands in the air. I don't know how he manages to move so many parts at once. There's a loud swallow, and, finally free of the biscuit, he turns to Mikey. "Ooh, that's the best part! Wanna dig for worms?"

Mikey nods, and a bit of egg flies off his chin and onto his pants. He doesn't notice. His face is beaming.

"I've got your shovels and buckets in the garage," Kathryn says.

"After breakfast, you boys can go on a worm expedition!" I say.

Mikey tilts his head and asks, "What's that?"

Jacob leans in and says, "Mommy *always* says that word. It means it's going to be fun!"

Everyone chuckles.

The front door opens. Kathryn is out of her chair and nearly running. Lauren, with her three-month-old cradled in her arm, comes around the corner as Kathryn crosses the family room. My mother-in-law throws her arms around them awkwardly, her five-six frame dwarfed by Lauren's six-foot height.

The scene sparks fear in me; Kathryn normally reserves her big hug for Travis. Her worry is now confirmed.

Nathan sets down his fork. He doesn't rise until Kathryn has released them, and then he does so slowly, one large hand on the table to help himself up. He lumbers toward them, then silently encases them, Lauren with her head resting on his chest, her eyes closed.

Her husband, Brent, enters next, laden with bags.

"Thank you, Jesus. Y'all made it here safely," Kathryn declares. "Y'all hungry? We've got biscuits! Maybe a few eggs and bacon left."

"We've already eaten," Brent says as he shrugs off their luggage.

Travis tosses his last bite of biscuit into his mouth and rises, carrying his plate to the sink. "Y'all got more than that, right?" he says as he approaches Brent and shakes his hand.

Lauren releases her dad, and the three men head outside.

"Looks like a five-star breakfast requires a five-star cleanup," Kelly says as she stands and collects plates. Since I saw her earlier this morning, she's pulled her hair into a ponytail and put on a gym outfit: black yoga pants with neon-pink designs along the sides, with a pink-and-black top, completed with screaming neon tennis shoes. She's intolerably thin, making me regret the two biscuits I've eaten.

I sneak away from Everett to give Lauren a quick hug. "So glad you made it," I manage between Kathryn's questions.

"What was your neighborhood like?" she asks. "Did you talk to anyone? How did the stores look on your way here?"

I listen to Lauren's answers as I head back toward Everett, grabbing the baby wipes off the kitchen island as I approach him.

"Most of our neighbors are staying put. Brent thought we should stay home, but I wanted to be with family. He says we packed all our things just to go home tomorrow."

As I'm wiping Everett's face and hands, Lauren continues. "When Brent saw so many stores with boarded windows, and the empty parking lots, I think he agreed that a few days at the cabin was a good idea. Remember that really old gas station near our neighborhood? It was still open! The old man who owns it was sitting outside in a chair with his shotgun across his lap. We stopped to chat with him for a bit. He didn't have much left on his shelves."

"Did you see any looters?" Kathryn asks.

"No, none at all. Just boarded-up stores. But we took back roads mostly."

Kelly is at the sink, rinsing plates. The three boys are still at the table finishing their food, a radius of eggs, bread, and bacon on the table, the floor, their chairs, and themselves.

"I'm so sorry, Kelly, where are my manners?" Kathryn says as I pull Everett from his chair. "This is my daughter, Lauren, and my granddaughter Kaitlyn." Kait is already in her arms, and Kathryn turns so Kelly can see her face. Kait's tufts of wavy ginger curls, just like her dad's, have nearly doubled since last I saw her.

"She's beautiful," Kelly says.

"Thank you," Lauren replies. "Um, don't mean to be rude, but who are you exactly?"

Kelly's mouth flaps open and closed as she searches for an answer. Kathryn answers for her. "She's Travis and Jenna's neighbor. And these are her sons, Mikey and Caden."

Lauren gives her mother a questioning look before turning to smile at Kelly. "It's nice to meet you," she says, strolling toward the table and grabbing a biscuit.

"You too."

"The dishwasher is here, dear, if you don't mind," Kathryn says to Kelly as she comes around the island and motions toward it.

"Where's your family?" Lauren asks Kelly while buttering her biscuit and looking at me.

Kelly is leaning over, putting plates in the dishwasher. As she straightens, Nathan comes in carrying a load of suitcases. He strides toward the women and says, "I'm sorry, ladies, but I think we should hand-wash for the time being."

Kathryn puts her hands on her hips and turns to him. "Are the men going to be doing the dishes?" she asks.

Nathan sighs. "The propane tank is at 50 percent. We get it filled every two and a half years."

"I know that," she replies. "Which is why 50 percent should be plenty."

"But we're only here on weekends, typically. And typically it's only the two of us, or even eight of us, at a time. We've never spent more than two weeks straight here. I'm just not sure how quickly we'll run out with this many people."

"We're only going to be here a few days, a week at most. I'm sure we'll have plenty to last us months." Kathryn waves her hand at Kelly to continue, but Kelly stands still, plate in hand.

"I think we should err on the side of caution, Mom. The men can help with the dishes," Travis says. I want to hug him. I agree with Nathan.

"Speak for yourself," Nathan says, but he smiles at Kathryn and shrugs. Travis has settled their argument. Kathryn always agrees with her favored son.

"Should we start rationing food then too?" she asks Travis.

"I don't know if we should go that far," he says with a chuckle. "I don't wanna fight Lauren for the last biscuit."

"Oh, you!" Lauren throws a chunk of biscuit at him.

Travis puts his hands up in defeat. "I don't want to return to childhood, all I'm saying."

Everyone chuckles. A common family story told around dinner is from Kathryn and Nathan's "poor" days, when the children fought for second helpings and there wasn't quite enough to eat. It's hard to imagine, since Nathan's company employs four people and Kathryn was a head nurse at the hospital.

As I reach Everett's bouncy seat, Travis stops me and takes him. I go back to Jacob and Kelly's boys with my baby wipes in hand.

Lauren sits down at the table, her blond hair cut fashionably short like her mother's, and looks at the boys. "And what are your names again?"

Caden looks to Mikey to answer.

"I'm Mikey. This is Caden."

I've finished with Jacob's face and hands. He hops off his seat and runs to Aunt Lauren.

She scoops him onto her lap and gives him a hug. "My lovebug," she says, tickling him. Then, turning to Caden and Mikey, she says, "Nice to meet you. My name is Miss Lauren."

I'm finishing up Mikey's hands, then shift toward Caden. He flinches as my hand nears his face. I look at Lauren, whose eyes widen. She raises an eyebrow. I frown and shake my head but switch on my smile as I turn back to Caden. His hair isn't dark like Mikey's. It's bright blond like his mother's. He has his back pressed against the chair, getting as far away from me as he can.

"It's okay, sweetie, just going to wipe your face," I say.

He holds his hands together in his lap and looks down at them, considering. Then he lifts his chin and meets my gaze. His eyes are haunting—a deep, dark blue. But there's something else about them—like he's searching for a safe place to land. He nods, and I take it as a sign that he's given his permission. I wipe his mouth, cheeks, and chin as gently as I can.

"Can I do your hands now?"

He nods again and looks down at his hands as he holds them out for me. I wipe his tiny fingers and realize he seems small for his age. How old is he again? Three and a half?

"You're all done, bud," I say. But he doesn't move, staying in his seat and clasping his hands again in his lap.

Mikey rests one hand on his brother's shoulder.

"Aunt Lauren, we're going fishin'! With my new friends!" Jacob says, still in Lauren's lap.

"How exciting!" she replies.

"Mommy, can we dig now?" He slides off Lauren's lap and pretends to hold a shovel, making digging movements. "For worms?"

"Let me finish cleaning up breakfast first," I tell him. "How about you show Mikey and Caden your Lego set?"

"Ooh, yeah!" Jacob shoots across the family room at breakneck speed. He stops so suddenly he slides several feet in his socks on the hardwood floor, lands on his bottom, and throws his head back in laughter. "That was fun!" He jumps up, runs back and forth, and slides again.

Mikey's and Caden's heads move back and forth, watching with wide, envious eyes.

"Not in the house, buddy. Too many people around to knock into. We'll run around outside later," Travis says.

"Yes, sir," Jacob says, stopping mid-run. He scratches his head. "Where are the Legos, Mommy?"

I'm on my hands and knees with a wet paper towel, wiping up their crumbs. I sit back on my heels. Where did I put them?

"They're in the mudroom, sweetie. Back left corner." I get the last few crumbs and stand. I grab the last three plates and bring them to the kitchen, where Kathryn has produced a drying basket for the dishes, one I've never seen before. Kelly is almost finished with the plates. "They're big Lego pieces," I say, as I hand her the last dishes. "No choking hazard."

Kelly looks up, almost startled, like she was in a trance. "Oh, okay." She takes the plates and nods but doesn't look at me.

Once I pack up the leftovers, I offer to finish up.

"Thank you." She thrusts her shoulders back like she's shrugging off a burden, then touches her low back with one hand. "I forgot how much work that is."

She wipes her hands and looks at me. Her eyes are a shade or two darker than my husband's. She says, "You're an amazing cook," as she hands the towel to me. "I've never had the patience for it."

"Thanks."

"Thank you for taking over. I'd love a cigarette about now."

As she gets to the door, Nathan says, "I put a tin can out there for your butts. Please don't throw them in the woods."

~

The three little boys carry plastic buckets—two orange, one green. Jacob is the tallest, though younger than Mikey, and is leading the way, pointing.

There's a small clearing of flat land next to the cabin. Beyond that, the land is forested and slopes down steeply to the lake. The level area has patchy grass and open dirt—Georgia red clay.

Kelly walks silently beside me. She's put on a black jacket that matches her black-and-pink yoga pants. She must be cold in that outfit. I'm in a thick sweater and my favorite pair of worn, comfy blue jeans. I'm so glad they fit again. Jacob resisted wearing his wool hat, so I put mine on too.

"This looks like a good place," Jacob declares and starts digging.

I'm carrying a bucket of fresh water and Kathryn's watering can, which contains soapy water. The boys know their first job is filling their buckets halfway with dirt.

"Is your husband tall like you?" I ask as I look up slightly at Kelly. I'm five foot three, and I'm guessing she's around five eight.

"I don't really consider myself tall," she says, looking toward me. "But I guess compared to you." She smiles. "No, he's not tall. He's barely six feet."

"You said he was in Colorado on business, right? What does he do?"

She looks out toward the lake. "Yeah, business," she says, pulling a cigarette out of her jacket pocket and lighting it.

"Mommy! I found one already!" Jacob holds up a squirming worm with pride.

"Good job, buddy! Y'all have enough dirt?" I bend over to look in their buckets. "Good job, boys."

"But we've only found one worm," Mikey says from where he squats on the ground.

"Let's try that big spot over there," I say, pointing.

Jacob charges ahead of me, but Mikey digs on, determined.

"C'mon guys!" Jacob looks back and hollers, much too loudly.

Mikey looks up, looks back at his hole, and reluctantly stands, taking his brother's hand.

Kelly walks away from us to where the ground slopes off and looks out at the mountains. As she stands with one hand on her hip, a line of smoke lingers around her head before snaking up into the air.

"Watch the magic," I say and start pouring the soapy water over the dirt. Little soap bubbles glisten in the sunlight.

Caden drops his bucket and squats to get a closer look. "Bubbles!" He looks up at me with a wide smile.

"That's not magic, that's just bubbles," Mikey says, cocking his head and looking at me like I'm no longer to be trusted.

"But it is magic. Just wait," Jacob says, and he squats beside Caden, studying the dirt.

Mikey looks back at his mother, her back turned to us. She pinches off the burning end of her cigarette, and then flicks the butt into the woods.

Mikey looks at me, and I smile and squat next to the boys. "Any minute now."

One by one, tiny little worm heads start wriggling to the surface.

Mikey leans over. "There are so many!"

I point to the bucket of clean water. "Before you put the worms into your own buckets, we'll need to bathe them first in that water there. We need to rinse the bubbles off, or it will make them sick."

"We don't want sick worms," Jacob says. "Then the fish we catch will be sick too."

I chuckle at Jacob's logic. I want to pull him close in a hug and smother him with kisses, but I resist. He'll only squirm away. I hope it's just a phase.

"Mommy!" Mikey shouts. "Mommy! Come look! There's so many!"

"In a minute!"

Mikey turns his attention back to the worm cupped in his hand. He lowers the worm until it's barely covered with water and rubs one small finger up and down its body.

"Can worms drown?" he asks me.

"They can. But it takes a long time. They can swim for days."

"Really?"

"Yep"

"So I can let him swim?"

"Yes, you can."

His whole body shakes for a minute as he lets the worm go. It wriggles around in the water, just like Mikey in his excitement.

Jacob and Caden scoot closer to watch.

Kelly saunters over, hands on her hips. "This is really a beautiful piece of property. That view," she says, looking over her shoulder. "It's breathtaking."

"Mommy, my worm is swimming!" Mikey says.

I stand up so she can get a look. She glances down and says, "Awesome. He's really swimming. Don't get too dirty. I just washed y'all up this morning."

"Mommy! Mommy!" Caden says, "Look! So many!" he points to the ground, where the worms slide over each other and the orange-red soil.

"There must be hundreds," she says. Then she looks at Caden. "You should count them."

"He can't count that high yet," Mikey says, scooping his worm from the water.

"Can you?" She juts her hip out and leans over. "Can you?"

He drops his eyes to her knees. "No."

"And why not?"

"I can count to one hundred," he replies proudly. "Not everybody in class can. But I can."

"So can I!" Jacob pipes in from his spot by the water bucket.

Kelly straightens, looks at her Fitbit.

"But you're not in kindergarten yet," Mikey says, plopping his clean worm in his bucket and eyeing the ground to find another big one.

"We have our own preschool, and Mommy is the teacher. Ooh, and we go to camp on Wednesdays, where we get to play in the woods." Jacob looks at me. "Will we go to camp this week, Mommy?"

"Buddy, today is Wednesday," I tell him.

"Really? Already? When did the lights go out?" he asks.

"Sunday," I answer.

"They've been out a really long time."

Mikey comes to the bucket and drops a fresh worm in the water. "A really long time," he says.

Mikey looks over at his mother while Jacob asks, "How long will they be out?"

Kelly puts a hand up to shield her eyes, again. She blinks rapidly a few times, then closes them.

"Oh no, Mommy, not another one," Mikey says and reaches for her hand.

"Just the lightning so far, but I'm afraid so." She shifts her head in my direction and says, "Migraines. Always worse when I'm stressed."

"Lauren gets migraines too. We've got Excedrin if you need it," I offer.

"I have medicine, prescription, but thank you. Sometimes just an hour in the dark is enough. Boys, we need to go to our room now."

"But, Mommy," Mikey says, tugging her hand and looking at Caden's crumpling face, tears gathering in his own eyes.

"I can watch them," I offer.

"I don't want to put you out. I just need to go now, before my vision gets worse. If I wait too long, I'll be useless for hours."

"It's no problem, really. Go. Get out of this sun." Then I

turn to her little ones. "That sound good with you boys?" Caden looks from me to his mom to Mikey. Mikey nods.

Kelly sighs. "Be good boys."

"Yes, Mommy," they say in unison.

"I mean it." She turns toward me, with squinting eyes, even though her hand still shields them. They look icy blue. "Thank you so much. I hate to miss all the fun."

For a moment we watch her walk away, ponytail swinging. I ask Mikey, "Does your mommy get a lot of migraines?"

He rolls his eyes. "Lots and lots." He puts his hands on his hips, watching her, then turns to me and shrugs. "Didn't have to walk her to her bedroom this time, like a gentleman."

"Well, that's very sweet of you to do for your mommy when she doesn't feel well."

Caden and Jacob are plucking their clean worms from the water. Mikey squats and picks up a worm, turning it over in his hand. "Just wish it wasn't all the time."

I send the men, boys, and dog to the lake with a cooler of sandwiches, snacks, and Gatorade. Caden is yawning as they leave, and I wonder what his nap schedule is. But Kelly is still in her room, and I don't want to bother her.

Kathryn, Lauren, and I stand on the back deck and watch them disappear into the woods. There's a trail that winds around the left side of the cabin, crisscrossing back and forth through the steep terrain. I have a feeling Travis will return with Caden sleeping in his arms.

Everett whines.

"Time for lunch," Kathryn says.

A cold wind picks up and rattles through the trees.

"I think I'll feed him by the fire," I say.

We go inside and pick our spots in the great room. I peel off my wool sweater and sit in Nathan's recliner, nearest the hearth. I unbutton my shirt halfway, drape a blanket over my shoulder and half of Everett's head, then neatly tuck it around his face.

"You know, it's just the women now. You don't have to cover yourself," Kathryn says as she settles in her plaid recliner next to me.

I blush. "I know."

"So modest." Kathryn smiles at me. "It's not a bad thing, my dear. Not at all."

Lauren sits on the plush red couch, kicks off her shoes, swings her legs up, and stretches them out. Kaitlyn is napping in her crib.

"So, what do we know about this stranger in our house?" Lauren asks.

"I'm beginning to regret letting her follow us," I say in a hushed tone. "Except for the boys. They're so sweet."

"They are very sweet and well-behaved," Kathryn adds.

"Almost too well-behaved," I reply.

Both women nod in agreement.

"Where's her husband? I saw a very large ring on her finger," Lauren says.

"She said he's in Colorado on business. I asked what he does, but she didn't answer." I pause, trying to recall the moment. "Actually, she might have answered, but one of the boys said something to interrupt us, and she lit a cigarette."

"She didn't smoke around my grandson, did she?" Kathryn asks, crossing her arms and staring at me in one frightful, fluid motion.

"No, no. She walked to the edge of the clearing." I picture her standing there, tall and poised, crowned by tendrils of smoke. I picture Mikey's face after she walked away, the slightest strain loosening, though not all of it. But he stopped looking in her direction once she was gone, and stayed with us while we scooped in the earth with our hands and wondered over its creatures.

"Well?" Lauren says, crossing her arms. "You didn't get any more info? About her husband? Who she is? Nothing?"

I picture her flicking her cigarette butt into the woods. I shrug. "The boys were pretty talkative. She did say he was six feet tall."

"Shorty Jenna has to find out his height before anything else," Lauren says, picking up a pillow and pretending she's going to throw it.

"I asked what he did. She just didn't answer!"

Kathryn puts a finger to her lips, indicating we're too loud, but she's smiling along with us. A drawback to an open room with high ceilings and bedrooms off a loft nearby—if we're too loud, Kelly will hear every word.

Kathryn settles back into her chair and looks up at the railing. "She must be worried sick about her husband. No way to call anyone or text. I never thought I'd get used to Facebook, and now here we are, without even a telephone."

She picks up the Bible from the table between us and lays it across her lap. I don't think she's aware she's done it, even as her hand rests on the cover and her shoulders relax.

Lauren looks at her mother with a stern glint. "Mama," she says. Then she waits until Kathryn can't stand the silence and looks at her. "Have faith. Chris is fine. They're coming. They have farther to drive and Amanda's family to check on."

How could anyone doubt Lauren? There's something

about her. When I first met her, I thought it was just her build—so solid and sturdy. There's no way it wasn't anchored to the earth. After a while though, it became indisputable. She has a certainty about her that people come to depend on.

I still can't help marveling over them—Kathryn, six inches shorter than her daughter, but both with the same clipped blond bob and piercing blue eyes. Both opinionated and bossy. But at times, one cedes to the other, and vice versa. I often try to bet, just to myself, who will win. I've developed a high accuracy rate but still find myself surprised. I never won with my mother, whether I was arguing or obedient.

Kathryn looks toward the fireplace, where the fire has died down to burning coals. She pulls a throw blanket across her lap and settles her hand on her Bible once more.

"I'm so thankful we have this property," she says. "I didn't want to leave our house until I realized this was the place my children would come to."

"I'm thankful we have this place too," I say and stop myself from making the sign of the cross. It's a leftover habit, like biting my cuticles, that's resurfaced in the last few days. "I don't know what I'd do in Kelly's position. She barely had any food, and what she did have would have gone rotten soon enough. She didn't have any firewood. She had to make sure her kids were taken care of."

"Well, she's certainly making sure we take care of them," Lauren says, rolling her eyes.

"Mikey said she gets migraines a lot."

"That sounds like quite a bit when it's said by a five-year-old," Lauren says.

"Children are prone to exaggerating though," Kathryn replies.

"That's true, but he said she gets them all the time, with a big emphasis on *all*." Everett has had his fill, so I button my nursing bra and lean him against my shoulder, patting his back.

"Well, the Lord put her in your path for a reason, Jenna," Kathryn says. "In time, we'll understand His plan."

Kelly stays locked in her room until the boys arrive home. She comes down wearing skinny jeans and a long turquoise sweater that accents her eyes. She doesn't look like Lauren does after a migraine—puffy from sleeping and still squinting in anticipation of pain. Instead, her makeup looks freshly applied, and her hair falls in soft curls around her shoulders.

The boys sit in front of the fire with fifty puzzle pieces of the USA strewn around them.

"Mommy, we caught so many fish!" Mikey says. He's sitting next to Jacob, a puzzle piece in his hand.

"Was it fun?" Kelly asks as she sits on the edge of the stone hearth. She leans her elbows on her knees and clasps her hands. Her nails have a fresh new coat of bright-pink polish.

"So much fun!"

She looks up at Travis, who sits across from her. "Did they behave?"

I don't like the way she looks at my husband. I pace behind the couch, bouncing Everett, who's fussy. I haven't been able to put him down for almost an hour. My arms ache.

Mikey watches Travis, waiting.

"They did. They were awesome."

I can't see what kind of face Travis makes at the boys, but Mikey's face beams. Flustered, he tries to jam Illinois next to Michigan.

"That doesn't go there!" Jacob says with a giggle. "That's Michigan! See the Great Lake next to it?"

"The Great Lake?"

"Yeah, there are five Great Lakes, all around Michigan." Jacob puts his hand out, and Mikey gives him the piece. "Look, fits right here."

My heart swells with pride.

"Good job working together, boys!" I say. They don't look at me but at each other, grinning. I smile with them as I pace another round with the baby. They could all be brothers if they had the chance to be.

"Aren't you a smarty-pants?" Kelly says as she stands. She picks up the cigarettes she had laid beside her on the hearth, as well as a metal Arctic cup I hadn't noticed.

"Dinner will be ready soon," Kathryn announces from the kitchen.

"Smells divine," Travis replies.

CHAPTER FOUR

KELLY

TWO DAYS EARLIER

I don't know what to do.

I blacked out again last night, and I woke to Mikey pulling on my arm. I feel pissed immediately. I want to slap him, but I don't. What happened last night?

I sit up and reach for my phone. Dead.

Mikey pulls on my arm again, saying, "It's cold."

"Of course it's goddamn cold," I say. "The power is out."

Fuck. I didn't mean to say that. I sit up a bit more, wipe my eyes. It doesn't help. They're still blurry. His freezing fingers still grasp at me. I'm not in pajamas. I'm in yesterday's clothes.

Mikey shifts from one foot to another, a move his dad often did. I thought it was cute once. Now I recognize it for what it is—an inability to make up his mind. Or worse, an unwillingness to stick with what he first decided.

I can picture my husband standing with my copycat, her hand in his back pocket, as if that wouldn't bother me, as if our life hadn't happened. Had never counted. I wanted to scream. Not at him. At her. I still wanted him then, in that moment. I wanted to erase her, make him see me again. I wanted her to know how much of him I'd claimed, how much of his life I could stake. Of all the things I could have told her, I wanted to say that he went to his first prom with me. He came home to my parents' house and sat on the family room floor and pulled forty-two bobby pins from my hair.

Mikey pulls on my arm again, and my vision focuses. His dark hair falls over one eye just like his father's does.

I want to claw at his face.

No, I don't want to claw his face. He's my son. He's my son. He's not his father.

Caden comes toddling in. Or maybe I'm just now noticing him. His colorful parrot is tucked under one arm; his thumb is in his mouth.

With reinforcements, Mikey asks, "Can we get in your bed?"

It's so cold. Caden's lips look blue.

"Of course, baby. Come here."

I grab him and toss him next to me. I see the surprise, delight, and terror flash across his face. He's watching me, his jaw tense, always watching.

I whisper, "Don't judge me," as I grab Caden and pull him close.

By afternoon, I'm quite sure I'll lose it, stuck here with them with no help in sight. I make a drink for courage, sip it slowly, watching the fire burn from where I sit at the dining room table. It's the last of our firewood. The boys play in front of it, oblivious.

I still want to kill him, but it's dull now, this want. I've taken a pill and drunk a glass of vodka, so it's just a scene, played over and over in my mind, without the wrenching need to see it done.

In the corner of my mind, I know I can't continue this way. We're in real danger. It's not just my sorrow and revenge to consider now. It's this. This darkness.

I try to control it, I do. I have one more glass, sipping slowly, watching the fire die. When it does, I pull on a thick sweat-shirt, avoiding the mirror above my dresser. The boys find me, tell me they're cold.

I'm at the perfect place—the brief window of content-ment—so I tickle Caden and chase them to Mikey's room, laughing and playing, as I layer them up with clothing.

"Are we getting ready for bed?" Mikey asks.

I lean forward. "Shh." I wait a count. "Hear that?"

They both stop moving and listen intently, their bodies frozen and faces expectant.

"Hear it yet?"

Their solemn faces show more wrinkles now, trying to hear it.

I fall back in laughter on Mikey's bed. I feel dizzy for a minute, then sit back up.

I reach for a sip of vodka.

The happy place is fading so fast.

Mikey watches the drink in my hand as it comes to my lips, as I place it back on his bedside table.

"Hear what?" he asks, arms crossing against his chest, his dark eyes pinning me down.

I put my finger to my lips. "Shh." I put my arms out, and Caden comes instantly, laying his head on my shoulder. Mikey doesn't move. I beckon again. He comes, but his shoulders don't relax. He stands stiffly inside the bend of my arm. I want to pull him closer, make him cuddle close to me, but I don't. Instead, I put my face in Caden's thick blond hair and breathe him in.

"You boys hear it yet?"

Mikey shakes his head.

"No TV. No phone. No airplanes. No buzzing lights even. Just, silence."

Mikey nods and looks down at his feet.

"It's scary," he whispers.

When I set Lunchables in front of them for dinner again and they whine, I lose it.

I throw my empty glass, my third, across the kitchen. It shatters into a hundred sharp pieces. Caden hides under the small two-person table, covering his ears and sobbing.

"Shut up!" I scream, all my fury and fear falling out of me, but it makes him cry harder. Mikey goes to him, holding him and staring at me with those damn eyes.

I flee down the hall to my room, where I slam the door. It's so cold and getting dark. I light a candle by the bed with shaky hands.

How could he leave me? Us? He might as well have left us for dead.

I lie on the bed and stare at the ceiling. If I close my eyes, I'll see him and his new plaything. I try to catch my breath. I've loved him since I was fifteen. Most of my life, given to him. I roll onto my side, clutching the sheets, focusing on the flickering candle.

Where are you?

I wake, confused, flickering light on the ceiling and my breath visible, barely, in the shadows.

My boys.

I stumble from bed, trip on trailing sheets, and fall forward. I land on my hands and knees, crying out, "My boys!" and the tears start, blurring my vision.

I'm the worst mother. I should take all my pills at once: the Valium, given by the kindly doctor when I broke down in his office, blubbering like a fool; the Vicodin, given by the distracted doctor whom I convinced my back injury was debilitating, despite the X-rays showing otherwise; the Ambien, left behind by my disloyal husband, prescribed for the insomnia he'd suddenly developed from guilt he wasn't self-aware enough to diagnose. Take them all and be done with it.

Still on my hands and knees, my tears and nose dripping, and shaking with cold, I lie flat on my stomach; feel the plush carpet against my cheek. It's the expensive kind I insisted upon, before I knew that I wouldn't care, not at all, how soft it was or how luxurious it looked, back when I still hoped to make my sister jealous of my fine house.

I see Caden's face in my mind's eye, so beautiful, my favorite being on the planet the moment they put him into my arms. I see him crying and his lips turning purple, shaking with cold like I am. It's his face that forces me back to my knees and then to my feet. For him, I fumble for a flashlight, open the door, grope down the hallway, searching and praying.

I find them in front of the fireplace, where a few embers still glow. Mikey has dragged four chairs into the room and laid a blanket across them. He's set up pillows around the chair legs. I get on my knees and pull a pillow away to find them curled up together in a nest of blankets, holding each other and sleeping.

I replace the pillow.

Pulling on a scarf and coat, I take one swig of vodka before I step out into the night in search of warmth. The ground crunches beneath my feet. I pick up stick after stick, twigs really, knowing they'll last mere moments. After bringing the first armful to the back deck and dumping them in a pile, I go back for more. I find larger branches under the trees at the back of the property and bring back two loads. My fourth trip out, I venture into the neighbor's yard. I watch for lights going on until I realize they won't. Not unless I've been delivered from this nightmare.

Back inside, I build the fire as quietly as I can. I have no idea what time it is, but after my outburst in front of the boys, I don't want to wake them. Once the fire is built, I bring my heavy down bedspread to the family room and tuck it over them. Caden stirs and his eyes flutter, but I kiss his forehead, and he rolls back toward Mikey, still hugging his stuffed parrot.

As I sit on the floor next to them and the fire, watching their sweet sleeping faces, guilt surges through me and lodges in my throat. Who have I been the past six months? I barely remember them. I've gotten the boys to school and back. I've managed the grocery store. Fresh shame hits me as I remember the recent night when I was so drunk I watched their bedtime cartoons with one eye closed because I couldn't see with both eyes open.

Starting tomorrow, I won't touch it again. Not a single drop. Not a single pill. I'll pull myself together and figure out how we're going to get out of this mess.

And then I pour myself another drink.

Mikey shakes me awake. I'm shivering.

The boys are still in their nest—I'm outside it, between them and the fireplace, which is now cold and dark. My empty glass sits on the hearth. Sunlight fills the room. My stomach rumbles. Did I eat yesterday?

"Mommy," Caden says as he crawls out of the blankets and comes to me.

"Come in here, Mommy. It's warm," Mikey offers, and my eyes fill with tears. We huddle together, lending each other warmth.

"Hungry," Caden says sleepily, curled up with his head on my chest. I try to remember what we have left to eat.

We have to get out of here.

The feeling jolts me out of my stupor. I can't pretend anymore. I have to do something.

After dry cereal for breakfast, because our milk has soured, I bundle them up, layer after layer. I feed them cookies for each layer of protection I give them. With their mouths full of sugar, they don't complain, and they don't ask questions. I gather the thickest blankets and make them a nest in the car. I tell God I'm sorry I haven't asked for Him sooner. I ask for a miracle in return.

I've been pacing for hours, turning the car off to save gas, then starting it again to warm the boys up once more. No one has driven by our street. I can see smoke escaping from a few chimneys, and I consider knocking on their doors, begging for help. Are they any better off than us?

We're down to seven bottles of water. We have no source of heat. As I pace, I consider finding the nearest shelter. Atlanta makes me nervous—I imagine overcrowding and squalid conditions. Would they have any beds left? Where's the next closest shelter? Do I have enough gas to make it there?

I can't help but think of a drink as I pace. Just a sip. One sip can't hurt. It'll calm my nerves. It'll help me think straight. My hands are shaking. I can't drive with shaky hands.

"Fuck!" I scream in the middle of the garage, the sound echoing around me. The tears start, and I wipe them away in anger. I look out the square windows at the car. The boys huddle together, their faces close, conspiratorial.

I bolt upstairs to the kitchen, grab a bottle of vodka from the freezer, run back downstairs, breathless. I look out at the boys again before taking a swig.

I spot my ski bag at the back of the garage, raid it, and find gloves, scarves, and hand warmers. I bring the hand warmers to the boys and show them how to shake them up.

"Don't eat them," I say with a firm tone, looking directly at Mikey.

He nods.

Back in the garage, I pace some more and consider the shelter again. They'll have food and warmth at least. Anything is better than this, better than me, right now. And I take another swig.

I run upstairs and grab my black satchel, throw in two bottles of vodka. I run to my bathroom and open the medicine cabinet, scooping up bottles of pills and dropping them into the bag. In my bedroom, I open my jewelry box. I put my wedding ring back on. I might be able to trade diamonds for food and water. A rock in exchange for wood. I dig further, grab my diamond earrings and the large emerald ring set among diamonds. My grandmother's. For a moment, I see her standing at my dresser, hand on her hip, polished and poised. She was my favorite, and I was hers. She would know what to do right now. She wouldn't be a trembling mess with shaking hands.

I put the jewels in a small bag, then deposit them in a pocket within my satchel. I pull one of the bottles of vodka back out.

"Save them," I whisper as the cold lip of the bottle touches my lips. But by the time the scorch reaches my throat, I can't remember whether or not I've said it aloud.

I grab two Lunchables and bring them to the boys. Mikey only nods and begins tearing open the packaging of one, then hands it to Caden. Once Caden begins eating, Mikey looks up at me and asks, "Mama, what are we doing? Are we going somewhere?"

We're getting out of here.

Caden's eyes, dark blue in this light, look from me to Mikey, and back to me. I look beyond them.

"We're waiting for a friend."

Mikey tilts his head. "What friend?"

I bite the inside of my lip.

"Who, Mama? Who?"

"I'm not sure who!" I snap, and they both jump. Caden stops chewing and pushes himself against Mikey, burying his face in his brother's shoulder. I let out a sob and cover my face.

I try to hold in my fear, my desperation. The effort makes my whole body shake. I take a deep breath and look up. "I'm sorry."

Caden has his thumb in his mouth, and his slurp, slurp, slurping fills the car with its erratic, panicked rhythm.

"We'll be okay." I need another swig, just one more.

"Can we go inside? Please? Mama?"

A moving object. A glimpse of metal. I stand so quickly I knock my head on the roof of the car. I hold my throbbing head as I run to the street, then outstretch my arms as the SUV rounds the corner.

As we pull onto the highway, I try to remember how many sips of vodka I've taken today. I try to remember what I've packed, or the name of the woman who's rescuing us.

The highway is eerie with so few other travelers. The boys fall asleep ten minutes into the ride, and I take the opportunity to pour some vodka—just a little—into my Arctic cup. With one hand on the wheel, I dig with the other in my black satchel and pull out my armor, arranging it on the seat next to me. I start with a makeup wipe, cleaning my face first, then primer, then lotion. Within twenty minutes, I've covered my tired skin, blotchy from cold and crying, with a rejuvenating caffeinated spray, then green anti-redness lotion, then concealer and foundation. Finally, I use contouring and blush, and a translucent shimmer finish. I put in eye drops and cover my red eyelids with a light dusting of color, apply mascara in the rearview mirror, and take another sip. The warmth of the vodka settles pleasantly in my stomach. I'm no longer shaking.

I apply perfume and pull my hair from my ponytail.

First, I use dry shampoo, then volumizer, then coat my hair with shimmer spray. All that remains to be done is lip gloss and breath mints, which I do as we turn onto the gravel road that winds through the mountains.

I'm ready.

The woman's husband jumps out of the car and hugs his mother. He's tall, taller than Patrick, with nice, broad shoulders.

I move the rearview mirror from my face to the boys. They're stirring.

I look back to the garage and see the mother eyeing me over her son's shoulder.

The lights in the kitchen are too bright, but it's a nice place, better than I was expecting. I can hear Patrick whistling next to me, as if he were here. But if he were, I wouldn't be here at all. There's a gorgeous view—the first thing you see, even at twilight. Next is the fireplace, spanning two levels.

They're all a flutter of activity, but I feel removed—somewhere just outside their chatter and comfort. My boys, thankfully, sit silently on the couch. One dark head and one light, bowed toward one another, almost touching.

I drum the countertop, wondering where and when I can sneak off to take a swig or smoke a cigarette. Or both.

The matriarch speaks to me. What do they call her again? She sounds muffled, and I know my response is as well, but it's so loud in this room with high ceilings. She doesn't seem to notice.

She nods absently and waves her hand when I ask about the back deck. Thank God.

The mountains are slowly fading into the night sky as I

light up and breathe deeply. I remember the Valium in my pocket and pop it in my mouth. It's a sorry substitute, and I force it down, dry and scratchy.

Jenna is in the kitchen when I come back inside. I watch her go back and forth, opening cupboards and drawers, pulling bread and meat out of packages, calling for sandwich orders. I wander past them all, toward the front door.

The house is grand in scale, but plain. Except for one piece of furniture—the red couch in the middle of the room—there's no color or flair. It's all wood and bland landscape paintings, family photos, and angel statues.

When we sit down to our deli sandwiches, potato chips, nuggets, pickles, and pickled jalapeños—as Mikey's hand reaches for the ketchup—the family bow their heads and close their eyes. Kathryn says the blessing.

"Thank you, Jesus, for the food we're about to eat. Thank you for bringing Travis and Jenna, Jacob and Everett home to safety. Please keep all my children under your protection and bring them home. Thank you for the neighbors you've brought to our table. May we treat them as Jesus would. Please gather my family under this roof and under your protection. In Jesus's name, Amen."

I wake to the smell of piss. Mikey stands next to my bed, silently staring at me with wide, guilty eyes.

"Why aren't you in bed with your brother?" I demand, although I know why, and my voice is harsh to my own ears. Mikey backs up so quickly that he trips on toy soldiers and falls backward with a crash and a whimper.

"Shut up," I snarl, my head pounding with fear and yesterday's vodka. How long till they figure out I'm an unfit mother?

He doesn't move, and neither does Caden, who's huddled in the corner of their wet bed. I sit up and cradle my face with shaky hands.

"I'm sorry, Mama," Mikey whispers.

"I'm sorry, Mama," Caden echoes.

Their voices are grating.

"To the bathroom. Now."

There's a voice inside, hardly audible, but still there, urging me to find tenderness, to apologize to my boys. I want them to hold out their little arms to me instead of shrinking from me. I don't want to see the fear in Caden's eyes as he pushes himself against the wall, his stuffed parrot squeezed tightly to his chest. But the voice isn't loud enough. It's nowhere near loud enough to drown out the other noise—their father leaving, their constant neediness, the feigned kindness on Jenna's face, the desperation that led me here.

My throbbing head and shaking hands demand vodka and a cigarette, and right now the boys stand in the way of that. I can't get them moving quickly enough. I'm so irritable I could claw my own skin, and then I'm slapping Mikey, and any chance that voice had disappears.

I invigorate my appearance as Mikey cleans first Caden and then himself in the bath. I steady my hands with a few swigs from my Arctic cup while I spread my arsenal of makeup on the bathroom vanity. I slide a Xanax into the pocket of my yoga pants for the panic that has appeared on the periphery, the kind that can bring pure terror at a moment's notice for no reason.

Once we're all clean and presentable, we go downstairs to face family breakfast. The boys are subdued and obedient; I make sure Kathryn sees me ruffle Mikey's hair with affection.

We're once again assigned seats like schoolchildren. We pray again before eating. There's the clink of utensils, murmurs of appreciation. A low fire burns in the fireplace, and a brisk winter light fills the room. My hand shakes when I try to eat, so I push my food around, hoping no one will notice. But I feel Jenna watching me. Her gaze makes my throat feel tight and my heart race. I slip my fingers into my pocket, pinch the pill in half, and hold it in my hand for comfort.

Avoiding Jenna's eyes, I look at Kathryn and ask, "Do you live here full-time?"

"No, this is our weekend getaway. I haven't retired yet."

She takes a bite of biscuit and turns toward Jenna, and I slip the pill into my mouth, taking a gulp of orange juice. When I look up, Travis is watching me. Did he catch me? I straighten, and his eyes flicker to my breasts.

In my periphery, I see Jenna bow her head, deflecting Kathryn's compliment. Poor, clueless woman. Has she even looked in a mirror?

Emboldened, I say, "This is quite the five-star breakfast." Jenna's eyes dart toward me and then my plate. She really should do something about those bags under her eyes.

I turn to Kathryn. "What do you do?"

"I'm a nurse."

"Head nurse," Travis says, showing the food in his mouth, just a little. "ER." He raises an eyebrow at me, and he's so damn cute with that thick, wavy hair that I forgive him.

I remember the Xanax I've taken, and the few sips of vodka, so I force down a few bites of egg and biscuit. It's not as good as my grandmother's, but it's better than most. As the conversation wraps up about the boys fishing, I can feel a loosening at the edges. My shoulders relax, and I almost feel like smiling.

Travis's sister arrives as breakfast is ending. She's a massive woman; I try not to stare. She's not overweight, exactly. She's built like an athlete—a male athlete. She's as tall as the men, except for her towering father. Even her feet are as big as a man's.

I stand and offer to clean up breakfast, now that my hands are steady. It also gives me the opportunity to watch them all. Kathryn badgers her daughter with questions before introducing me to her grandbaby.

The men come back with bags and start an argument about dishes as I stand with one hand held over the dishwasher, waiting for the family to make up their minds. If they say hand wash, I'm never offering again.

They decide on hand-washing. Lauren and Travis go back and forth teasing each other, and I feel a pang of envy. My sister and I meant only one thing to each other—competition. Jenna squats down in front of my boys, talking to them with a sickeningly syrupy tone. I need a cigarette.

By the time I'm relieved of my duties, Nathan, who I'd started to think never speaks unless spoken to, kindly asks me to discard my butts in the tin he's provided. I nod but don't look at him. I can't get outside quickly enough.

I get glittery sparkles first, in my periphery, and then the translucent zigzag lightning bolts. They're terrifying. One moment, reality is as it should be, and the next, the air itself pulsates in an incandescent, wavering form. If I wait too long, these invisible worms will take over my vision.

I shield my eyes, just like I would if a migraine really was coming on. On cue, Jenna offers to look after my boys. I try to subdue the swing in my step as I head back toward the cabin. I wonder what Travis is doing and whether I can spare a minute to chat with him before retreating to my room under the guise of distress.

He's nowhere to be found as I come into the great room. I hear Lauren and Kathryn talking, but thankfully they're in Lauren's room, and I sneak past them to the stairs. Once in my room, I grab my black bag and plop on my bed. I open a small bottle of orange juice and pour half, top it off with vodka. I grab my phone, wanting to check Instagram and Facebook, since Patrick is too stupid to change his log-ins. I haven't missed a single day of checking them, until now, but there's no internet. My palm itches. I drop my phone and sigh, taking a sip and leaning my head against the wall. Where is he? Where did he and his little bitch run to for safety? Did he even think of me? Or his sons? Did he try to reach us and couldn't? I take another sip, open my phone, and find a game that doesn't require cell service.

When I hear the boys come in from their silly, fucking worm expedition, I stash my drink and lie down with a scarf over my eyes. The boys don't come up. When I'm certain they've left again, I get back up, pop in my earbuds, and play the Amazon music downloaded on my phone.

I unpack my light-up mirror and open my makeup case. I have at least a couple of hours to give myself a mini spa day, starting with my eyebrows. It's going to be easy to fool them, especially Jenna. With that tone of hers, she's practically begging to watch my children.

Once my stray eyebrow hairs are plucked, I open my bedroom door to listen, hoping I can sneak across the upstairs landing to the bathroom. All three women are downstairs talking in hushed tones—about me, no doubt. I close my door as quietly as I can, cursing the open landing. Instead of washing my face, I use makeup wipes, then apply my rejuvenating skin mask.

Time for nails. I only have a few colors in my traveling makeup case, and I settle on a light, feminine pink.

I can't believe we've ended up here, really. We could be in an overcrowded shelter. We could still be at home, eating cold canned food and holding each other for warmth. I stop painting to look around our room. We could have done much worse. It's a tiny, plain room, yes, but it's ours. We have warmth and food and our own little private space. And there's a built-in babysitter.

I'm smiling, and I don't remember the last time that happened. I take another drink and finish my nails.

And then there's Travis. He's not gorgeous, but a few key attributes make him sexier than he should be. I can't figure out what he sees in Jenna, or how loyal he is. He looks at me, of course. He's a man. Most men stare, even with their woman on their arm. But Travis doesn't look at me long enough, not yet. I'll just have to try harder.

I pick out my slimmest blue jeans and my favorite turquoise sweater for dinner. I spend over an hour perfecting my makeup and hair. I take selfies, examine them, take a few more. Snack on almonds and try to limit my drinking. I want to take my other half Xanax but remind myself that I have to charm them. And more importantly, I'm on a limited supply now. I consider opening the window to smoke a cigarette but decide it's not worth the risk. If I want them to buy the migraines, I can't be caught lounging and smoking.

When I finally hear Travis's loud voice echoing their return, I'm pacing the tiny bedroom, sipping and sipping some more. I hide my drink underneath the bed and shove a few crackers in my mouth. I take a swig of water and dig in my purse for breath mints. I hear Jenna laughing and one of the boys shrieking in delight. Her son or mine, I can't tell. I change my mind about my drink. I'm bringing it with me.

I don't expect the nervousness I feel as I come down the stairs, and my fingers curl too tightly around my cup. My legs even feel a bit shaky, but as I reach the last few stairs, Travis looks up and takes in the sight of me just long enough.

He's on the couch, and the boys are on the floor, playing with a giant puzzle. I take a seat on the hearth, directly in front of him.

"Mommy, we caught so many fish!"

"Was it fun?" I ask as I lean forward, elbows resting on my knees, hoping Travis will take a look.

He does. *See, Patrick? See what you gave up?*

"So much fun!" Caden says.

"Did they behave?" I don't look at him for more than a second. Let him think I'm not interested.

Jenna paces behind him, not savvy enough to hide that she's watching me, again. I pull my elbows in, just enough to plump my boobs a tiny bit more. It works. She glances at them, then away, then bites her lip and bounces her baby a bit higher.

"They did. They were awesome." Travis smiles at me before turning his attention to the boys.

I take a sip while he's not looking. My drink is warm, but Kathryn and Lauren are in the kitchen, and I don't know how to slip past them for ice. I need a cigarette too, badly. How many hours has it been?

The boys talk about their puzzle, and I hear Jenna droning with that sickening tone of hers. I turn back toward her as she beams at her son with pride and says, "Good job working together, boys!"

"Aren't you a smarty-pants?" It falls out of my mouth before I can stop it. I smile at Travis, but I feel wobbly. Cigarette. Now.

From the kitchen, Kathryn says, "Dinner will be ready soon," and I sneak another glance at Travis. He looks right back and says, "Smells divine."

I stand up slowly, hoping he'll take in the view one more time before I strut to the glass door and slip out.

It's frigid, but I welcome the cold blast. I know I'm not imagining the way he just looked at me.

CHAPTER FIVE

JENNA

The fishing trip yields two walleye bass and one striped, and over a dozen bream. Kathryn makes corn bread and canned green beans with onions and vegetable oil.

The boys are so tired at dinner. Caden keeps nodding off at the table, his little chin falling toward his chest, only to snap back up again. Jacob mutters incoherently, until Nathan gently picks him up and carries him to their bed. Comes back whispering, "He's out."

Kelly lets me carry a sleeping Caden upstairs, his warm face nestled into the crook of my neck.

She orders Mikey, "To the bathroom! Go pee!" and swats him on the butt. It's hard enough that he wobbles, then extends his left arm for balance and scampers, crookedly, to the bathroom. He closes the door with a quietness uncharacteristic of children. My heart aches for him. I too know the value of keeping all my actions silent.

She turns to me and takes Caden with her right arm, placing her left hand on the banister, her long, slender fingers grasping the wood as if she wants to pull it off.

"Thank you," she says, without smiling, and turns toward their bedroom.

The heat has been off for hours, and the house is chilly. Nathan said the heat would go back on at eleven and get turned off again in the morning. Then he went around the house turning off every unneeded light and appliance. Kathryn insisted on night-lights in every room with a sleeping child.

Nathan sits in his chair, fiddling with the radio. I want to plug my ears. I don't want Everett to sense my fear.

Fuzz. Fuzz. More fuzz.

Brent comes out of their bedroom, where he'd been putting Kaitlyn to sleep, and joins Lauren on the couch. She leans in for a kiss as soon as he's landed, expecting it. He whispers something, and she smiles, making me blush and look away.

"Should we wait for Travis?" Kathryn asks. He's showering upstairs.

Nathan's brow wrinkles as he turns knobs and adjusts the antennas. Fuzz.

Everett's eyes are drooping. I switch him to my other breast. I lean back and take in the scene of the room—crackling fire and dancing shadows, a gray-haired man bent over his radio, his worrying wife next to him with her beloved Bible in her lap, a young couple cuddling on the couch, a satisfied baby in my arms—but still my heart won't quiet.

I know we're safer than most, tucked out in the forested mountains, the nearest town a thirty-minute drive, and the town a tiny one, with a population of less than three thousand. My family is with me, healthy and safe—except my mother and brother, but that thought goes as quickly as it comes. Even if this blackout—this inexplicable, unexpected thing—drags on for weeks or even months, we'll survive. But if it does last any considerable amount of time, desperate people may make their way to our quiet woods, searching for food, for shelter. And what then? Will we have enough to serve others, or will we have to turn them away? Will they get violent in their desperation once they see what we have?

And Kelly, and her desperation. The unnerving way she looked at Travis all evening, by the fire and at the dinner table, hooded eyes peeking up at him. She'd rather pant over my husband than care for her children with any kind of gentleness or kindness.

Travis comes downstairs, still shaking water from his hair.

"You need a haircut," Kathryn says.

"I know."

"I'll give you one tomorrow."

I talked him into going to a salon, once. He scoffed at the price and the overdone decor; tilted his head at the colorful, lopsided dos of the hairdressers. His stylist underestimated the utter rebellion of his cowlick, and he never returned.

I tried once with newly bought shears, undeterred by the failure. I spent an hour and a half making tentative cuts, the story of Samson from the Bible in the back of my mind as I tried to keep my hands from shaking. It looked decent when I was finished, but it had taken too long. I ceded haircutting rights to Kathryn.

"Do you think Chris and Amanda went to be with her family?" Travis asks.

Nathan continues playing with his radio.

Everett has fallen asleep in my arms, and I shift carefully so I don't wake him.

"I wish I knew," Kathryn answers.

The radio hisses to life. "... not declared warfare, though we are under attack. Widespread power grid and communication disruptions continue nationwide. If possible, shelter in place. Assistance is coming through FEMA and the American Red Cross, and foreign nations are assisting with supplies and emergency power infrastructure. Shelters are available in major metropolitan areas. Travel cautiously. Sheltering in place is advised. Boil your water before using it for drinking or bathing. Use generators outdoors only; conserve your fuel. Dispose of sanitation by burying or securely bagging your waste. Some waste can be safely burned to provide heat: paper products, cardboard. The president urges, "Take care of yourselves, take care of your neighbors, America will overcome ..."

Static.

Nathan fiddles. The static persists. The silence grows across the great room until the fire, snapping and rushing, grows not only in sound, but presence.

Kathryn and Nathan go to bed, whispering to each other.

As soon as their bedroom door closes, Lauren sits up and says, "It can't be as bad as it sounds."

"Definitely not," Brent agrees.

"Were you able to reach your mother, Jenna?" Lauren asks, leaning back against Brent's shoulder.

Travis scoffs. "She was impossible to get in touch with

before this. What makes you think we'd be able to reach her now?"

I lie in bed, thoughts climbing like vines in a fast-forwarded video, crisscrossing and twirling with a million tiny offshoot tendrils. I didn't think about her right away, that first day. The first day, I got home with a car full of groceries and a sweaty, squealing baby accompanied by his short, whiny sidekick.

I didn't think about her, on that day, until I tried to call Travis. He always answers when I call. Always. He knows I don't like phone calls. If I make one, it's for a reason. He answers the phone the same way, every time: "Wow, what's going on? You called me? Must be something major!"

But this time, he didn't answer. He didn't answer, and I heard Mama whispering in my ear, *Poison. He's gone because of you.*

The groceries had been unloaded and put away.

Jacob paced in the family room.

I sat in my chair, attempting to nurse Everett, but he sensed my tension. He kept pulling away in frustration.

I held the phone in my hand, staring at it in disbelief. I tried again.

No answer.

I stood and paced alongside Jacob.

"Why are the lights out, Mommy?"

"I don't know, sweetheart."

"When they coming back?"

"I'm sorry, but I don't know that either."

Everett's whimpering turned into full-blown hysterics.

I laid him on the floor, and Jacob and I sang and made funny faces until the shrieking subsided.

"Try now, Mommy." Jacob put his hand on my knee, looking from his little brother to me, nodding.

I kissed his forehead and told him he was the best big brother in the world.

Everett finally settled in and nursed happily, until I opened my phone and saw I had no service. I still tried to call Travis, despite no bars at the top of my screen.

Nothing. It didn't even ring.

I opened Facebook, but it was blank. News—blank. Text messages—spinning, not sending. Back to contacts. Hit every one, and waited for a ring that didn't come. Spinning. Black screen, then another. The faster my heart beat, the harder Everett cried.

Please come home to me, Travis.

I decide to pray, but after the Lord's Prayer, my thoughts stray again. Prayer isn't working, so I turn on my reading light and open my book, *Raising an Emotionally Intelligent Child.* It's a difficult read. It's not only teaching me how to mother my sons, it's showing me what my mother didn't give me. It screams out at me, *This you will have to learn alongside them!*

Dreams of gurgling water, a creek, completely clear, rushing around rocks. The water grows louder, swirling, gurgling.

No, that's Everett. He's awake. I open my eyes and look

at the crib. He isn't there. I bolt upright, and Travis laughs beside me in the bed.

"He's right here."

His blue eyes are so bright in this light that they take my breath away.

"He's right here."

I take the baby into my arms, unbutton my night-gown, and settle him in. Then I drape his blanket over him.

"Jenna. Why are you covering yourself?"

"I'm not." Everett's blanket is tucked luxuriously around his beautiful face, and just so happens to cover most of me.

"But you are." He reaches out and slowly pulls the blanket away. My heavy breasts are now visible.

"You're beautiful."

I make a funny face.

"Still beautiful."

He leans in and kisses me, barely touching my lips. He pulls away slightly, only to press his mouth against mine again, harder this time.

When he pulls away, I ask, "Do you think she's pretty?"

He shifts his weight and leans back against the pillows, sighing.

"I think you're pretty."

"But do you think she is?"

"She's an attractive woman, Jenna. But she's not my type."

I pull Everett's blanket back over myself. "But chubby and saggy is?" I don't look at him. I don't want him to see the tears in my eyes.

"Way to ruin the mood, Jenna." He flicks the blankets back and gets out of bed.

A tear escapes and drips onto Everett's forehead. He opens his eyes and looks at me as I wipe the tear away.

"I'm sorry. She's just so skinny. And pretty."

"You're the one who invited her here." He's pulling on his jeans, his back to me. "Now you have to deal with it."

"She makes me feel so fat."

"Jesus, Jenna, then lose some weight. Go for a walk. I'm so tired of hearing about how fat you are. How many times do I have to say I love you just the way you are for you to actually believe it?"

Everett pulls away and whimpers. I refrain from scolding Travis for saying the Lord's name in vain.

"Give him to me," he says.

I hand him the baby and the burp cloth.

"I'm bringing him down. Pull yourself together."

I nod and bite the inside of my cheek. As he gets to the door, I whisper, "I love you."

He stops and looks at me. "I love you too, Jenna. I need you to believe it." But I see Mama, standing just behind him, looking at me over his shoulder.

Breakfast is Nathan's famous pancakes with blueberries and bananas, and even though he's made six for himself, he's the last to eat.

Between Travis's and Lauren's sugar addictions and the children's, we go through a whole bottle of maple syrup. I don't rely on baby wipes for this breakfast; I order the children into the bathroom for a full washing.

Jacob can't resist the running faucet and splashes water in Mikey's face. Mikey splashes back. They giggle, but it's not just with their mouths. Their whole bodies move, squiggling, swaying, and shaking, while their laughter reverberates in the small half bathroom.

"What do I do with you boys?" I smile as I try to catch their laughing faces.

~

We aren't quite sure what to do with ourselves once breakfast is over and the kitchen is clean. We want to check our phones, but we can't. There wasn't much service here before the outage, no way to know now whether it's the mountains or the enemy. Nathan picks up the TV remote, remembers, and puts it down again. He goes to the tall wall of windows and doors, and looks out toward the lake. Without a word, he slips out the door.

Lauren lounges on the couch, still in her pajamas, feeding Kaitlyn. As the woman with the youngest baby in the house—Kait is only three months—she seems to be taking advantage of resting as often as she can.

The boys are running around playing a game of hide-and-seek. I decide not to send them outside until they get in someone's way. Everett is getting his tummy time in the pack-n-play we've tucked in the corner. My sweet Beauty lies on the floor next to him, guarding him.

Rambling around the kitchen, I notice dust on the spice lids in the circular spice rack. Taking them out one by one, I run a warm cloth over them while Kelly sits on a stool at the island, watching all of us. Or maybe I'm just imagining she's watching us. It's what I would do if I found myself in her situation—constantly gauge the people around me. I search for things to say. A question to start the conversation. What her husband does for a living. Whether she has any siblings. But I don't want her to feel that I'm interrogating her.

Travis, who's been sitting in his mother's chair, stands and goes outside. He walks to the railing and leans against it. Kelly doesn't skip a beat; she grabs her cigarettes and joins him. I watch in horror as he takes one from her and leans toward her as she lights it.

He quit smoking when we were planning our wedding. He vowed to never touch one again. I want to run out to them and snatch it from his lips. I want to grab her pretty blond hair and demand she leave, find someone else to shelter her. Instead, I take a deep breath and go to the mudroom to put the wash in the dryer.

When I come back into the great room, they still lean on the railing, facing the mountains and lake. I see her throw her head back in laughter and shift her hip to the left, toward him. Travis is a very comical man. He loves taking center stage and telling jokes, doing impersonations, reveling in his audience's laughter.

Lauren, her perception as sharp as Travis's, says, "Jenna, don't stand there like that, spying on them. Travis loves you. You have nothing to worry about."

I nod and give her a grateful smile, but her words don't make me feel any better. She's a beautiful woman, with full, pink lips and the same startling blue eyes as her brother. She commands the room just like Travis does, only in a different way, with a sort of certainty and sturdiness. She tells it exactly like it is, and I wonder if she's ever had a moment of insecurity in her life.

I sit in a chair opposite Kathryn's and Nathan's so I can face the view of my husband and Kelly. They've put their cigarettes out. He nods at her and walks around the side of the house. Kelly comes back inside with a smirk.

"How can you stand how terrible those things make you smell? I can smell you from here," Lauren says from her spot on the couch, and I want to hug her. I've never been quick-witted enough for the thinly veiled insults women hurl at each other.

Kelly stops, right in front of the fireplace, and slowly turns to face Lauren. Her jaw is tense, and her hand goes to her hip.

"I know. It's awful, right? I wish I could quit. I've tried so many times." The venom in her voice is thick, even as she smiles.

Lauren smiles back.

"Maybe we should all take a little hike in the woods today, get some fresh air. I think we're all going a little stir-crazy," Brent suggests. He's a quiet man, like his father-in-law, thoughtful and generous, too much so for his own good. Lauren walks all over him when she's in the mood to.

"That would be nice. I love hiking," I offer, picking up Brent's attempt at peacemaking.

"I didn't bring any hiking boots," Kelly says, and then walks toward the stairs. But just as she's getting to the edge of the fireplace, Mikey comes zooming around the corner from Kathryn's bedroom. He's the seeker, intent on his mission, and he plows right into his mother. She nearly falls.

"Michael Anthony! You stop running in the house this instant!" She grabs him by his collar and drags him to the stairs.

"We were playing, Mommy. I wasn't the only one running!" He whimpers and twists to get free.

Kelly bends toward his face, grasping his chin roughly with one hand, his collar still in the other, pulling back so tightly his shirt looks like it will choke him. She hesitates and seems to remember she has an audience. She lets him go and squats down in front of him.

"I'm so sorry, baby."

Her back is to me, so I can see his face, wet with tears. He has a confused expression, his whole body tense, waiting to see what comes next.

"You just scared me to death! I'm sorry I got so angry."

He nods but takes a step back. She grabs him by the shoulders and forces him into an embrace.

"I love you, baby. It's okay."

He looks at me over her shoulder.

She lets him go, and he takes another step back.

"Where's Caden?" she asks, sweetly.

"He's hiding." Mikey takes one step to the left so he's no longer in line with his mother's body. "We're playing hide-and-seek." He puts his hands behind his back and looks down at his feet.

"There's no reason to run in hide-and-seek."

Mikey nods but doesn't look up.

"No more running." Kelly sighs and stands up. "Watch where you're going."

Again, Mikey nods.

Kelly doesn't turn back to acknowledge us and continues past Mikey, up the stairs.

Mikey stays in his spot, shifting from one foot to the other, hands still behind his back. When his mother reaches the loft, he looks up, listening. She crosses the landing to their bedroom. He exhales and frees his hands. He looks at me but seems frozen to his spot.

Everett shrieks. Mikey and I startle, still looking at one another.

I smile. Mikey's shoulders drop an inch, but when I

stand, he straightens his posture, pulling his hands once again behind his back.

Everett, in his pack-n-play, shrieks again.

"Well, he wanted to be found," I say.

Mikey looks puzzled, then slowly smiles. He looks back down at his red Converse.

"I think you have two more to find." I wink at him.

He doesn't move from his spot.

"Jacob is an expert at hide-and-seek. He's been known to switch his hiding place in the middle of the game." I turn away and head toward Everett, silently sending Mikey the courage to move.

I hear footsteps as I hold my hands out to Everett, who smiles and slaps the railing of his pack-n-play, triumphant; he's pulled himself upright.

Kelly reemerges after Mikey has found Jacob and Caden hiding together in the storage closet under the basement stairs. Caden was too scared to hide by himself. I feel a surge of pride that Jacob understood and swallowed his normal competitive streak to accommodate him.

She comes back downstairs as Jacob kneels at the fireplace, his hands on the hearth, his head resting on his arms, counting. Everett is on my hip and my hand on the door-knob. I want to know where Travis has gone, and Nathan.

"Are they okay under your watch for a few minutes?" I ask Lauren and Brent, still in their spots on the couch.

They nod.

"Eighteen ... nineteen ... twenty ..." Jacob says.

I don't look back at Kelly as I hear her getting to the bottom of the stairs. I push open the back door and step out.

I cross the level ground next to the house. Pausing at the edge of the clearing, I take my wool hat off and put it on Everett, folding it back several times until the edge lands just above his eyebrows; it feels colder today than it has since we arrived. I think of checking the weather on my phone and remember that I can't. There isn't a cloud in the sky, and I pause to look up, letting the sun warm my face.

I look across the mile or so to the only house visible from this spot. It's a log cabin, nearly identical to Kathryn and Nathan's, tucked into the hillside among trees. The owners are a decade younger than Kathryn and Nathan; the woman is a lawyer, and I can't remember what the man does. My in-laws met them shortly after they built their weekend getaway; they're Northerners and not Baptist, and therefore suspect on two counts. Before we were married, Travis promised he couldn't care less whether I was Catholic or Baptist, as long as we got married in his mother's church. But I wanted his family to accept me completely. And I needed Jesus to wash away the sins my mother lashed into me—the real wounds—and the accusations.

As I'm considering whether Travis and Nathan headed off in that direction without letting us know, I hear their voices behind me. I turn around as they're coming up the slight incline of the gravel driveway.

Everett coos, and I give him a bounce with my arm. "Should we go see what Daddy and Papa are up to?"

By the time I reach the house, the men are in the garage, tinkering with something.

"Where did y'all sneak off to?" I ask as I approach.

"Just checking the perimeter," Travis says and winks.

"All clear?"

"Yes, ma'am, no signs of trouble." Travis takes off his baseball cap and tips it like it's a cowboy hat.

His dad has taken whatever they were working on to the workbench, opening and closing drawers in his tool shelf, looking for something.

Travis looks from me to his dad and back to me. He walks toward me, and I melt, just a little.

"I need to go to my hunting site and throw down some corn if you want to join me. I'm sure my mom will watch the kids."

I nod and smile as he leans in for a kiss. He's playful, flicking my lips with just a hint of tongue.

"I'll ask her," I manage.

The boys play on the back deck until their cheeks are pink and their noses runny. I call them in for lunch, serving sandwiches with the last of our deli meat. Kelly has retreated to her room again, so I ask Mikey to help me in the kitchen. He points to the mayonnaise.

"We like that one," he says.

"And how do you like your sandwich cut?" I ask, pressing the knife into the bread without cutting.

"That way," he says, indicating diagonal.

He helps me carry the plates to the table.

"Thank you for your help, sir," I whisper to him, squatting down to meet his eyes.

His cheeks flush and he looks down. I grab his hand and gently squeeze three times.

After lunch, I put Everett down for his nap and haul out Jacob's railroad track and trains.

Once the boys are playing happily, I give Travis a look that says, "I'm ready."

"Hey, Mom. Do you mind keeping an eye on the kids for an hour so, so Jenna can join me in the woods? I'm going to throw some corn out. Ya know, call in the deer."

Kathryn looks over, her knitwork paused in her hands. "As long as you bring me back a buck for steaks and stew," she says and smiles at Travis.

"I just put Everett down. Shouldn't hear from him before I get back," I say as I pick up my jacket and slide it on. I go to her chair and put my hand lightly on her arm. "Thanks for the break," I whisper, trying to hide my excitement.

She sets down her knitting and squeezes my hand. "Just don't stay gone too long, my dear. Don't worry me."

As we head into the woods, Travis carrying the bag of corn, he says, "Dad and I have decided we should walk the property boundary every day, just in case."

"For what? Looters? Way out here?"

I expect him to chuckle, because of course there wouldn't be looters out here, I realize as soon as it comes out of my mouth.

But he doesn't laugh. "Better to be safe than sorry," he answers. He holds a branch of brambles so I can pass.

"Do you think there will be trouble, way out here?"

I'd thought it would be weeks or even months before we

had to worry about anything reaching us. That it would take a while for people to get desperate, to use what gas they have left to flee big cities, seeking the refuge of wilderness. Then again, I hadn't really pictured what it might be like in cities, where everyone is on top of one another, where they don't have heat and have to boil their water. Where would you boil your water in an apartment or condo? In the suburbs, like our neighborhood, I picture women bent over campfires, boiling their tap water, and carrying it inside, storing it in containers for drinking. If they don't have generators or camping stoves, they have to cook over the campfire. If Sunday wasn't their shopping day, would they still have enough to cook over their campfire? Or were people already digging into their pantries for canned vegetables and soup?

I'm hit with a rush of gratitude that I'm here. I'm walking behind my husband in the forest, headed to his deer stand, the solid shadow of the cabin behind me. My son plays happily in front of a fire, and my other sleeps soundly in his crib. Tonight, they will be warm and fed. And safe. And even if it gets dire, my husband will hunt to feed us.

The ground gets steeper. Travis reaches his hand back, and I take it. We're almost there. His deer stand is placed twelve feet up, permanently installed. It looks out over a level spot in the landscape, hardly twelve by twelve, but just enough room to regularly spread a bit of corn. It's not technically legal, but even without the corn, it offers a good vantage point for spotting deer. We reach it, and Travis heaves the sack off his shoulder. It lands on the ground with a thud. He unties it, takes a handful of corn, and tosses it. He takes another handful and extends it to me.

I've never spread corn with him before. We've walked

these woods together plenty of times, but hunting was always his domain.

I hold out my hand, and he pours the dried kernels into it. I walk to the edge of the little clearing, open my hand, and flick it outward like I'm tossing a Frisbee. The sound of raining pellets echoes around me.

We continue until the sack is gone, Travis covering the ground closest to his stand, me scattering tiny yellow flakes around the perimeter, drawing them in.

He takes me into his arms when we're finished and kisses me like he hasn't done in days. I feel my body leaning further and further into his embrace; my lips open to his exploration, his need. Before long, I feel him harden against my thigh.

He pulls away and looks at me. I want him. I want to feel his skin and his hands and his lips, but I feel shy, and I close my eyes so he'll kiss me again. He does, but now his hands are fumbling to unzip my jacket and find their way under my shirt. I suck my belly in, and he whispers, "Breathe," as his hands find my bare skin and stroke my sides, my back. Then he reaches up for my breasts. He's inside my bra and taking my nipples into his fingers as I bury my mouth in his neck, trying to silence my moan even out here, where no one can hear us.

As we approach the cabin, holding hands, my worry kicks back in. I squeeze Travis's hand to stop him.

"What is it?" he asks as he turns to look at me.

"How long do you think this is going to last?"

"I don't know," he says, readjusting his baseball cap.

"Why don't they have the power back on yet? What's taking them so long?"

We stand at the edge of the forest, on the driveway side of the cabin. In front of us is the small grassy hill, which leads up to the little square front porch.

"Whoever is responsible must have crashed the entire system. I don't really know how it all works, but there are so many different companies responsible for creating and distributing power, they're probably scrambling to coordinate. And with communication down, it might be next to impossible."

"So, you think this could go on for ..."

Travis scratches at his stubbly chin. "The foreseeable future," he says, then tucks a wayward strand of my hair behind my ear. He drops my hand and pulls me into an embrace. "Don't worry, honey. We'll be fine out here. I'd be worried if we were stuck in Atlanta, but we aren't. We have supplies, and food, and well water."

"But there are so many of us to feed."

"Even if we get low on food, we can fish and hunt. We'll be fine."

I smell cigarette smoke. I pull away and peer over his shoulder, spotting the lingering cloud of smoke around the corner of the house.

"Please don't smoke with her again." I look up into his clear blue eyes.

"Jenna." He smooths my hair again, but because I see him set his jaw, resisting his frustration, I, in turn, resist the urge to pull away. "Honey, I love you. You're the only one for me."

"Promise?"

"Pinkie promise." He leans in for a short but tender kiss. "Now, what excuse can I use tomorrow to get you back into the woods with me?" He laughs, a mischievous smile across his face.

"So, boys," Brent says, waiting until they stop moving and look at him. "This is how we make magic meatballs."

Jacob lowers his hands, nearly touching the mound of Play-Doh he's been allotted.

Mikey looks at Jacob, then back to Brent, who holds his hands above his bowl like he's holding something small and round.

"Pick up your eggs. Next to your bowls." He nods. "They're invisible. Just put your hands out and feel for your egg. It's there."

The boys look at each other, giggling, then feel around the counter.

"There! There! You've got it! Grab your egg!" Brent holds his hands over his bowl and crushes his egg, wringing his hands like they're covered in goo. "Do it! Break your eggs!"

The boys follow suit, adding sound effects.

"Mush it in!" Brent suggests, and the boys reach their hands into their clay, squishing, squeezing, and giggling.

The three boys sit at the kitchen counter, feet dangling off the high stools. Holding Everett on my hip, I stand back to watch Uncle Brent, smiling as the boys erupt in laughter at his antics.

I take my time grabbing plates and silverware, listening in.

"Roll them around, like this," Brent says, and the boys follow with their Play-Doh, making little meatballs on their own tinfoil platters.

"You're such a good teacher, Uncle Brent. I think you should change jobs," Lauren says, striding into the kitchen with Kaitlyn in one arm. Sliding the other around him, she continues. "I believe I told you that the first day we met."

Neither of them knows I set them up. I asked Lauren to pick me up from Sunday school for a lunch date, with the sole intention of stopping by Brent's classroom. When we did, he was wrapping up a puppet show for his five-year-olds. That was all it took.

"You might have," he says, then returns to the boys. "Those magic meatballs ready yet?"

"Almost!" Jacob shouts.

Everett shrieks and slaps my chest in response, kicking his legs.

In my periphery, a figure appears at the loft railing. I glance up to see Kelly looking down at us.

"Keep on rolling them," Brent says as he slides his own sheet into the oven.

Jacob jumps off his stool. "Mine are ready!" he shouts.

"Okay, okay, leave them there. I'll help you." Brent motions to the second oven, which isn't turned on. "Pull open that door there."

"This?" Jacob asks, pointing.

They pull the door open together.

Nathan comes into the great room, turns off a lamp, dims another, reminding me we aren't on vacation. It descends and colors everything, this feeling of darkness closing in on me. I can't, I won't give into it. Everything is okay, right now. Right now, everything is okay. We can pretend the uncertainty lives out there, across the mountains. That we aren't within its reach. I can pretend. I look toward Brent, watching as he helps Jacob and then Mikey slide their Play-Doh creations into the unlit oven.

Travis comes out of the upstairs bathroom, towel around his neck. I look up as Kelly turns to him and smiles. The way she tilts her head reminds me of my mother, when her lipstick was fresh and she had on one of her favorite dresses.

"To your room, and not a sound," she'd say, her long finger pointed at me.

But I can't hear what they're saying. I can't control my heart beating faster as I watch Travis linger, then lean against the railing, then run his hands through his wet hair. She bends forward, so interested in what he's saying.

Everett slaps my chest again, and I grab his hand, hold it in my mine.

Please, shush, for just a moment. Please, let me hear what they're saying.

She laughs again, and he leans in, a tiny bit more, breaking the space between them.

CHAPTER SIX

JENNA

My sleep is plagued by dreams of my mother. She holds a smoking, bubbling vial to my brother's lips, urging him to drink. He drinks, and the scene shifts. Now my brother stands over me as my mother joins him.

Me, huddling in the corner. I peer up at them, trapped, as they point and laugh.

They begin chanting, "Look at her! She thinks she's pretty!" Louder and louder, until they pull at my hair, yanking and yanking. They pull out chunks, holding them up, howling. They turn into crows, squawking and pecking and tearing at my flesh with their claws. More and more birds join them until all I can see is black. All I can hear is the deafening whir of their wings while I feel the blood dripping down my arms.

I sit straight up, panting.

The boys sleep peacefully on either side of me. My Fitbit says 4:52 a.m.

I take a hot shower, trying to relax. Every part of me aches. I miss my home and my own space. I miss my morning cuddles and stories with the boys. I miss our routines. I miss the tiny act of walking Travis to the door every morning. That minute we get, when our eyes meet, when he kisses me, when I pray for him as he walks away.

I clear the fog on the bathroom mirror, still feeling a weight bearing down on my shoulders. Her eyes, her mouth, stare back at me. Mama. And the men watching Mama, turning their heads to see her. Men coming to our house, a new one, then another and another, at all hours.

Mama found me once when I was wearing her high, high heels, teetering, arms stretched wide. She hit me so hard I flew sideways, broke an ankle.

Look at her. She thinks she's pretty.

I want to smash the glass. I close my eyes and take a deep breath, envisioning my fortress springing up around me—the walls of stone thicker than the width of my body, with their metallic gleam and smooth, cold feel beneath my hand. The walls grow higher and higher into turrets and towers guarded by sentries of my own making. And down below, beneath us, the rows and rows of pikes and barbed wire keep circling the perimeter, tighter and tighter.

They cannot reach me here.

After checking on Everett, I slip to the kitchen, where I go to work cataloging our food supplies. There's enough bread for two to three days at most, and only eight eggs. The last of our milk expires in four days.

I pace a lap around the kitchen, chewing on my pen, stopping to look at the horizon.

We have eleven pounds of beef, seven pounds of

chicken, three turkey tenderloins, plus several packs of bacon, boxes of corn dogs and nuggets, and frozen fish.

I open the fridge, close it again. We need to cook the last of the fresh vegetables before they spoil.

I pull everything out for pancakes; syrup is getting low. I mix up a batch and put it in the fridge, then go upstairs to check on Everett. I find Travis and Everett giggling in bed. My shoulders instantly relax.

"Hey, Mommy, where ya been?" Travis asks.

I sit on the edge of the bed. "Checking our food supply."

His eyebrows go up. "And?"

"We have meat for dinner for ten to fourteen days. After that, no meat. We only have enough bread for four more days of sandwiches, and we're running low on breakfast stuff too."

Everett makes the hand sign for "hungry," and Travis passes him to me. The red sweater I put on this morning was a silly choice. Without buttons, it will be hard to breastfeed in.

Reading my thoughts, Travis says, "Just take it off," and winks at me.

I roll my eyes but do it anyways, folding the shirt across my middle to hide my belly rolls.

Travis yanks it away. "How many times do I have to tell you you're beautiful, every part of you, even your cute little belly rolls?"

"You're so annoying," I say, but I can't help but smile.

"Your back is gonna hurt if you sit at the edge of the bed like that," Travis says, then scoots down the bed. He slides his left leg around the side of me and hugs me from behind. I lean into him and get Everett situated.

"Comfortable?" he asks.

"Yes." I nestle my head against his shoulder and whisper, "I love you."

"I love you more."

I sigh and look at Everett, who holds my gaze with his dark-brown eyes. He looks straight into me, and I feel like he knows me better than I know myself, even while he's watching my face to learn every nuance of life and the world, from me. Such a heavy task—to be what he sees in my eyes—and such a privilege to be his guide, and his safe place.

"We're low on food already," I remind Travis.

"We'll figure it out."

"But we're low on milk, bread, fresh fruit, vegetables."

"We still have plenty."

"You don't have to feed little boys cereal without milk, or lunch without sandwiches."

"Don't worry about the food, Jenna. We'll figure something out."

"I can't help but worry. What if this thing lasts another month?"

"I can't imagine that happening. I mean, the US has seen a few blackouts, and we've always got the power back up."

"It's never been out this long."

"True." He rests his head on my shoulder and reaches his left arm around to rub Everett's head.

"And if it is a terrorist attack, or Russia, or North Korea, this could be just the beginning."

"Seriously, honey? You're going with North Korea?"

I don't answer.

"Anyways," he says, "I wonder how the rest of civilization is doing out there."

Everett murmurs, grabs my chin.

Travis continues. "I'm thinking about riding into town and checking things out."

"No."

"Jenna."

"Absolutely not."

"Jenna, come on. I don't even have to get out of the car. I'll bring my gun. Hell, I'll bring two guns."

"What good would it do?"

"Maybe things aren't that bad. Maybe there's information in town. Maybe they have an idea of when the power will come back. We're not exactly close to civilization out here."

"Yeah, that's the point," I tell him. "That's what's keeping us safe."

"We can't stay out here forever, not knowing what's happening with the rest of the country."

"But what if you're ambushed by a mob of angry, armed men who've set up barricades and traps right on Main Street?"

"You've watched way too much *Walking Dead,* Jenna. Seriously."

Everyone is awake and gathering around the kitchen table, drawn to the smell of hot pancakes on the griddle. Travis, spatula in hand, makes silly sounds and dances a little jig every time he flips one, sending Jacob into spasms of laughter.

I sit on a stool at the high counter, Everett in my lap, watching my sweet boys, when Kathryn approaches and whispers in my ear, "Any sounds from the guests this morning?"

I shake my head. She looks up toward the second floor.

"I'll go up," I say.

I wish I didn't feel so responsible for bringing them here. I know in my heart it was the right choice, the Christian choice, but I wonder where the line gets drawn between taking care of others and ensuring your own family is provided for. I hand Everett to Kathryn and make my way to the stairs. I'm quiet in my thick, plush socks, my funky red-and-white striped favorites. Unwanted images flood my mind from dinner last night—the way she absently twirled her hair around her finger, how even her laughter is flirtatious.

I pause at the door and listen. I think I can hear Mikey and Caden talking in hushed tones. I raise my hand to knock but change my mind and tap lightly with my nails. A few seconds later, the door cracks, and Mikey's dark-brown eyes appear.

I squat down and smile at him. "Good morning, bud."

"Morning," he mouths, but no sound comes out.

"Mommy awake?"

He shakes his head.

"Come on down for pancakes, then, and let her sleep a little longer."

He nods and opens the door wider. Caden sits on the floor between the twin beds, an assortment of toy soldiers and cars strewn in front of him. Kelly sleeps in the bed against the left wall, her long golden hair spread out across her pillow. Her black leather bag is right next to the bed, the long neck of a vodka bottle sticking out. The two bottles I saw her grab when we packed together are in the freezer downstairs, untouched.

Is that what she went back for when she said she needed to check the house one more time, and came back out with that same black bag? How many bottles did she grab? I try to remember exactly how many she had in her freezer at home, but then I recall seeing a liquor cabinet in the dining room as well.

I sigh and look back at Caden, who's tiptoeing over the toys. As soon as he gets near, I can smell the urine in his diaper.

"Grab a fresh diaper, Mikey," I whisper.

After breakfast, I layer the boys up for some outdoor play, even though there's barely a dusting of snow. As I do, Travis announces to the room, "I think we should have a family meeting on the porch while the boys play."

Lauren looks at me with her characteristic "What's up?" face—head tilted slightly to the left, left eyebrow shooting up in an extreme point above her startingly blue eyes. She's the kind of woman who needs to know everything, and needs to know it five minutes before anyone else.

I shrug at her, even though I know what's coming.

"Jacob, go to the mudroom and grab your buckets and shovels, please," I say.

"Mommy, there's no snow," he whines, his hands and face pressed to the window.

"I want buckets!" Caden says.

"Okay, okay," Jacob says, turning and trudging toward the mudroom.

We file onto the porch, Caden happily swinging his bucket, and leave behind a still sleeping Kelly and two babies put down for their morning naps.

"Stay within sight, boys!" I call as they run around the side of the house, Beauty bounding alongside them.

We pull the chairs into a semicircle and sit, except for Travis, who paces, tugging at his growing beard. Nathan stoops low, lighting the propane on the table, which has a firepit at its center.

"What's this about?" Lauren asks.

Travis stops and faces his family. "I think it's time I go into town and check things out."

"I knew you were going to say that!" Lauren says, nodding and beaming as if she's won a prize.

Kathryn is shaking her head. "No, Travis, it's too dangerous. We have no idea what's happening."

"That's exactly the point, Mom," Travis says. "We need to know how bad—or how good—things are going. We need to get an idea of how long this is going to last. And we need to figure out if we can get more supplies, or if we're going to have to start hunting, seriously hunting, for any kind of meat we can get."

"They have to have the power back up soon," Brent says. "We just need to hold out a little longer. I mean, we just got here, what? Two days ago? I really can't believe it's gone on this long, but surely it won't be more than another day, two tops."

"No one can believe this happened at all," Nathan interjects. "No one saw this coming. We know this is an attack of some sort. They said so on every broadcast we've heard. For all we know, it wasn't just a hack of the power grid. They may have hacked other systems. They may have sent missiles and blown up the capitol. We really have no idea what's going on out there."

"Oh c'mon, no one has bombed us. That's absurd," Brent says, stroking his ginger beard and shaking his head.

"Is it, though?" Lauren asks. "It's absurd that the power has been out five full days, going on the sixth. If it was just a hack of the power grid, why haven't they found the problem and fixed it yet?"

"Ya know, I saw a special report a year or so ago, I think it was," Nathan says, leaning forward, his elbows on his knees. "They were talking about how vulnerable our power grid was to attack—how old the infrastructure is, how power companies weren't doing enough for cybersecurity. The expert they had on, some famous journalist, I don't remember his name ... I'm pretty sure he said if the attack was bad enough, power might be off for years before they could piece it all back together again."

"Again, that's absurd," Brent says. "We're the biggest superpower in the world. How could we have a blackout that lasts years? We're not a third-world nation."

"I don't know. I thought the same thing when I saw the special. But this guy was adamant. He cited an awful lot of experts—engineers, military men, what have you. I didn't realize they're still using the same system—grid—that was built when electricity was invented. How long ago was that? A hundred years at least, I think they said. I guess it's not streamlined. Bunch of different companies piecing the whole system together. Small companies and big ones, the big ones have the money for cybersecurity. But the small ones ..." Nathan drifts off, but we wait in silence. When he speaks, everyone listens. Responding, I suppose, to the rarity of hearing his mind. "Anyways, he said one little mistake, and the whole system could go into chaos."

Kathryn shakes her head again. "I still don't think it's a good idea. We can hole up here forever if we need to." She turns toward her husband. "Nathan, didn't we just watch something on the news about the updates they were making to cybersecurity?"

He shakes his head and stands, goes to the railing, and puts one hand there. "That was cybersecurity for government computers. Entirely different."

"And this is exactly why I need to go to town," Travis says. "We need to know what's happening." He starts pacing again. "I mean, we need to know how long this'll last. Two more weeks? A month? We need to be prepared. Know whether we've got to ration, hunt, use less electricity. I'd love to find some ammo, some real supplies."

"I agree," Nathan says quietly, looking down at his hands. He looks up at Kathryn. "I know it's dangerous, but we need to know."

"What do we need to know?" Jacob asks, coming around the corner of the porch.

I hear Caden's and Mikey's footsteps, and then they appear alongside Jacob.

"You need to know," Travis says loudly, bending over and waving his arms around like a gorilla, "that Daddy has been waiting to capture you!"

Jacob shrieks and runs toward him, bending over as he gets close and ducking right between Travis's legs. Travis stands up, laughing, head thrown back.

"You clever, tiny human, you! Next victim, then!" He lunges toward Mikey, whose face registers surprise first, then delight. He's giggling so much, he forgets to move, and Travis sweeps him up in his arms and buries his face in Mikey's neck, tickling him with his beard.

"Down with the ogre!" Jacob cries and grabs his dad

from the back in a futile effort. He barely reaches Travis's waist. Caden stands, watching, wide-eyed, with a bewildered smile on his face.

Travis sets Mikey down, then reaches back and grabs Jacob with one arm. "No one can take down the mighty ogre!" he roars, grabbing Mikey again with his free arm. Then he gallops down the porch, a boy under each arm.

Caden walks toward me and puts his hand on my leg without looking at me, transfixed by Travis playing with the boys.

"Does your daddy play with you in this silly way?" I ask him.

He looks up at me and shakes his head.

"Don't 'member," he says. Then, "Me, up?" He holds up his arms, and I pull him onto my lap and wrap my shawl around him. He puts his thumb in his mouth and cuddles into my shoulder. I look up just as Lauren raises an eyebrow and motions toward the house with her eyes.

Kelly stands at the door, arms crossed, watching. When we make eye contact, she opens the door, putting a smile on her face, holding her hand up against the sun.

"Good morning, y'all. Or should I say afternoon? I'm so sorry I slept so late." She smiles apologetically at Kathryn before turning her attention to Travis, who's still running around with the boys at the other end of the porch. "I forgot to charge my phone since I'm hardly using it. Never imagined I'd sleep this late without an alarm."

She looks at Caden, takes a step forward, but stops, resting her hand on the back of an empty chair. "Good morning, sweetheart," she coos at him before turning back to Kathryn. "I hope they were behaved." Her southern accent is deeper today, sounding forced, the syllables held just a second too long, like someone trying to imitate Scarlett O'Hara.

"Of course they were. Each ate a whole stack of hotcakes," Kathryn says.

Kelly nods, looks again toward Travis. Her lips glimmer with a soft pink gloss in the sunlight. Today she's chosen black leggings with high boots and a thick wool sweater that hugs her breasts, paired with an elegant scarf. If I were staying with strangers, I would check on my sons before I showered, let alone curled my hair and applied eyeliner and foundation. Then again, I wouldn't sleep in either, leaving my boys for someone else to look after.

"Sometimes, migraines just wipe me out for days," she says as Travis and the boys, winded, rejoin our circle.

"Mommy!" Mikey says. "We've been playing! Having so much fun!" He throws his arms around her legs, grinning up at her.

"Mikey!" she shrieks, pushing him off as he leaves behind a smear of orange clay on her black pants.

"I'm sorry," he whimpers, lowering his head and slapping himself, hard.

"Oh, Mikey." Kelly grabs his hands to stop him. "I'm sorry, bud." She falters, shaky, and almost stumbles. "You just surprised me, baby, and startled me." She runs her hands down his face, wiping away his tears. "And then I scared you back! What a mess we are!" She puts her hands out, offering to pick him up, but he backs away a step.

"I'm dirty. I'm sorry, Mommy, I didn't know. I didn't know I was dirty."

"They've been playing with their buckets in the dirt," Travis says, motioning to the side of the house.

She smiles at Travis and says, "Boys," shrugging.

He nods back and answers, "Boys," chuckling along

with her. I wait for him to look at me and roll his eyes, but he doesn't. He just keeps looking at her.

And then I see it.

The way the men looked at my mama.

Travis and his dad do another perimeter check after lunch, and a knot forms in my stomach. I know they're discussing Travis's idea. Once I get Everett down for his afternoon nap, I slip outside and find them loading a tote into our car.

"What's that for?" I put my hand on my hip and hold my breath.

"Supplies for my morning trip," Travis answers without turning around.

Nathan holds a rifle in one hand and a box of ammunition in the other. "Front seat?" he asks.

"Yes, sir," Travis says.

Nathan walks to the passenger door, and I move closer, next to Travis, and peer into the tote. He has three gallons of water, jerky, granola bars, two cans of soup, his one-burner camping stove and accompanying kitchenware, a crowbar, flashlights, headlamp, and batteries. Beside the tote, his other supplies include a one-man tent, sleeping bag, canvas bags, empty totes, and three gas cans.

"Is it safe to have so much gas in the car?" I ask. "What if you get in an accident? Or someone rear-ends you?"

"Only one has gas, in case I need it to get home. The other two are empty, in case I find some more."

"In case you need it to get home?" My face betrays me. I can't stop my chin from quivering.

"I know you don't want me to do this," Travis says, turning me gently toward him, my arms crossed against my chest. He pulls me in, untangling my arms, forcing them open. "Baby, you worry too much. You know you do. I'll be fine. You'll see."

I cling to him even though I don't want to, even as I try to hold the walls steady in my mind, their weight and texture, their cool, comforting feel beneath my hand. A crow sounds, and I peek over his shoulder just as the dark bird swooshes up and out of sight, his cawing carrying on the wind.

I shiver.

Travis pulls away to look at me. "You trust me, right? You know I'll be safe."

I bite the inside of my cheek and nod, scanning the horizon behind him.

I'm thankful for the reprieve cooking dinner brings. My chili recipe, the only recipe I've created on my own, requires eight cans of beans and various states of tomatoes. I open all sixteen cans and line them up. Then I drag three stools over to the stove and call the boys.

I tuck a large cloth napkin into the necks of their shirts. "Don't pour too fast, but a little splattering is okay."

They happily take turns emptying the cans into the pot, giggling at the sprays of sauce and crushed tomatoes. I stand behind them, touching their hands lightly if they pour too fast. Everett, who has graduated to a walker Kathryn pulled from storage, does laps around the kitchen island, gurgling and calling out "Achoo! Achoo!" which I've come to believe means "Jacob."

"It smells like ketchup!" Mikey says.

"Yep. Ketchup is made from tomatoes, and so is our chili."

I haven't turned the burner on yet, so I don't have to worry about their little hands resting near the stove as they giggle at every new splash. The stove needed a scouring anyways, I realize, as I greedily watch their exalted faces. After the final can, Mikey and Jacob high-five, then giggle as Caden tries to join in. They all end up grabbing hold of each other's hands. Their laughter drowns out the whispers in my mind, and I feel a tugging in my belly. As Everett makes another round, I wonder: Is this what I could have had?

The Lord put her in your path for a reason, Jenna. In time you'll understand His plan.

I'm pouring the corn bread batter into the cast iron skillet when Travis comes downstairs, barefoot, in jeans and a black T-shirt that makes his eyes stand out from across the room.

"Chili's smelling good," he says as he reaches me and puts his hand on my low back, leaning in for a quick kiss. I tense, against my will, even as I raise my face to his.

"Hmmm, Mom's corn bread." He nods, kisses my forehead, and walks away.

When I straighten from putting the corn bread in the oven, Travis is at the set of doors to the right, pulling on a jacket and looking toward where Kelly is lounging, one long leg bent. He steps onto the porch, and I step forward, wiping my hands on Kathryn's apron. Kelly puts her magazine down the second the door closes, then pushes her sunglasses up to make a crown in her perfect hair.

They exchange a few words.

"Set the timer, Jenna!" Lauren calls from the couch.

Kelly rests her chin on her hand, smiling up at Travis.

"Jenna. You hate yourself when you burn your corn bread, your biscuits ..."

"Broom! Broom!" Caden calls out, trying to mimic Jacob's sound effects as they drive trucks around the family room.

Look at her. She thinks she's pretty! Mama, looking at me, sidelong, says. *He's gone because of you.*

"Jenna," Lauren says again.

I move toward the oven, saying over my shoulder, "Correction, little sister, your mother's corn bread, your mother's biscuits."

"Just because it's Mom's recipe doesn't mean they're hers and hers alone."

The timer set, I turn back toward the lake. I watch in horror as Kelly smirks, flicking her sunglasses back down and returning to her magazine in one swift, graceful movement. Travis laughs and holds out his hands, shrugging.

"You cooked them. They're at least a hybrid," Lauren continues, holding Kaitlyn up. "Right, Kait? Mama's right. Aunt Jenna is the most annoying little sister ever."

I put my hands on my hips. "I am not your little sister."

"Yes, you are."

I look back to the porch, and he's gone.

Kelly leans against the railing, smoking a cigarette.

CHAPTER SEVEN

KELLY

We sit down to another of Jenna's masterpieces. This time it's chili. The family makes the appropriate oohs and aahs, then the even more tedious thanking-Jesus ritual, before we can begin eating.

There's a tension today between them. Jenna's eyes look puffy, and Travis seemed relieved, earlier, to make light of our situation. He lingered, made sure he didn't look at me too often.

"This is another one of your recipes, isn't it?" I ask Kathryn, holding up the corn bread.

"Yes. Thankfully, my daughter-in-law tries to master my recipes, since my own daughter won't."

Jenna smiles and looks away, feeding Everett a spoonful of goo.

"They're even better than Mom's," Lauren says.

"They're just as good, I agree," Nathan says, not looking up.

"My grandmother put honey from her own hives in her biscuits. She tried to teach me her magic, but I was a mess in the kitchen," I say. I smile at Lauren first. "We all have different gifts, right?"

Lauren nods but doesn't even attempt a smile.

"I did learn my love of houses from my grandmother. That one caught on."

"Oh?" Kathryn says, being polite.

There's a silence around the table, except for Nathan slurping his chili next to me.

I clear my throat, my hand clenched in a fist between my thighs. "I'm a real estate agent."

"Mommy sells houses," Caden says, waving his chicken nugget in the air.

"Well, isn't that lovely," Kathryn says.

"And yours is especially beautiful," I add, taking another helping of corn bread that I don't want.

This is complete shit. I'm not winning them over at all. Nathan murmurs again, beside me, his lips open and moist.

CHAPTER EIGHT
JENNA

We gather in the family room once the children are asleep. Nathan cranks his radio. Fuzz.

Travis puts another log in the fireplace, reaches down to scratch behind Beauty's ear. Nathan keeps cranking.

I wish I had something to do with my hands. It's too dark to color. I resist the urge to bite my nails. I want Travis to sit down, sit next to me, but he lingers near the fireplace. She sits on the hearth, stealing glances at him, repositioning herself every few minutes.

A voice breaks through the silence. "State-run community shelters are organizing on their own, so we cannot report on their readiness. Repeat: the federal government is not responsible for state shelters. Federal resources remain committed to national and homeland security. Federal aid is going to major cities, and FEMA and Red Cross continue to assist. Foreign nations continue to send aid and promise more to come. Reports of state-run shelters are being added daily. At the end of this broadcast, we will read a list of open shelters across the United States, in alphabetical order. The White House has declared a shelter-in-place policy. Do not travel unless it is a life-threatening emergency. Looters at large, and they are armed.

"Water sources are unsafe. Boil your water before drinking. Do not run generators inside your homes. Conserve fuel. Fuel sources are down and inaccessible. National stockpiles are dedicated to government and military operations. Repeat: conserve your fuel and potable water.

The president has requested that all active and retired military, first responders, and medical professionals report to their nearest army base.

"We need all Americans to stand together to overcome this, the worst ..."

Fuzz.

Nathan cranks some more, stops, tries again. We sit in silence, and the darkness of the room seems to deepen.

"I wish you wouldn't go to town tomorrow," Kathryn says, holding Travis with her gaze.

"It doesn't sound good," Brent says, his arm draped around Lauren on the couch.

The radio crackles. Nathan turns the handle some more.

"... pull together. Help our neighbors. We will ..." Fuzz.

He holds the radio up to the left, then the right.

We wait, listening. Crank. Static. Repeat.

"Turn it off, Dad." Travis says, digging around in the woodbin. "There's no way I'm not going, after that broadcast. We need supplies. We need to know what it's like in town."

"I'll go with you," Brent says, quietly.

"No." Lauren swings her legs around and sits up, turning to face him. "No."

"I can go by myself. I prefer to." Travis throws a log onto

the fire. "No offense. I'll be faster by myself. In and out. See what I can see, grab what I can, and get back home." He turns and looks at his mother. "Safely."

He's in my arms. Lifeless. Still. Such tiny features formed with such perfection, angelic and pure.

Hands grasping for him, pulling at my arms, my hands. I open my mouth to scream, but I can't. My throat won't work, it won't make sound.

No No No No No No No.

The scream stuck in my throat, choking me with its force.

They add hands to the grasping and yanking until there are too many. They've taken him. He's gone.

I fall to the ground, to my hands and knees, and that's when I see her.

Mama. Mama on the floor, puking and crying, crawling toward me, her lipstick smeared. Her hand reaching out, finger pointing.

"Gone! Gone because of you! Gone! Gone!"

She's howling, her eyes ringed black, smudged.

I back away, but she crawls faster, spider-like, spitting and screaming, "You!"

I wipe her saliva from my face again and again, but it won't come off.

I wake with a start, heart racing. Forcing my breath to slow, my chest rising and falling painfully, I roll toward Travis. I make out the faintest line of his shoulder in the dark.

Please. Please hold me. Please make me safe.

It aches. How it aches. How it hollows me—this need to

reach for him. But I hear Mama's voice, stopping me with a whisper.

"You don't deserve to."

He gets up while it's still dark. I stay in bed. I know he doesn't want me getting up, extending his departure with a long goodbye. Still, I cling to him when he bends to hug me, praying and murmuring against his neck, beseeching Mary, the one true Mother, to bring him back to me.

After the door clicks shut, I whisper, "Glory be to the Father, and to the Son, and to the Holy Spirit, as it was in the beginning, is now, and ever shall be ..."

I can't sleep. By the time Everett wakes, I'm dressed and pacing the room, ready with a thick blanket.

I've put on my grandmother's sweater, her rosary tucked in my left pocket.

Beauty's nails click-clack down the stairs as we head to the porch, ready for the sunrise.

"Da-Da!" Everett smacks my chest with his open hand. I hold it in mine and kiss his palm.

Are your brothers looking down on us from Heaven right now? I wonder.

Everett grabs my chin with his other hand, smiling up at me.

Is that a yes?

But instead, I say, "Hungry, bubby?" as I step out onto the porch.

The first loss was hard, maybe harder than it should have been. But I'd already had Jacob. I knew what I was losing.

I started spotting at eight weeks. By the time I got to the doctor's office, she'd left for an emergency surgery. The elderly midwife attempted an ultrasound, failed to find the baby, and sent me to the emergency room.

I knew he was gone before they told me. There's such a certainty in death. Before they spread the jelly and ask if you're comfortable, you know. They'll move their wand around again and again, wanting to be certain and wanting to be wrong. And as tomorrow hangs in the balance and your heart gets stretched, further and further, you ask them, silently, to keep searching, to avoid the words, "No heartbeat."

I watch Everett's face and pray, moving the rosary beads through my fingers, one by one. I never got to meet my grandmother. I know her from Mama's pictures, before she married Daddy and Jed was born, before she moved south. In my favorite photo, Grandma looks both respectable and elegant, standing by a glistening lake with a large-brimmed hat, her arm flung around a beautiful young woman, so radiant she takes your breath away.

What happened to you, Mama?

I'm pacing with Everett when Kathryn comes bustling into the room, dressed in sweats and tennis shoes.

"Chris and Amanda will be here any time now, and we've been slack around here for days," she says. She sets a plastic bin on the counter, full of cleaning supplies. "Vacuuming or scrubbing?"

She's furious in her scrubbing, attacking the counters like they're a crystal ball that will reveal some truth once they're clean enough. Perhaps she's attempting to divine Chris's location or steal a glimpse of Travis in town. I find that I'm grateful to push the heavy old cabin vacuum around and around the old braided rugs—anything to keep me from biting my nails.

But I'm exhausted by lunch, with tight shoulders and a throbbing head. I can't seem to stop checking the time every ten minutes, even with the nonstop chores Kathryn keeps calling out.

"The glass doors need a Windexing! Why don't you do the oven doors as well!"

"The bird feeder is empty!"

"Why don't we wash all the bathroom rugs?"

Jacob senses my tension and is the worst behaved he's been all week. After lunch, when I ask him to collect plates, he stands on his chair and throws his sippy cup across the room.

"No!" he shouts.

"Jacob!"

"No!" He stomps and crosses his arms. "Someone else's turn!" He stomps again, his eyes brimming with tears.

"You do not speak to me like that ..." My voice sounds weak to my own ears.

"No more!" he shouts, then jumps off the chair, running to Kathryn and Nathan's bedroom and slamming the door.

I stand dumbfounded, not noticing the food sliding off

the plate I hold in midair until Kathryn gently takes it. "Don't worry about it, Jenna. We all have our moments."

Kelly chortles and pushes back from the table. "Plates, boys," she says, and they snap to action.

I never talked back to my mother either.

"Jenna," Kathryn says, a little louder. "You're exhausted. Go lie down. I've got the boys for a little while."

I feel weighted, my feet stuck to the ground. All I can hear is Jacob slamming the door.

"Jenna," Kathryn urges.

I nod dumbly and head for the stairs.

I lie down on Travis's side of the bed, burying my face in his pillow, breathing him in. And then I roll over to my own and pull his up against my lips. I don't want to spoil his scent.

I startle and sit straight up, panicked. My Fitbit reads 12:52 p.m. My heart beats wildly as I scramble to the window and look down toward the driveway.

Empty. He still isn't home.

Pulling the blinds all the way up for an unobstructed view, I collapse in the window seat, pull the afghan over me. Squeeze my hands between my knees, hard. The gravel drive inclines away from me and then forks—to the left and out of sight or disappearing down, only to rise again in the distance before fading into forest. A sloping hill of dead wild grasses and bare brambles hugs the forking path. I watch the birds darting by, my hand pressed to the glass. I let my eyes follow the sunlight slanting through the trees and the shadows stretching beyond them.

He will come back to me. He isn't Daddy, the man

who was never mine at all. He belonged to Jed. Jed remembered playing ball with him in front of the brick house, the one we had to leave when I was born. Jed knew that Daddy had a size-twelve shoe and smoked Camel Lights. He had a picture too, of him sitting on Daddy's knee on the porch of that nice brick house. I remember Jed, spitting and kicking and rattling the trailer as I huddled under the table. *Gone because of you. You made him leave!*

And me, hands cupped over ears and eyes squeezed shut, too little to remember all the lines but calling for her anyways, whispering, "Hail Mary, Mother Mary, one, two, three, four, fix, six, seven, Hail Mary, Mother Mary."

I take the fastest shower I can manage, after cracking the bedroom door and hearing cartoons and silence. Afterward, I straighten my hair with the bathroom door open, listening as the boys encourage Thomas the Tank Engine, urging him on. I haven't heard Kelly's voice.

Beauty starts barking and turning in circles as I come downstairs.

"Daddy!" Jacob hollers, rushing to his feet.

I move toward Kathryn, who holds Everett. "Go on," she says, smiling and holding a palm up in hallelujah. "God is good."

As I round the corner of the mudroom and go through the open door, Jacob is jumping into his daddy's arms.

Travis's smile lights up his whole face as he says, "You'd think I'd been gone a week!"

He makes his roaring "I'm gonna eat you" sounds as he gobbles Jacob's neck, sending him into a fit of giggles.

Once he's calmed down and caught his breath, Jacob says, "Daddy, is the power coming back now?"

Travis shakes his head. "I'm afraid not, buddy. I think it's going to be out for an awfully long time."

"Really?" Kathryn says as she comes to stand beside me.

"Yes," Travis says, looking at Jacob and making a silly face.

"So, we aren't going home?" our son asks.

"No, bud, not for a little while more, at least."

"That's okay, Daddy. I like living with Nana and Papa. Can we live here forever?"

Travis chuckles and puts him down, saying, "Look what I found." He pulls out a stack of DVDs.

"What are those?" Jacob asks.

Travis laughs. "Movies."

"Movies?"

"Yep, and I don't think you've seen most of these. Let's bring them inside, and you and Mikey can pick something to watch." He turns to Nathan. "We haven't used the DVD player yet. Does it use too much electricity?"

"I'm sure we've got power for some movies!" Nathan says, taking the stack from Travis, then taking Jacob's hand, "Let's go get one set up."

Once the boys are snuggled up with pillows and stuffed animals and watching *Cars 2,* the adults assemble on the porch, chairs in a circle. Nathan has lit the propane firepit. Kelly is in yet another stylish ensemble: brown leggings with tall boots and a dark-brown-and-green sweater that hugs her in all the right places. She smiles at me, open and friendly, and gushes, "Thank goodness your husband found movies," as she takes a seat next to him. I want to dump her from her chair.

"Ma-Ma!" Everett slaps his thigh, waiting. I reach into my loaded tote bag and hand him the first toy in my arsenal. "Da-Da," he says as he swats at the toy's blinking lights. "Da da ba ba ba dadaaa."

Lauren is the last to sit, and before her bottom has hit the chair, she's asking, "So, what's it like out there?"

"Not good." Travis leans forward on his knees and clasps his hands, looking beyond me, toward the mountains and sky.

He looks down, takes a deep breath.

"Most places are completely looted. All the windows at the Ingle's—smashed, broken. The shelves are bare, just a few odds and ends on the floor. I managed to get a couple cans of vegetables and condensed milk. My best finds were a few bags of dry beans and rice."

"Oh my," Kathryn says.

"Every single store was looted?" Lauren asks. "How far past town did you go?"

"I didn't say every store. The ones I went by, at least."

"Did you see anyone?" Kathryn asks.

"Now, just hold on y'all, and let the boy speak," Nathan says.

Travis takes off his ball cap, runs his hand through his hair, looking at his dad. "Right?"

He settles back in his chair and waits until we've all stopped moving, including Kelly, who's leaning another inch toward him. "There's a shelter in town, at the high school. It's guarded by a dozen or so men. Said they're sheriff's department or military, but I bet a few of 'em are ROTC from the damn school they're standing in front of. They wouldn't let me inside. Said if I came with my family to take shelter, then I could. There were people sitting around outside in camping chairs, their kids playing in the field by the school. A few hundred cars in the parking lot, I'd guess."

"Did they have food or supplies to give out?" Kelly asks.

"Definitely not. Friendly enough, though."

"Any of 'em old enough to be in charge?" Nathan asks.

"Yeah, there were a few older guys. I'd say one or two were vets, maybe National Guard. They said the hospital down the road has one wing still up and running, somewhat, managing on generators for now."

"See, society hasn't collapsed completely," Nathan says, looking to Kathryn and nodding.

"For now ..." she says quietly, her eyes searching Travis's face.

"For now." He shrugs. "One young man, still got his pimples, started saying they should pack up the whole shelter and head to Dobbins Air Force Base, since the broadcast was calling on all army and first responders." Travis shakes his head. "He'd heard there were cities burning, though how he'd heard that, I don't know. Maybe just blabbering out of fear, till an older guy shut him up and sent him on an errand."

Adjusting his ball cap again, he adds, "Older guy told me they were staying put, taking care of their own."

"Well, shit." Lauren says.

I hand Everett his fifth toy, forcing myself to breathe against the pressure squeezing my chest. We are safe. My family is with me, and we are safe.

Please, please keep us safe.

Brent takes Lauren's hand and says, "Shit, exactly. Why didn't we grab all our food?"

"Or our toilet paper," she replies.

"But those supplies in the truck ..." Nathan stalls to

silence. We wait. Travis stands, walks away from the circle and leans on the railing.

I shiver and pull my shawl closer around us. Everett smiles up at me, grabs at the blanket, catches my hair instead.

"I got plenty," Travis says.

"Travis?" Kathryn leans forward as Nathan places his large hand on her knee.

My husband clears his throat. "I'm not sure I acted as a Christian should."

I sit up straighter, eyes on his profile.

"What do you mean?" Kathryn asks.

"I feel a bit guilty. Technically, I looted."

"I thought that's why you went to town. To get supplies," Lauren says, crossing her arms.

"Still felt wrong. It was the Walgreens just out of town. Boarded up nice and tight. They had everything."

Lauren stands and joins her brother at the railing. "You went to town to take care of your family."

"I took a fair portion and left the rest. And I left a hundred bucks on the counter, not that that covers it."

"For the next looter to grab," she says, elbowing him.

"No, you did good," Nathan says, "and left some for your neighbor."

I can't help myself. I read the food inventory list again and again, chuckling every time I pass over "ketchup, twelve," picturing Travis in a boarded-up Walgreens, grabbing bottle after bottle. And yet he left some, for whoever came after him.

Brent uses an ungodly amount of ketchup and brown

sugar in his meat loaf, one of his many mouthwatering specialties. Kathryn drowns the last of our fresh vegetables in butter and minced garlic since they aren't looking so fresh. We carve sprouts out of potatoes, our last, and decide to make them mashed, with lots of butter.

As Brent puts the loaves into the oven, Travis announces, "I got beer." He goes to the garage and comes back grinning, a six-pack in each hand. "Chef gets first pick."

"Thank you, sir," Brent says. He bows, one arm crossing his midsection, the other plucking a bottle. "I gladly accept."

"I thought y'all didn't drink," Kelly says from her perch on a kitchen stool.

"What would you like us to say? That even Jesus drank wine?" Lauren says, walking into the kitchen and punching Travis on the arm. "Ya got me some cheap wine, right?"

"Only the best for you, lil' sis," Travis says, going back to the garage.

"What's for dinner?" Jacob shouts, his voice bouncing off the high ceilings. "I'm starving!" He clutches his stomach while sinking to his knees, moaning, and falling backward.

Caden falls apart giggling, while Mikey stands straight and still, scanning the adults' faces one by one. When he decides it's safe, he falls beside his brother, mimicking Jacob's hungry growls.

Kathryn laughs and shakes her head. "Just like his daddy!"

"Only much cuter, and much, much less annoying," Lauren adds.

Sensing that he's losing the crowd's attention, Jacob

stands and storms into the kitchen, hands on hips. "I smell food. Feed me!" He juts his chin out at Travis.

Travis rounds his shoulders, lets his arms dangle like a gorilla looking like he's about to charge. "Children who speak like that get put in the stew for supper!"

Jacob squeals and turns to run, but Travis grabs him and tosses him over his shoulder.

"Where's the chopping block?" Travis bellows.

"No, ogre, no!" Jacob yells, beating on his daddy's back.

"I'll save you!" Mikey yells, then runs for Travis, only to be scooped up and swung onto Travis's free shoulder.

"You prefer white, right Jenna?" Lauren is holding out a glass of rosé wine. I start to shake my head, but she says, "Oh, c'mon, Jenna. Loosen up. One glass won't kill you."

"But I have to breastfeed Everett later."

"I distinctly recall seeing some pumped breastmilk in the fridge and thinking, *Yuck*, earlier today," she says.

I hate to admit she's right. I have built a small reserve. I've read about women not producing enough milk during times of stress, so I've been pumping once a day to make sure my supply stays high. I still don't want wine though.

"Jenna," she says, grabbing my chin. "Let's have some fun."

She kisses me on the forehead, which she likes to do from time to time, since she's seven inches taller than me. Usually, it annoys me and makes me feel like a child. But in this instant, I want to hug her.

"Fine," I say and take the wine.

The noise from Travis and the boys reaches deafening volume, and Kathryn says, "Time to simmer down or take it outside, boys!"

"Outside, Daddy, outside!" Jacob insists.

"Just for a few minutes. It's almost time for supper,"

Travis says in a serious tone, then sprints to the door with a grin on his face. The boys chase after him, shrieking and shouting.

"I'm glad I have a daughter," Brent says as he mashes the potatoes by hand.

"Don't think your daughter won't be loud. Mine was louder than both my boys," Kathryn says as she rummages in the fridge. "This shredded cheese won't last much longer." She passes two half bags to Brent. "Always hollering about something."

"When'll that meat loaf be done?" Nathan asks, groaning as he stands.

Brent instinctively reaches toward the oven, like a parent protecting a child in lieu of a seat belt. "Don't open it yet."

"Would you like me to set the table?" Kelly asks.

I look at Lauren and open my eyes as wide as I can. She rolls hers and mouths, "Kiss up."

I suppress a giggle and take a sip of my wine. It tastes better than I remember.

Kathryn points to a cupboard. "Plates are there. Let's get our place mats out for this meal. What the heck—the fancy ones. We don't know when we'll have fresh potatoes again."

Fresh potatoes. The last of our fresh vegetables too. No more fruit either, save a few canned or jarred. I set my wine down and retrieve the mats, kept in the antique dresser, which is often overlooked where it sits in the foyer. It belonged to Kathryn's grandmother. There are two levels of "fancy" place mats. The first set, which I retrieve, are a deep red and sewn with an intricate floral pattern that's dizzying if you look straight at it. The other set is off-white antique lace—much too delicate for children.

I lay them on the table as Kelly follows me with the plates. Her sickeningly sweet perfume creates a cloud around us.

"I wish we could play music!" Lauren says, interrupting my thoughts and grabbing my hand. She twirls me until I laugh, then sweeps up my glass and hands it to me.

Why not, I think as I take a swig. Kelly moves in my periphery, grabbing a wineglass, pouring. Taking something from her pocket and washing it down.

"Should we play a game tonight?" Lauren asks. "What did you bring?"

Kelly grabs a handful of silverware but leaves it in a pile, her attention caught by something outside. She watches the boys for a moment before grabbing her jacket and slipping it on.

"Um, I'm not sure," I say.

How long will we be here? How long will *she* be here?

Kelly opens the door quietly and slides out.

"Surely you brought games," Lauren says.

I pick up the silverware Kelly left and begin my circle around the table. "They're in a tote in the garage, if you wanna go look."

The flash of Kelly's lighter sparks in my periphery.

"Seriously?" Lauren sits down on a stool, glaring at me.

"Not yet, Papa!" Brent says, swatting a towel toward Nathan, who's reaching for the oven handle.

"She certainly likes to watch Travis, doesn't she?" Kathryn says, coming to stand beside her daughter.

The boys run around on the porch, lunging and laughing. The last light of the day illuminates Kelly's hair as she stands in the corner, smoking and watching.

"Yes, she does," Lauren says from her stool, where she's swiveled to watch too.

"So, I'm not the only one who's noticed," I add.

"At least she's not drunk today," Brent says as he finally pulls the loaves out of the oven.

"The night isn't over yet," Lauren says. "But maybe we should all get drunk, so she won't seem so obnoxious."

"Baptists don't get drunk," Nathan says, watching Brent. "That done yet?"

Lauren swivels toward me as I put down my last fork and knife. "Not drunk then. How about tipsy?" She raises her glass to me. I've always envied her sass and confidence. She never worries about what anyone thinks. She just speaks her mind. She's also the only person who's successfully gotten me intoxicated.

I shake my head no.

"Oh, Jenna!" She grabs my glass and hands it to me as she slips her arm around my waist. "Let's have some fun!"

"Sure, but ..."

"But what? We're stuck here until who knows when. And, therefore, we're obligated to have some fun."

"But everyone isn't accounted for." I say it under my breath so Kathryn won't hear, even though she's gone across the kitchen to retrieve Kaitlyn from her pack-n-play.

"Jenna."

"Well."

"They'll show up. Tonight. Tomorrow. The next day. We won't think about how many days we might be stuck here. But what we will do is have fun."

"It seems—"

"Did you bring a speaker?"

"Travis might have, but would it work without Internet?"

"Ugh." She rolls her eyes and takes a chug, eyeing me over her glass.

"Drink!" She gives an upward nod of her chin, and I do as I'm told.

I sneak a glance outside and find Travis has stopped playing with the boys. He stands against the railing, his body turned toward her.

Kathryn walks toward us, sensing a conspiracy. "Are we still watching her?" she asks as she gets to us, Kaitlyn lying happily in the crook of her arm.

They can't see us watching them, at this hour. The sunlight hits the doors at the perfect angle, instantly blinding, so anyone outside looks away. The boys play, oblivious. Kelly flips her hair and toys with a cigarette, pulling it out of her pack, putting it back, considering. Travis laughs and looks out toward the mountains, pulls his right hand out of his pocket, and scratches his neck, looking back at her while the smile lingers on his face.

As the last of the sunlight fades beyond the mountains, the boys stream in with red cheeks.

"Did you get all your shrieks out?" Kathryn asks.

"Yes, ma'am!" Jacob says, standing perfectly still and giving her his best salute.

"That's my boy."

Kelly comes in, also with red cheeks and nose. But somehow, the pink makes her blue eyes stand out and sparkle even more than usual. She walks up to Travis, who went straight for the fireplace, hands extended in front of the fire, and puts her hand on his arm.

Caden tugs on my jeans, saying, "Ms. Jenna, Ms. Jenna," so I can't hear what Kelly is saying to my husband.

"Yes, sweetheart?" I set down my wine and hold out my hands. He nods, and I pick him up.

"What's for dinner?" he says, then puts his thumb in his mouth.

"Meat loaf. Have you had meat loaf before?"

He tilts his head, considering. Mikey, who I hadn't noticed, pipes in, "Yes, Caden, the dark meat with ketchup."

Caden takes his thumb out. "Ketchup?"

I nod, and he smiles, reinserting his thumb and laying his head on my shoulder. I rub his back with my free hand and hold him a little closer, feel his small body relaxing against my own. He could be my son. He could be. I glance back toward the fireplace, and there's Brent, his arm around Travis, raising his beer in a toast and pulling Travis along with him and back to us.

Once we're all settled around the table, and Kathryn has served everyone a thick slice of meat, she exclaims, "I just love this recipe, Brent. Best darn meat loaf, hands down."

Nathan nods and helps himself to a second slice before he's even started his first.

"Do you like it, boys?" I ask Mikey and Caden.

They nod in unison.

"Can I get more ketchup, please?" Mikey asks.

"Of course, sweetheart." I reach for the ketchup and nearly knock over my wine. Travis shoots me a look. I give him a sheepish smile. As I'm passing the ketchup, Mikey looks at my wine and asks, "Does that make you mean?"

"Hey, boys!" Travis says loudly. "Wanna go fishing again tomorrow?"

"Yes!" they all say at once. Jacob wiggles his bottom,

and Caden clasps his hands under his chin with a huge smile. Mikey looks down at his lap before turning to his mother and saying softly, "Can we?"

"Well, of course. Why not?" She smiles and ruffles his hair. It was a tiny movement, so slight that if you blinked, you'd miss it. But just as she was raising her hand, Mikey flinched.

Lauren and I do the dishes and have so much fun whispering jokes to each other that, at least for a little while, I forget to pay attention to our houseguest. When Everett signals it's time for his nightcap, Travis takes my pumped milk from the fridge, warms it, and settles in to feed him. We let the boys stay up a little later than usual, and they play happily in front of the fire, building a city out of Legos. Jacob is in charge, of course, and has named the city, the buildings, and the roads that he's carefully marked off with his Lincoln Logs.

As we finish the dishes, Lauren leans in and whispers, "Just one more." She giggles. "Okay, maybe two more," she says and refills our glasses.

Lauren saunters—her telltale wine walk—into the family room and plops in a wingback chair next to Kelly. I grab a pillow and join the boys on the floor. Their city stretches across the family room rug.

Lauren picks up her wine, staring at me dramatically over the rim, still giggling.

Kelly, eyeing her, picks up her empty glass.

"Oh, I'm sorry. I didn't think to ask if you needed more," Lauren says, laying on the Southern belle accent.

"Anyone else?" Kelly asks as she stands.

Kathryn shakes her head.

Caden's eyes are drooping, and he starts falling right toward downtown. I lean forward and stick my arm out to keep him upright. He startles, sees me, and crawls toward me and right into my lap.

"Thanks for saving the heart of the city, Mommy," Jacob says, his eyes on his precious buildings.

Caden snuggles into my chest and falls right to sleep.

Mikey scoots over and pats his brother's back. "He okay sleeping here?"

"Yep." I smile at him.

He smiles back and returns to fiddling with his plastic creation.

Travis stands up and comes over to me. "I'm going to put this one down in his crib."

"I can do it."

"That's alright; you've got your hands full. Besides, I need another beer anyways."

"I'll get one for you!" Kelly calls out from the kitchen.

"Um, thanks," Travis says and heads upstairs.

"What the heck? Can you get me one too?" Brent says as he also stands. He stops by Lauren's chair, where she kisses Kait's brow, then goes on to their room with his sleeping bundle.

"Bedtime in five, Mikey," Kelly says, as she heads to the porch for a cigarette.

"Does that mean me too?" Jacob asks.

The wine swimming in my head wants to answer, "Stay up as late as you want!" But I know that means a cranky five-year-old tomorrow.

"It's getting pretty late, bud."

"Uh," Jacob whines, setting down his Lego piece and

crossing his arms. "But we've been working so hard! And we aren't finished yet!"

"Maybe if you ask Nana nicely, she'll let you leave the city up overnight so you can work on it more tomorrow."

Jacob's eyes light up, and he swivels around to face Kathryn. "Can we?"

She sets down her needlework. "If I say yes, I have one rule."

"Anything, Nana!"

"You boys have to clean it all up by dinner tomorrow."

"Yes, ma'am! Thank you, Nana!" Jacob scrambles to his feet and rushes over to hug her.

"Thank you," Mikey says quietly from his spot.

"Well, don't I get a hug from you too?" she asks.

"You want one?" Mikey fiddles with his shoelaces.

"Yes, I do," Kathryn says, releasing Jacob.

Mikey, pushing his hair out of his eyes and peeking up at her, stands and hesitates before walking to her and into her arms. She kisses the top of his head. When he returns to his spot, his head is down and he's looking at the floor, but his cheeks are bright red and he's smiling.

Kelly reenters and heads to the fridge, retrieving two Bud Lights. She walks toward the far sink and sets the beers on the counter, her back to us, but I can see her reflection in the window above the sink. She reaches into the V-neck of her sweater and readjusts her cleavage, swaying slightly as she does so. Grabbing the beers with one hand, she strolls back toward us and grabs her wine on the way. Sitting on the arm of the couch, she waits for the men, her eyes on the stairs.

"Look, Mommy, at all our buildings!" Mikey says, turning to look at her. "Do you like our city?"

Kelly glances in his direction. "It's amazing."

"But you didn't really look, Mommy," he says quietly.

"I did look. I've been seeing them all night." She doesn't bother to take her eyes off the stairs.

Lauren looks at me with narrowed eyes, and I'm not sure if I want her to unleash her anger on Kelly or not.

"It really is amazing, Mikey," Lauren says. "I love y'all's creativity. Maybe you'll be city designers one day!"

Kelly scoffs, but Jacob doesn't hear her. "That would be so cool!" he says. He stands to survey their creation.

"Time for bed," Kelly says as Travis descends the stairs.

Mikey's hands stall on his building, and his head falls to his chest.

Jacob stands up, hands on hips as he says, "Mommy said we could finish our buildings, and Mikey isn't done yet." He looks straight at her. "And Mommy is the boss."

Kelly stands, glaring at him. "She's not the boss of Mikey. I am."

"In this house, Nana is the boss, and Mommy is second in charge," Jacob says. "Get used to it."

I'm aware of my mouth falling open and my wine-laden mind racing, but words escape me.

Kelly's face is turning red, and she takes a step toward Jacob.

"Is that how we speak to adults, Jacob?" Kathryn's stern voice rings above the fire and the angry silence.

"But, Nana."

"Jacob Lawrence!" Travis snaps from the stairs as he descends, which makes Jacob startle. "We do not speak back to Nana, or any adult."

Jacob's face collapses, and he starts to cry. "I'm sorry, Daddy." His breathing is already heavy, and he turns to Kathryn. "I'm sorry. It's just. It's just ..."

"I know, baby, come here." I put down my wine and hold out my free hand.

Jacob doesn't move. He balls his hands into fists at his side and sobs, tears dripping off his chin.

I glance at Travis. "I did tell them they could finish their buildings," I manage.

Nathan stands. "Just the case of too many cooks in the kitchen."

No one speaks.

"What I mean is," Nathan says, scratching his head, "too many mamas in one house, making different rules." He takes a few steps toward Jacob and extends his hand. "It's alright, bud. I'm proud of you for sticking up for your friend, but your daddy is right. You can't talk back, and especially not to your nana."

"Breathe, buddy, breathe," I say. I hate it when he gets this upset. I want to stand and go to him, but I don't know if I have the coordination with a heavy three-year-old asleep on my lap. I glance at Kelly. Her eyes are getting that familiar glazed look. Lauren sits on the edge of her chair, and I notice her hands are also balled into fists.

Mikey, so quietly it's hard to hear, says, "I'm sorry I got you in trouble." He doesn't look up. His eyes are fixed on the building, still unfinished in his hands.

Nathan leans over and grabs Jacob. Holding him and looking straight into his eyes, he says, "It's late, bud. Everyone is tired. Let's you and me go to bed, and we can talk it over some more if you want."

Jacob nods, puts his arms around Nathan's neck, and lays down his head, his tiny shoulders bobbing up and down as he tries to catch his breath.

As they pass by me, I say, "Goodnight, baby. I love you."

Nathan stops at the bottom of the stairs, and Travis

tousles Jacob's hair, whispers something in his ear, and kisses him. Grandpa and grandson go to their shared room.

For a moment, it's quiet, save for the popping of burning wood.

"Well, that was some unexpected entertainment!" Kelly says and holds the beer out toward Travis. "Here's your beer." Her cheerful voice sounds brittle and matches the strange, forced smile she gives Travis.

"I think I'm good, thanks. I'll put them back in the fridge." Travis takes the beers and heads toward the kitchen.

I watch in horror as Kelly stands straighter, the smile gone, her eyes suddenly narrow and glinting, her wine sloshing and spilling down her hand. One uneven step, a slight sway, and then her heavy boot is kicking Mikey's building, sending it flying into the stone hearth.

She leans into his face and snarls, "Way to ruin the night, Mikey."

He curls into a ball and shields his head with his arms, hiccupping with sobs.

She bends over and grabs his hair, yanking him upright.

"Don't you dare," Lauren says as she takes a step toward them.

Travis strides in. "What's going on?"

Kelly lets go of Mikey's hair. Her expressions change so quickly—blind wrath, recognition, embarrassment. And a familiar thump, thump, thumping starts in my head.

"Nothing," Kelly says. "I'm sorry we caused a scene." She looks down at Mikey. "Come on, baby, let's go to bed."

"I'm thinking maybe the boys should sleep down here. We'll make them a comfy spot in front of the fire," Lauren says.

"No." Kelly attempts a smile at Travis, but her mouth

contorts instead. "I'm sorry I got angry. Really. We've just been stuck in this house too many days ..." She looks at Lauren. "I'm really sorry. Won't happen again." She holds her hand out to Mikey. "Come on, baby, let's go to bed."

Mikey, still trying to catch his breath and face wet with tears, keeps his eyes trained on the floor while he takes his mother's hand.

Please don't let her take him. She's breaking him. Please, she's breaking him.

I struggle to control my own breathing and shaking hands. Caden sighs contentedly in my lap, unaware of my racing heart.

Kathryn stands and extends a hand to Kelly. "I'll take the wineglass to the kitchen for you."

Kelly hesitates, looks at her glass, and hands it to her.

"I'll carry Caden up to y'all's room," Travis says, and he lifts the sweet boy from my arms.

I wobble a bit as I stand and put my hand on the hearth to steady myself. I want to follow them up the stairs, but Lauren puts her hand on my arm and gives me her raised eyebrow, her "what the hell is wrong with that woman?" face. Instead, we follow Kathryn into the kitchen, where she dumps the wine and rinses the glass. We stand around in a circle at the farthest end of the kitchen, against the sink, where only moments ago, Kelly spruced herself up for my husband.

"Did you see how hard she yanked his hair?" Lauren whispers.

"Did you see how Mikey curled into a ball, immediately?" I fold my arms across my chest.

Kathryn shakes her head and whispers, "It was obviously instinct. I bet that bruise he had on his face the first day y'all got here was from her."

"I just don't understand how you could hit a child," Lauren says.

I see my mother and the way her face would change, all the lines in her profile suddenly sharper somehow. That sideways glance before she faced me full on. She'd grab whatever was closest, and eventually I learned that running and hiding was worse. She wanted me to cower, and I did. I always did.

"She's a poisonous woman, just like my mother." I don't look at either of them when I say it. I look past them, out the window, into the darkness.

"I don't know how much longer we can keep her in this house," Kathryn says. "I wasn't sure 'bout sending her away when Lauren said it earlier today, but she just looked like she was gonna beat Jacob. And no one touches my family, especially not my grandbabies."

Lauren puts a hand on my shoulder and stoops to make sure I'm looking her in the eyes. "I know you're worried about Mikey and Caden. But, Jenna, she'll be at a shelter with hundreds of other people, and soldiers. Surely they'll step in if she starts beating on the boys."

"Can't we just send her away and not the boys? I love those boys. I'll look after them."

"Jenna, we cannot send her away without her children," Lauren says. "She'd just keep showing up on our doorstep, shouting her head off, and she'd attract any wandering idiot with a gun looking for supper."

"How do you know she wouldn't be glad to be rid of them? Without having to take care of them, she can sleep with every soldier at the shelter!"

We startle as Travis comes into the kitchen.

"Don't worry, ladies, it's not the enemy." He holds up his hands like he's surrendering, then runs his hand through his thick blond hair and shakes his head in disbelief.

He joins our circle. I face Kathryn and the mountains, and Travis faces Lauren and the window behind her. The fire is dying in the fireplace, and with it, the warmth.

"Did she do something else?" Lauren asks.

Travis looks at the floor and runs his hands through his hair again. He looks up at his sister and crosses his arms. "That was the most bizarre interaction I've ever had."

My throat catches.

"She came onto you, didn't she?" Lauren says.

"I guess you could call it that." He scratches his head.

"What do you mean?" I hold my breath.

He shifts from one foot to another. "She told Mikey to go to bed, then followed me out to the hallway, where she threw her arms around my neck and started crying. Crying and apologizing."

I can't take my eyes off Travis, even though he's not looking at any of us. I look for signs of makeup on his face, then his collar, and finally his shoulders—his beautiful, broad shoulders. No signs, but it wasn't freshly applied. I bite the inside of my cheek. He loves me. *He loves me.*

"I didn't know what to do," he says. "She's ..."

"You didn't hug her back, did you?" Lauren leans forward, puts her hand on her hip.

"No, of course not." He speaks to her in a tone he never uses with me as he takes the smallest step forward.

Kathryn holds up her hands. "Don't let the serpent come between us."

They straighten simultaneously.

"I wasn't trying to accuse him," Lauren says. "She's just that sort of woman, Mama, and you know what I mean."

Kathryn nods.

"I know the difference, Lauren." Travis uncrosses his arms, shrugging and holding out his hands. "I didn't hug her back, but I didn't push her away either."

He glances in my direction, strokes his beard while shaking his head. "She's so lit, no telling how she'd react. I was worried she'd start screaming or worse, and the boys have seen enough for the night."

"Yes, they have," I say. I want to touch him. I want him to reach for me. I stay where I am.

"I told her to get some rest and ..."

"And?" Lauren has both hands on her hips now, though she maintains her distance. I can feel Kathryn watching me.

"She kissed me. Or tried to." He looks at me directly for the first time. "I pulled away fast enough that she just slobbered all over my cheek."

I want to charge past them and out into the cold winter air, but I can't move.

"Then?" Lauren hisses.

"Then I grabbed her arms and told her it was time she went to bed."

"And she listened?"

"Yes."

"Are you ready for her to leave now, Jenna?" Lauren leans against the counter, eyes on me, jaw set in a sharp line.

I don't know what to say. Yes, I want her to leave. I want to march up there right now and drag her by the hair into the dark, cold forest, screaming, me and her both. I want to tie her to a tree and leave bait around her neck.

"I refuse to abandon the boys," I finally say.

Travis huffs. "They're not yours to abandon!" He turns his back on me and strides away.

CHAPTER NINE

JENNA

I'm startled awake in the middle of the night. My first thought is a bad dream, until I realize Travis is also awake, sitting up, and listening. I peer at him in the dark. His hair sticks up in random spikes, and when I see how still he is, I hold my breath. There are unmistakable sounds of people downstairs.

Silently, he swings his legs out of bed and twists the doorknob, opening a small crack between us and whoever is downstairs.

He slips through the door. I scramble across the bed after him. He's at the railing as I get to my feet. He turns to me, tears in his eyes, and says, "It's Chris."

He doesn't even put pants on. I follow, and as I'm rounding the landing, Travis and Chris are embracing.

"Where are your pants, bro? You can't be that excited to see me," Chris says.

I slip into Kathryn and Nathan's bedroom, then grab a bathrobe off their door. I hand it to Travis as I go straight for Amanda and hug her tightly.

"You're finally here," I say.

"Mom, where am I putting my stuff?" Ava stands with her arms crossed and a book bag on her slender shoulders. She's nearly Amanda's height, and she's only thirteen. I look around her and see Henry sitting on the hearth, slumped over with his chin in his hands. Drew sits next to him, head resting on his older brother's shoulder.

"Henry, Drew, and Ava, take the upstairs bedroom with the bunk beds," Amanda says.

"No way, Mom. Gross. I am not sharing a room with either of those idiots," Ava replies.

"They're getting a bit old to be sharing a room, hon. We just bought Henry his first razor," Chris says.

"I'm afraid that bedroom isn't available anyway." I feel guilty as I say it, knowing it's my fault the room is occupied.

"We have houseguests," Travis finishes for me.

"Houseguests?" Drew asks, his voice cracking and jumping an octave.

He gets up and joins the rest of us, while Henry stays seated, watching us warily. Ava rolls her eyes and slips the bag from her shoulders.

Travis continues. "On our way up here, we were stopped by a woman crying in the street, begging for help."

"So you brought her here? Are y'all crazy?" Chris asks, taking off his baseball cap and slapping his thigh several times.

"We didn't know what else to do." I realize I've already said this once before, to Kathryn. "She has two small children."

Chris scratches his beard roughly. "How long have y'all been here?"

Travis looks up, as if the number will magically appear.

I clear my throat. "We headed up here on day three of the blackout, so we've been here almost five full days."

"Lucky you. It's hell out there," Ava says.

"Ava Grace!" her mother says, her face immediately red.

Ava shrugs and looks at me. "So, that means we're sleeping where?"

"Y'all get to have a slumber party in the basement!" I say, trying my biggest smile.

"Seriously?"

"Nana already made up the spare bed down there for your parents," I tell her. "And there's the pull-out couch and the blow-up mattress. It won't take a minute to get it all set up."

I grab the two closest bags on the floor and head downstairs without looking at their expressions, but I hear Chris echoing his daughter. "Seriously? We get the basement?"

A whirlwind of activity ensues. Amanda and I get busy setting up mattresses, putting on sheets, fielding questions, and stuffing pillows into cases, while the men unload suitcases, duffel bags, and totes of food from the car, and the three sleepy children wander, discuss, and stop to watch, thinking their own thoughts.

We head back up to the first floor, with Henry and Drew discreetly kicking each other on the sofa pull-out and Ava writing in her journal by flashlight, sighing loudly on her air mattress.

Upstairs, we pull chairs closer to the fire. Chris adds a few logs and puts a foot up on the hearth, halfheartedly poking and adjusting the wood. I feel a chill and pull my robe tighter.

What time is it? I try to remember what time we were woken by their arrival; I don't remember looking at the time. My Fitbit is charging upstairs, although I noticed yesterday it's four minutes behind the analog clock in the kitchen.

"Why'd it take y'all so long to get here?" Travis leans forward with his elbows on his knees. I marvel at how long his beard is after seven days of growth. His random red hairs are coming in.

"We couldn't decide what to do," Chris says, his eyes flitting in Amanda's direction.

"We went to get my father," she says.

We wait in silence for more. Amanda stares at the fire; Chris turns to look at us and says softly, "He wanted to be with his son."

Amanda lifts her chin. "So we dropped him off at my brother's house. My brother—who couldn't be bothered to drive an hour to check on him—when we went five hours in the opposite direction to make sure Dad was okay."

I've only met Amanda's father a handful of times, and yet every time, my understanding of my sister-in-law has grown. It's shocking, almost, watching how quickly her sass and sarcasm evaporate in the face of his meanness.

"We ended up staying a night with them. But it was cramped, and they didn't have much food," Amanda says.

"Not to mention, no power or heat," Chris adds.

I have the sudden urge to scream, "I didn't know it would last this long!" I look down at my lap, spread my hands out on my lavender robe. Was impressing everyone with my cooking so important that I needed to waste food we now direly need? What was I thinking? I bite the inside of my cheek until I taste blood.

"This is pretty much the best place to weather this storm," Travis says. Looking at Amanda, he says, "I'm sorry your father chose not to come. And your brother."

She waves dismissively. "They're stubborn."

"I'm sure they'll be fine." Chris reaches over to take Amanda's hand. "You watch. In a day or two, the power will be back on, and we'll be packing all this shit up again and driving home."

"That's what Lauren and Brent said when they got here," I say.

"I'm glad they're here already," Chris says.

"When did they arrive?" Amanda asks.

Travis looks at me.

"Four days ago," I answer.

A swoosh echoes through the great room as a log falls in the fire.

"What were the roads like?" Travis asks.

Chris's brow wrinkles as he looks in surprise at his brother. "Y'all haven't been out to see?"

"I went to town today. First time we've left the house since Jenna and I got here."

"On day three of the blackout," I offer.

"They've got a shelter set up in town, at the high school, with a small group of men who claim they're soldiers standing guard," Travis says.

"Same situation at home, except it was the community college, and everyone was crammed into the cafeteria," Chris tells us.

I shiver. I can't imagine being stuck with a bunch of strangers in one central space, guarded by a hodgepodge of boys and men playing soldier.

"We avoided the main highway here. I wasn't sure how many people would be trying to get out of Dodge," Chris says. "So that added time. Saw lots of stores with either broken windows, or they were boarded up. Didn't see a whole lotta cars on the back roads, but the ones we did see were fully loaded. Reminded me of *Walking Dead*, to be honest."

"I still can't believe this is real," Amanda says and puts her hand to her mouth. "Did you hear the latest broadcast? And now they're calling on doctors and police officers to leave their families and help the military? It's just so ..."

"Unbelievable," Chris finishes. "How could we be taken down by cyber warfare, of all things?"

"Who says we've been taken down?" Travis asks, his gaze directed at the fire. "We're the greatest nation on earth. We'll have this fixed in no time. No time. You watch. And then we'll hunt down every last one of 'em."

CHAPTER TEN

KELLY

Where am I? What happened?

I don't open my eyes. Not yet. If I wait, maybe the void will offer some answers.

I have no idea where I am.

I open my eyes and see a shiny wooden wall.

Reality floods in. I'm staying with strangers, dependent on their charity, and I fucked up. I really fucked up.

Groaning, I roll over. The boys aren't in the room. I sit up, which makes my head throb and my stomach turn. I lie back down.

I've lost them. I lost him, and now I've lost them, and there's nothing left. There's nothing fucking left.

Sobbing, turning my face into the pillow, I'm annoyed by the coarseness of the cheap-ass pillowcase. Turning angrily away, I hold my breath against the wracking sobs until the pressure in my chest forces me to gasp and sputter. I force myself to slow my breathing.

Remember, remember what happened last night.

What's the last thing I remember? I press my palm flat against the wall.

I remember dinner. Meat loaf. The Baptists were actually drinking. Travis was chugging beer and cracking jokes, looking so cute with that mischievous grin of his. It was all going so well until Mikey asked Miss Perfect Jenna if wine made her mean.

It was almost salvaged though. Almost. I looked hot—my hair was amazing. Square Jenna was set for an early bedtime with all that wine she drank. It was going to be my night.

Another wave of nausea hits me. I roll over—slowly—reach for a bottle of water, take the tiniest sip, then another. No more red wine mixed with vodka.

I never want to move. Just let me stay here and sleep until I wake to something different.

I don't know how long I've slept when I hear crying. I tiptoe to the door and open it a crack. Bratty Jacob is whining.

"But Nana said we could keep our city! And now it's ruined!"

"I'm sorry it got knocked over, buddy. I really am."

That syrupy-sweet tone that makes me gag floats up to me. I hate her.

"It was dark when Uncle Chris and Aunt Amanda got here. They couldn't see it, bud. It was an accident."

"I'll help you rebuild an even better one downstairs. How about that?" says a voice I don't recognize.

The Baptists have multiplied.

CHAPTER ELEVEN
JENNA

Everyone is finally here, and it's total chaos. The cabin no longer seems large and airy; it now feels small and cramped. The tension is palpable—Everett is fussy, Jacob is snotty, and the sheer noise of so many people in one room with high ceilings makes my head pound.

We don't have enough flour to make pancakes for everyone, and we're out of packaged batter. Travis managed to scavenge six dozen eggs on his trip to town yesterday. But when added to our dwindling supply, that gives us eighty eggs for seventeen people. I wonder if they're safe to eat, but I decide it's best not to mention it. Kathryn takes two dozen and sticks them in the back of the fridge for cooking something other than breakfast.

We're down to fifty-six eggs.

I stand in the kitchen in a small group consisting of Kathryn, Lauren, Chris, and Amanda. We decide to cook seventeen eggs a day for breakfast for the next three days, which means one egg per person, and one piece of toast per person for the next two days. Day three—no toast. We decide on one cup of frozen hashbrowns each.

Kathryn goes to the pantry and pulls out two boxes of granola bars and two large cans of peaches. I rush to her and whisper, "Shouldn't we save that? Shouldn't we save as much as we can?"

She stops and looks at me with her bright-blue eyes. "I will not have Chris and his family go hungry their very first meal in this house."

I bite my cheek in the same tender spot from last night. In three days, we'll be eating granola bars, oatmeal without milk, or dry cereal. In three days, the children will be whining and crying, wondering why we don't have pancakes or biscuits. I see myself on our first morning here, running around the kitchen, whipping up bacon and eggs, biscuits and gravy. How could I be so shortsighted?

There are too many people now to fit around the table. Kathryn sets up a folding one for the children. Ava sighs loudly and often to let everyone know she should be sitting with the adults. Caden chatters happily, excited with the new arrivals, but Mikey is silent and stands off to the side, holding his arms across his belly as if it hurts.

I go to him and kneel. Holding him with my gaze, I slowly reach my hand toward his face and brush the hair out of his left eye, then trail my fingers down his soft cheek.

"I love you," I whisper.

His eyes glisten with tears. He nods. Looking up toward the loft, then back to me, he says, "Mommy."

A question? Or a statement?

"Don't worry. I'll take care of you."

~

Halfway through breakfast, Jacob reminds Travis of their fishing trip. But by the time everyone is finished eating, sleet falls in straight gray lines, coating the porch with ice. His disappointment is short-lived; he switches gears and asks his newly arrived cousins if they're ready to rebuild their epic city.

"Take it downstairs, boys. Too many people here now to build in the family room," Kathryn says.

The children begin scrambling, collecting plates and silverware. Jacob declares, "I'm chief city planner!"

Mikey seems glued to his chair. Everett still slurps on his last peach, so I go to Mikey and squat next to him. "Don't you want to rebuild the city?"

He looks down at his hands, held tightly in his lap, but he nods. Gently taking his chin in my hand, I turn his face toward mine.

"Don't worry about your mommy. I'll make sure she's okay."

"Okay." He nods, but his lower lip trembles. I take one of his hands, hold it, palm to palm.

"I'll take care of everything. I promise."

We're interrupted by Ava. "Where am I supposed to go while the babies play Legos?"

Mikey's hand tightens around mine.

"Ava!" Amanda says shrilly.

"What? Why are we stuck in the basement anyway? Daddy's the oldest! He should be on this floor, with Nana and Papa! The boys should be upstairs in their room, instead of these strangers!"

Mikey's head snaps down onto the table, his forehead hitting so forcefully that the sound echoes. Everyone stops.

"Ava! That's enough!" Chris bellows.

I lean forward and whisper in Mikey's ear, "It's okay, buddy. She's just used to having the basement to herself."

His eyes stay squeezed shut, and he doesn't move. His palm sweats against mine.

I look up to where Ava now stands with her arms crossed.

"You can hang out in our room, Ava," I say. "It's got the cute little window seat, remember?"

She reaches into her back pocket, pulls out her phone, and stares at it in her hand. She says, "I do have a couple of games that don't require Internet." Rolling her eyes and sighing, she flips her hair over her shoulder and grumbles, "Thanks."

"Ava! Attitude!" Amanda glares at her daughter, her high cheekbones red and flushed.

"I have a stack of coloring books up there, with fine-point markers and pencils," I tell my niece.

Ava pauses on her way to the stairs and turns to look at me. "The cool ones with the crazy, intricate designs?"

"Yep."

"Awesome. Thank you, Aunt Jenna." She gives one last spiteful stare at Mikey and Caden, throws one at her mother for good measure, and stomps up the stairs.

The drama passed, Jacob and his two older cousins thunder down the stairs to the basement. Caden puts his hand on Mikey's back and rubs in jerky, awkward movements. I smile at him.

"Mikey, it's okay. I promise. Go play."

"C'mon, Mikey," Caden says, then rests his head on his brother's shoulder.

Mikey sighs and raises his head. Caden giggles and points at his brother's forehead, at the long indentation from the table. Mikey touches it himself, then roughs up his brother's hair. "Let's go," he says. They take each other's hands and head toward the stairs.

When they get to them, Mikey stops, then comes running back to me. As I lower myself to his eye level, he throws his arms around me.

"I love you too, Miss Jenna," he says, then he runs back to his brother and down the stairs.

The room grows blissfully silent, except for the clinking sounds of Lauren and Amanda washing, drying, and stacking dishes. Everett screeches, then wails. I grab him, and his sticky hands grab my face and make it sticky too.

"Shh, bubby." I bounce him on one hip while going to the kitchen drawer and grabbing a fresh rag. We still have baby wipes, but I've decided to save them for wiping bottoms instead of faces and hands. He pulls away angrily as I try to wipe his face.

"Here," Amanda says, wiping her hands on a towel and reaching for him. "You helped me with my monster. Let me help you with yours." She smiles, and I gratefully hand him over. I close my eyes and rub my temples. I might need two aspirin. Was it too much wine or no sleep? Or both?

Travis and Chris, huddled together with heads bent in a heated discussion, turn away from the fireplace and head toward the kitchen.

Travis says, "Mom," and motions with his hand. I lean against the counter as everyone finds their way into a circle.

"Seems like we're a little low on food," Chris says.

"Hopefully no one gets sick from the eggs. They weren't refrigerated when I found them," Travis says, crossing his arms. "It was pretty cold inside the store though."

"I'm sure it'll be fine," Kathryn says. "But you're right, we are low on food."

"How low?" Chris asks.

I look down at my feet.

"Didn't you have dinners planned, Jenna?" Kathryn asks.

I clear my throat and look up. "Just the main entrees. We had enough chicken left for three nights, but I think it'll only be enough for two nights now. We have two pounds of beef and two tenderloins, and some odds and ends I thought I could stretch ..."

Amanda says, "Don't forget, I brought three pounds of frozen chicken, three pounds of venison, and two pounds of beef. Plus that box of frozen shrimp. Oh, and a box of corn dogs!"

Nathan speaks up from where he sits near the fire. "There are several pounds of venison left in the small freezer in the garage. Maybe some tater tots and hash browns too. Not sure."

"I forgot about the garage freezer!" Travis says.

"I didn't," Kathryn says. "But I figured I'd leave that until we were out of food from the main fridge."

"Let's bring it in, then, and see what we've got," Travis says. "You ladies mind cataloging what's left in the pantry?"

"Y'all need help?" Brent asks, burping Kaitlyn. "This one is about ready for her morning nap."

"We've got it, thanks," Travis says as they head out to the garage.

Kathryn digs in a drawer and produces a pad of paper and pen. Lauren goes to the pantry and opens the double doors. She pushes some boxes aside and starts sliding cans around. I go to the counter and start grabbing dishes to put away.

"Ready, Mom?" Lauren asks.

"Ready."

"We have sixteen cans of green beans." She slides objects around. "Nine of corn, five peas, one each of lima and great northern beans, and one sixteen-ounce can of tomato sauce."

"Wait. We haven't unloaded my totes yet," Amanda says and hands Everett back to me. "They're still in the garage!" She hustles to the mudroom, calling, "Totes too! Grab our food totes!"

"It's a mess in here, Mom," Lauren says, pulling cereal boxes out and lining them on the counter.

"I meant to organize that," I say as Everett burps and vomits an orange glob down my shirt. It reeks of peaches.

Kathryn says, "Don't worry, sweetie. You've joined your pantry and mine, plus Lauren's. And with all these folks digging in here, how's it going to stay organized anyways?"

"Correction, Mom," Lauren says, stacking two boxes of oatmeal next to the cereal. "I only packed soup, chips, and a couple boxes of cereal. I left the rest at home."

Nathan shuffles into the kitchen, his head slightly bent in the stooped manner of someone who has always felt too tall. He takes Everett from my arm, my other hand busy scrubbing at peach goo with a kitchen washcloth.

"Don't be so hard on yourself," he says quietly before turning to head back to his chair, whispering to Everett on the way.

I look down at the orange circle on my white blouse, which is covered with dainty red roses. A Christmas present from Travis last year. I scrub harder.

"Honey," Kathryn says. "Honey." A little louder this time.

I look up to see Kathryn and Lauren watching me.

"Throw some OxiClean on that. It'll come out." Kathryn nods at me, and I feel like a child. "Actually, why don't you go and take a nap? Take a minute for yourself, Jenna." Kathryn smiles at me and nods again. "I'm sure Ava won't mind you napping while she colors. You're always so sweet to her."

"We've got this covered. Promise," Lauren says.

I'm not sure if I want to laugh or cry, so I just mumble, "Thank you," and head upstairs.

They think I'm out of earshot, but I hear them speaking in hushed tones as I close the bathroom door.

"She seems more fragile than normal," Kathryn says.

"I think our houseguest is triggering some mommy issues."

CHAPTER TWELVE

JENNA

A sense of calm washes over me as I look over the food list Lauren, Kathryn, and Amanda have created. They sorted through the random odds and ends Travis picked up yesterday, and Amanda contributed a significant amount to our dried goods as well.

<u>*Meat:*</u>

12.5 lbs chicken
8 lbs venison
3 pork tenderloins
5 lbs beef
2 lbs turkey
2 lbs salmon
1 lb shrimp
1 box corn dogs (12 count)
1 bag chicken wings
29 cans tuna

. . .

Frozen:

3 bags mixed vegetables
1 bag peas
1 bag broccoli
1 bag strawberries
1 bag assorted berries
5 packs dinner rolls
9 individual frozen dinners
1 family portion lasagna dinner

Canned goods:

28 soup
11 corn
3 creamed corns
9 peas
22 green bean
9 kidney bean
4 great northern bean
7 black bean
4 pinto bean
7 16-ounce tomato sauce
5 16-ounce diced tomatoes
10 8-ounce tomato paste
5 can black olives
23 boxes pasta
18 jars marinara sauce
5 jars alfredo sauce
3 jars vodka sauce

Dried goods:

33 boxes cereal (some half stale)

19 boxes crackers
22 bags chips
47 mini bags chips
11 boxes oatmeal
2 boxes blueberry muffins
4 boxes corn bread
6 boxes brownies
3 boxes banana bread
22 packs instant rice
10 boxes rice
19 boxes assorted granola bars
22 jars peanut butter
7 bags jerky
12 ketchup
2 boxes graham crackers
3 bags marshmallows

Refrigerated goods:

Assorted condiments
1 tub and 7 boxes butter
3 packs Kraft cheese
1 pack Italian shredded cheese
62 eggs
1½ gallon milk

Sweets:

14 Snickers bars
4 Hershey bars
9 Milky Way bars
2 bags chocolate chips
4 large bags assorted chocolate bars

1 large bag lollipops

We can stretch the meat for three weeks, maybe longer. We can get creative with ingredients, fillers. How many casseroles can we make with tuna, crackers, and dry cereal? I run my finger down the list and stop, picturing what we can scrounge together based on where my nail lands.

Travis and Chris take two thermoses of soup into the woods with them, as well as crackers and peanut butter. They walk out the door with Chris chiding Travis, "Can't believe you haven't hunted yet, bro."

The afternoon drags on endlessly. Kelly stays shut in her room. Brent dozes on the couch, and I want to push him off. It seems he's claimed it as his own personal space. Everett naps on Nathan, who's also snoozing. I keep finding myself wandering around, straightening, re-wiping clean counters, staring out windows. I remember there's laundry in the dryer; I fold it and distribute it to the proper owners. I wander some more. I consider divvying the cereal into breakfast portions and snack portions but decide that's a waste of sandwich bags. I stand at the double doors and look out over the mountains. Maybe I should go for a walk. I yawn.

Everett babbles behind me. I rush to retrieve him so he doesn't wake Nathan. Brent lets out a snore. I grab a blanket and spread it on the rug in front of the fire. I lay Everett on his belly and sit down, cross-legged, a few feet away from him. I hold out my hands.

"Come here, bubby!"

He kicks his legs and waves his arms, making him wobble back and forth on his belly. He smiles and gurgles, a line of drool spilling from his mouth and onto the blanket. He changes tactics, grabbing the blanket with his hands and pulling himself forward a few inches in a sort of army crawl.

"We're going to need to babyproof this room soon," Amanda says from her chair, where she's knitting gloves. I watch in envy for a moment as her hands move seamlessly before returning my attention to Everett.

He's no longer smiling. His mouth is puckering, and his face is red.

"Come here, hungry boy." I grab him before the crying starts.

The children are growing wild, and there's so many of them. They're like a pack of wild dogs. I wait for Amanda to take charge. She doesn't. Travis and Chris are still in the woods. Brent is busy with Kait, and Lauren is reading a magazine. None of them belong to her, I suppose. The children have Amanda and me outnumbered seven to two.

I'm so tired I can barely keep my eyes open.

By seven, I've lost patience and tell the boys they have thirty minutes till bedtime.

Kathryn and Nathan stand at seven thirty on the dot and shuffle into their bedroom.

Caden sleeps in a ball on the floor near the fire, his head resting on the pillow I slid there. Jacob, Mikey, and Drew still chase each around the kitchen, sliding on their socks. Henry has moved on and sits in a chair next to Lauren, tossing a small bouncy ball up and down, up and down, up and down.

"Jacob and Mikey, time for pajamas, toothbrushing, and bathroom," I say.

The boys stop and slide into a jumbled heap, elbows, knees, and feet in the air.

Mikey says between giggles, "Yes ma'am," but it sounds like he says, "Yes, Mom," and Jacob springs to his feet.

"She's not your mommy!" he hells.

Then he lunges at Mikey as I yell, "Jacob!"

I stand, holding Everett tightly, but Henry reaches them before I do and pulls Jacob away.

Big, fat tears slide down Mikey's cheeks as he shakes his head. "I didn't say 'Mom.' I said 'ma'am.' I pr-pr-promise." He shakes his head violently, his gorgeous wavy hair falling into his eyes.

"She's not your mom!" Jacob yells, louder this time, and I hear a door open upstairs.

The boys don't notice. Henry holds Jacob around the shoulders, gently but firmly, and I want to go to Mikey, but I don't want to push Jacob further over the edge. We're all exhausted.

"I know she isn't. I know she isn't," Mikey says, looking at his feet and pulling at his hair.

"I know your mommy is the worst mommy ever, but you still can't have mine!" Jacob spits.

"Jacob, that's enough!" I call.

"Don't you talk about my mommy!" Mikey yells back. "She gets bad headaches! She has to take all those pills!"

Amanda sucks in through her teeth.

"Mikey!" Kelly yells from the balcony. His head snaps up in terror.

"Bed, now!"

Mikey looks at the floor as he passes Jacob and then me.

"Caden!" she barks.

I turn to look up at her. "He's asleep by the fire."

"Oh. Can ... Can Travis carry him up?"

Amanda's eyebrows shoot up a mile. "The men are hunting," she says.

"I don't think I'm steady enough to carry him." She puts her hand to her face, and for the first time in five days, she seems embarrassed.

"I'll bring him up," I tell her.

I hand Everett to Amanda. Sliding my arms under Caden, I scoop him up. I should have changed his pull-up. Maybe I should find Jacob's old training potty in the attic. As I reach the top of the stairs, I hear Kelly zipping a bag. Mikey has already changed and is curled up in his bed. His chin quivers when he sees me, but he doesn't make a sound. I lay Caden next to him and tuck the blanket around them both. Mikey tucks Caden's colorful parrot into his arms.

"It's okay, bud," I whisper. Then I back out of the room, which reeks of alcohol.

Back downstairs, I find Jacob waiting on me. I kneel in front of him.

"I'm sorry, Mama,"

"Thank you for saying you're sorry. It's been a really long day for all of us." I hold out my arms, and he rushes in. "I love you, bud."

"I love you more."

"Impossible." I try to mimic Travis's exaggerated French accent and fail miserably.

"When is Daddy getting home?"

"Soon, baby, soon. Let's get some rest."

I pace with Everett in front of the doors, going from one end of the great room to the other, scanning the woods for a flashlight. There are plenty of bears in these woods. We've seen them on the trail cameras. Wild pigs and hogs as well.

Everett shows no signs of sleeping. Every time I make it to the end of the room and turn around, he throws his head back in gleeful laughter. It makes me miss Travis even more.

The men come home shortly after eight, carrying a medium-size doe. Amanda has long since gone downstairs, leaving Lauren and Brent cuddling on the couch. Lauren hoots and hollers when Chris and Travis come into the room, a strange combination of fresh air and blood wafting in with them.

Travis takes one look at my face and orders me to bed.

"I probably won't be able to sleep, and this one doesn't seem tired at all either," I say, nodding toward Everett.

"That's 'cause his mama is antsy. I'm back. I'm safe. We're gonna skin and dress this deer, and then I'll be right behind you."

"After a shower, right?" I smile and lean in for a kiss.

Everett takes a nightcap, which finally makes him drowsy. He falls asleep in my arms, and I move him to the crib. I leave the lamp on beside the bed. I can't be in the dark right now. I'm scared my thoughts will get too big. I close my eyes and recite, over and over, "Hail Mary full of Grace, the Lord is with thee. Blessed are thou amongst women, and blessed is the fruit of thy womb Jesus. Holy Mary Mother of God, pray for us sinners now and at the hour of our death. Amen."

CHAPTER THIRTEEN
KELLY

Jenna pretends she doesn't see me when she brings the boys in. She tucks them in like they're her own, leaning close to Mikey and whispering in his ear. The sight of his arms around her neck nearly breaks me.

Once she's gone, I sit on the edge of the bed, tucking Caden's parrot closer under his chin. He lets out a snore and rolls toward his brother. Mikey looks at my chest, waiting.

"I'm so sorry for last night, baby."

He nods, but his chin starts quivering, and still, he won't look up.

I close my eyes, take a deep breath. "Did you have a good day?"

He looks up, confused.

"What did you do?" I ask, trying.

He looks down, scratches his forehead, then looks up at me and finally holds my gaze. "New people came."

"Really?"

I know they did. I heard them. All day. More family, less room, more strain, and less forgiveness.

"Are they nice?" I try for my sweetest tone, but when I

look back at him, he's put his arm protectively over Caden, and his eyes are trained away from mine once more.

He nods.

I want to cry.

Patrick, why aren't you here? Why am I doing this alone?

"I love you, Mikey."

I kiss the top of his head as he mumbles, "I love you, Mommy."

I set three alarms on my phone and plug it in, resting it on the pillow beside my head.

I wake before dawn and crawl out of bed. Creeping along the silent landing, I pause and look across the great room to the tall windows that reach to the ceiling. The faintest hint of light beyond the mountains makes them stand stark and black before the shrouded expanse of the lake.

Panic grips me momentarily when I turn the faucet, but the house remains silent.

After my shower, I stand looking at my pill bottles lined up on the bed. I decide on two low-dose Valium. One for now, one for my pocket. No alcohol. Not today.

By the time the boys begin stirring, I'm ready.

CHAPTER FOURTEEN
JENNA

When I wake, Everett is already in our bed, babbling, "Da-Da, Da-Da," and belly laughing.

Travis, who's lying beside me, makes a funny face and echoes, "Da-Da!"

I reach out and put my hand over Travis's, which is on Everett's back.

"Finally awake, sleepyhead?" he asks.

"What time is it?"

"I have no idea. My phone is dead. Didn't there used to be an old-fashioned clock in here?"

Giggling, I answer, "It's called analog, honey."

"The one with the hands that spin around?"

"Yes." I sit up.

"Mama!" Everett gushes, pinching his fingers together and tapping his mouth with them, the baby sign language for *eat*. I unbutton my nightgown and take him into my arms.

"Aren't you tired of breastfeeding yet?"

"Getting there, but ..."

"But there's not enough milk to go around."

"If this doesn't end anytime soon, like they're suggesting, I'll be breastfeeding him until he's three."

"Don't be dramatic. It won't last that long. And besides, we'll just get this boy hooked on deer jerky instead of his mama."

"Then y'all need to hunt and fish until that freezer is full again." I flutter my fingertips through Everett's wispy hair and continue, "Got a good start on that last night though. Right?"

"Not as much as we hoped. After we dressed it, it was maybe forty pounds of meat, forty-five at best."

"That's a lot!"

"Not to feed seventeen people," Travis says.

I wince as Everett bites down and yanks his head back, looking at me with what I imagine is disdain. I switch him to the other breast.

Travis takes my hand in his and squeezes it.

"Jenna."

I look at him.

"We'll be okay." He leans over and kisses me gently. "Thank you for feeding our son."

I wait until the fear abates, then ask, "How long will it last?"

"The blackout?"

"The meat."

Travis turns and slides down under the covers, bending his arm and resting his head on his hand. He looks past me, thinking. "We've got enough steak for two nights, for sure. We set aside a good bit for breakfast sausage patties, since we're outta bacon 'n' eggs. Went ahead and seasoned it, added brown sugar, and shaped it. Shame we don't have any pork to add to it, but it'll still be good. With how few eggs we got left, probably only last for four or five breakfasts."

"Maybe we can spare some butter to make biscuits. That might stretch it."

Travis smiles and rubs Everett's head. "Like the way you're thinking." He winks at me.

I wish Everett would finish feeding. I want to snuggle up next to my husband, put my head on his chest, and absorb his strength, his certainty.

"We got enough meat to stretch three or four nights of burgers," he says, "but we don't have any buns. Maybe you ladies can create some sort of casserole with it."

"We've got some frozen dinner rolls. We could make mini burgers one night at least."

"That's why I love you. You know how to feed me." He rolls onto his back, head resting on his hands, arms akimbo.

"So basically, we've got another week of dinners and a few breakfasts out of one deer?"

"Pretty much."

"Seems like it should go further."

"We've got a lot of people, including two hungry teenagers. Hell, I remember I used to eat two or three burgers when I was Ava and Henry's age."

Everett finally finishes. I sit him up, grab a burp cloth from the table beside me, and lean him over my shoulder.

"Plus, we cut some strips of meat for jerky," he adds. "We're gonna cook that up today. Hopefully that'll last a week for snacking."

"It does seem like everyone's eating a lot more than normal."

"That's 'cause we're all bored out of our minds."

~

"Will we be graced with our houseguest's presence this morning?" Amanda asks as we sit at the high counter, watching the men cook sausage patties.

"I'm surprised she never came out yesterday." I glance at the clock hanging above the kitchen window. It points to eight ten, while my Fitbit reads eight fifteen. "I'm hoping her disappearing act means she's mortified by what she did," I add.

"She looked pretty rough last night, standing at the railing. Frail, almost." Amanda leans closer. "Is she that bad off?"

"I think so. She seems to take a lot of pills." Looking down at my folded hands, I add, "And I'm beginning to think she beats Mikey."

Amanda closes her eyes and shakes her head. "I just don't understand it." She looks at me. "What are we going to do?"

CHAPTER FIFTEEN

KELLY

Caden runs ahead into the great room while Mikey hangs back. For a moment, I think he'll cling to my thigh like he once did. I wish he would.

Kathryn sits in her usual chair, regarding me. Jenna and a woman I don't recognize sit at the high counter, eyeing me and whispering to each other.

Just as I look down, hoping to take Mikey's hand and wishing I'd chosen Xanax, Kathryn calls, "Good morning, Mikey!"

He darts away from me and goes to her, standing by her chair like a begging dog.

She glances at me. I nod and say, "Good morning." I force a smile in her direction but look beyond her, where Nathan stands, holding Everett. He turns and looks at me with kind eyes, and I want to run straight out the front door.

Then, for a second, I imagine that I see spotlights. And the vague outline of an audience—dark heads in row after row. Spine straight. Shoulders back. Chin up. I take one precise step, toes pointed, then another. Turn my smile up a notch.

I can do this.

As I approach the kitchen, Jenna and the other woman turn away from one another and swivel in my direction, neither of them smiling. The new arrival rests her face in her hand and stares at me, with large and surprisingly pretty green eyes. Jenna sits up straighter, looks me up and down, and says, "Amanda, this is the woman." She pauses, gives a tiny shrug, then, with a tight smile aimed in my direction, says, "The neighbor we're helping out in these unprecedented times."

Amanda nods. "Nice to meet you."

One deep breath, shoulders tensed back so tight they feel like they'll snap, breasts up and out. "I'm Kelly. Very nice to meet you too." I give a slight nod to Jenna. I'm still smiling but hoping my glare is boring holes into her stone heart. "Although I also wish it were under different circumstances."

By now I've felt the men's gazes settling on me, their breakfast task interrupted. I shift my body and my breasts directly toward them, then gracefully lift my left arm to grab my hair and pull it to one side, letting the whole heap rest on one shoulder. "You must be Chris," I say to the other newcomer. "Everyone has been so anxious for your arrival."

He looks perplexed for a moment, not expecting me, clearly.

I add, "The long-awaited firstborn."

Travis rolls his eyes and Amanda scoffs, but the faintest touch of color in Chris's cheeks indicates I've hit my mark. I give a dazzling smile and reach down to adjust the tongue on my sneaker. His eyes follow exactly where I want them to.

As we sit down for breakfast, I realize they've set up an extra table for the children, and I'm grateful for it. With my back to Mikey's watchful eyes, I can focus on salvaging this situation.

Our portions are noticeably smaller. Scrambled eggs, one piece of toast, and two small sausage patties. I'd hoped to put forth a good impression with the new arrivals, but everyone is speaking at once—so many voices colliding, yet in a familial rhythm. One that I don't know.

Chris dominates the conversation, even speaking over Travis several times, which surprises me.

Finally, a brief lull in the conversation, which I use to compliment the men. "Nice work on catching a doe. This sausage is so tender."

"My husband is an accomplished hunter. Won quite a few contests in our state," Amanda says, taking Chris's hand. "Does your husband hunt?"

"No, he's more of a golf and skiing kind of guy." I tilt my head and give my sweetest smile, with practiced, relaxed lips. "I'd say your husband's talents are much more appreciated in this situation."

"I'd say *needed*," she says, pursing her lips and looking around the table.

"Damn right. That's the gosh darn truth," Chris says, slapping his free hand on the table.

CHAPTER SIXTEEN

JENNA

As the women pass plates around the table, piling them in a stack—not quite ready to stand up and clean them—Jacob shouts from the children's table, "Daddy! Can we fish today?"

The weather looks as gray and dismal as yesterday, with a steady drizzle of rain and ice.

"Not looking good today, bud."

"Another day of boredom stretches infinitely in front of us," Henry laments.

"You can say that again," Drew says, copying his older brother's tone.

I stare past the table and outside to the mountains beyond, shrouded in gray. Then I say, "Nana, could we set up your scrapbooking table in the family room for arts and crafts?"

Jacob is out of his seat and hopping up and down before she can answer. "Arts and craps! Arts and craps!"

"How could I say no to arts and craps?" Kathryn says, laughing.

~

The women excuse me from cleanup duty so I can set up my supplies. Travis carries the six-foot table down from the loft, where it lives, folded up and leaned against the wall, unless Kathryn is actively scrapbooking.

Next, he carries in my tote: paper, glue, crayons, colored pencils, markers, washable paint, watercolor paint, regular clay, scented clay, child-sized scissors, and a durable plastic tablecloth. As I spread the tablecloth, I bite the inside of my cheek. What craft can I suggest that suits both a three-year-old and a thirteen-year-old? I wonder where my tablet is so I can consult Pinterest, and then remember that I can't.

A crashing sound reverberates across the great room. Everyone stops.

I turn around to see Kelly standing with her hands outstretched over shattered glass. Then, she covers her face with both hands. Was she finally helping with dishes? Beyond the first day here, she hasn't pitched in at all or even muttered a single thank you.

Everyone stands frozen and silent, watching her.

"I ... I ..." She falls to her knees and starts sweeping the glass with her hands. Amanda strides over, crouches beside her, and stops her.

"My nannie's dish," Kathryn says, her hand covering her mouth after the words have escaped. She takes a few steps forward and says again, "My nannie's dish." She lets out a low, anguished moan. Still holding her hand over her mouth, she shakes her head. "No."

Amanda blows glass off Kelly's palms.

Brent appears with the broom and dustpan.

"I'm so sorry," Kelly says as Amanda helps her to her feet. "I didn't mean ..."

Amanda herds her toward the stairs and takes her up, keeping an arm around her waist.

Kathryn walks toward the aftermath.

Brent stops sweeping.

Lauren walks toward her mother, saying, "It's just a dish, Mom ..."

Kathryn stops, and without looking at any of us, goes to her bedroom and quietly shuts the door. Brent carries the clinking box of broken glass to the garage.

Nathan stands near the fire, holding Everett. I hold my hands out, indicating I'll take him, but he shakes his head. The only sounds are the shrieks of playing children, who are in the basement, thank God. I can see Mikey's reaction if he'd been here to witness the scene—his little chin trembling, his wide eyes looking from me to his mom, debating how to fix yet another of her mistakes.

Brent comes back in and speaks much too loudly to the hushed room. "I labeled the box and put it on Nathan's workbench, in case Kathryn figures out some sort of project to do with the pieces. Maybe she can salvage them somehow."

"Good thinking, hubby," Lauren says. And then she says to Kait, who's in her arms, "Good job, Daddy, right?"

Amanda comes back down, pausing for a moment at the bottom of the stairs. "She's a wreck. Bawling her eyes out and shaking like a leaf. I hate to say it, but I encouraged her to take one of those pills she has. Hopefully it'll calm her down."

"Did you give her a drink to go with it?" Lauren says in a snarky tone. Then she hands Kaitlyn to Brent and offers, "Unless you want to finish the dishes, that is."

"No, thanks," he says and takes the baby.

"Should I still set up arts and crafts?" I ask.

"Yes, definitely, Jenna. The kids will be bored and running around us in circles before long, I'm sure," Amanda says, then heads back to the kitchen.

"Y'all going hunting again?" Brent asks as he settles in his spot on the couch.

Chris turns away from the doors, where he has been brooding. Of all the Covington children, he's most fiercely defensive of his mother, almost to the point of absurdity. Maybe it's something to do with being the eldest, like my brother.

"We plan on going at dusk. That was the magic hour yesterday," Chris says and takes a seat in his mother's chair, next to Nathan and Everett. "So, ladies, we're going to need an early supper tonight. I don't want crackers and soup again." He looks toward Travis, who stands at the fireplace. "I think we should go bright and early tomorrow morning too. Around four?"

"Works for me," Travis says. "Jenna, do you need any more help setting up?"

I shake my head and move toward the table to pull out supplies.

"Boys, I think we should cut up some firewood. The pile is lookin' a tad low," Travis says.

"Do you want help?" Henry asks.

"How about you fill up the woodboxes as they chop? The box in here and the one in the garage are nearly empty," Amanda says.

"I'm almost sixteen, I'm old enough to swing an axe, Mom."

"Next time, bud. But your mom is right about the boxes being low," Travis says, grabbing Henry's T-shirt and pulling him into a headlock.

~

By the time the children come thundering up the stairs, the table is set and ready.

"Mama, Mama! Are arts and craps ready?" Jacob's voice rings across the room.

"Dude, it's crafts. *C – R – A – F – T – S*." Henry says each letter and reiterates, "Crafts," speaking painstakingly slow.

Lauren speaks up from the couch. "Henry, I believe Aunt Jenna wasn't correcting him for a reason."

"What? Why?"

I shrug. "It's cute."

Henry rolls his eyes. "I suppose this is for the little kids?"

"Not at all. There's something for everyone."

Ava hangs back, arms crossed.

"What are we doing?" Jacob asks as he climbs into a chair. "What's this?" He picks up a fish cut out of construction paper.

Caden stands watching and sucking his thumb, waiting for Mikey to sit.

"Come on, boys, over here on this end." I pull out two chairs across from Jacob. They take their seats silently, holding their hands in their laps.

"Mama!" Jacob says, holding up the fish.

"What does it look like?" I ask

"A fish!"

"Yes, and can you count how many there are?"

"One, two ..."

"Ava, come look," I say. "I've got another book with the designs you like. But it's for painting."

"Really?" Her eyes perk up.

"Yep. I've got you all set up down on the other end."

She tucks her long hair behind her ear and comes closer. I flip through the pages of the book so she can see.

"Oh, Aunt Jenna, did you paint that one?" she asks, pointing to a page.

"Yeah, after Everett was born."

"It's so good."

"Thanks, sweetie. I've got a cup of water here for you to clean your brushes. Just make sure the boys don't get their hands on these paints though. They aren't washable."

Amanda, who has returned to her knitting, looks up and says, "You're not letting her use your good brushes are you, Jenna?"

"I'm sure she'll take good care of them."

"Are you sure, Aunt Jenna?" Ava asks hesitantly.

"Yes. Absolutely. Just wash them thoroughly when you're finished."

"Mama! What are the fish for?" Jacob has lost patience. I glance at Henry, but he's wandered to the doors, looking out over the lake, with Drew following behind him.

"Did you count them out?" I ask my son.

He raises his chin and declares, "There are fourteen fish total."

"Really close, buddy. Should we count them one more time?"

I walk to the other end of the table, take the first fish, and lay it down on the table.

"One," Jacob says.

I look at Caden and Mikey. "Join in, boys."

"One," they say in unison.

We all count together to twelve, and I sort four out to each boy as we do.

"Since y'all can't go fishing for the second day in a row, I thought we could paint the fish you'll catch when it's sunny again."

Mikey thanks me with a slow-growing grin that makes his eyes sparkle when it reaches them. It's a new smile I haven't seen yet. I squeeze his hand under the table, three times for *I love you*, like I do with Jacob.

"What'll we do with 'em after we've painted 'em?" Jacob asks.

"Why, hang them on some fishing line," I say, holding up my precut strings. "Just like fish you'd catch! Instead of eating them, we'll hang them up for decoration."

"That's a really cute idea, Aunt Jenna," Ava says.

Jacob opens the paint in front of him and grabs a brush. Mikey reaches his hand out slowly, and I nod. A hint of the grin comes back, and he opens his can and then Caden's, who's rocking back and forth with excitement.

I hold up a sheet of stickers. "And we have googly-eye stickers so your fish can have crazy eyes!"

"Googly!" Caden says, giggling.

"Googly!" Jacob answers. "Gooooogly!"

I leave them to their googlies and laughter and check Ava's work. She's picked a busy page of teacups, birds, and flowers. She's putting the first blue touches on a dainty teacup.

Looking up at me slyly, she says, "Did you find a way to get Wi-Fi and Pinterest and you're keeping it a secret?"

I laugh. "I wish!"

"Aunt Jenna was going to be a teacher. Remember, Ava?" Amanda says. Her mittens are already finished. Today she's working on socks.

"No, I don't remember that. Really?" she asks, looking up at me.

"Yeah, I was going to teach."

"Why didn't you? Did you go to college?"

"Yes, she did, and she graduated," Amanda answers for me.

"She had me!" Jacob shouts.

"Volume, baby," I say.

"Sorry, Mama."

"But lots of teachers have kids," Ava says.

"I don't want to miss out on the boys when they're so little. I'll start teaching when they start school."

"I wouldn't if Chris made what Travis does," Amanda says, still not looking up.

"Daddy works really hard," Henry says, turning away from the lake and looking at his mother with a hardness in his eyes.

"I know he does. And so do I."

"What does Uncle Travis do, anyway?" Henry asks.

"Mergers and acquisitions," I reply. "Business, basically."

Amanda chimes in, "Bigshot business guy, buying companies."

"He buys companies?" Henry says. "That's pretty cool."

"He's young to be so successful already, that's for sure," Amanda says.

I resist the urge to roll my eyes. All she sees are the fancy suits and money, not the weeks on end when I'm juggling everything because he's out wooing clients. "Henry, Drew," I start tentatively. "I don't know if y'all still like NASCAR ..."

"Heck, of course we do," Henry says, walking toward me, hands tucked into his blue jeans.

"Well, this isn't exactly NASCAR, but it is car related ..."

"Whatcha got, Aunt Jenna?" He's no nonsense, just like his dad.

"I've got two car model kits y'all could put together and paint."

Amanda lets out a loud breath, just short of a moan, and puts her knitting down. "Now, seriously, Jenna. Why do you have that in your art tote?"

"They were in the clearance bin, marked way down. I always grab little prizes for Sunday school students or toy drives, what have you."

"And that, children, is why Aunt Jenna's closets overflow onto your head when you open them." She chuckles.

She speaks from experience.

Henry picks up the box and turns it over in his hands. The box says ten plus, but I hope he won't mind.

"I might try it." He takes it with him back to the middle doors, looking at the box instead of out across the mountains. Drew takes his box, goes to the table, and opens it.

"Ooh, awesome! Henry, take a look at the decal stickers!"

Henry ambles back and glances over his brother's shoulder. He nods his approval. "Pretty cool, Aunt Jenna. Thanks."

Amanda says, "Wish they were that nice to me."

Henry's back is to his mother, so she doesn't see him roll his eyes.

The boys' fish turn out beautifully. Kathryn emerges from the bedroom as I start clearing off the table. Drew and Henry are still bent over their cars.

"Leave the tablecloth and table, Jenna," she says.

I tuck my papers into their folder. "Are you sure? It's right in the middle of the room."

"Have the men move it to the foyer. It's wasted space. That way, y'all can bring it over whenever you wanna do arts 'n' crafts, or even some board games. I know the kids are getting bored."

She smiles at Jacob, who has his pointer finger pressed against his mouth in the "Shh" motion. It's a trick I taught him to keep him from interrupting adults. It doesn't usually work, but maybe he's being polite, having noticed Kathryn's face, puffy from crying. "You got something to show me, bud?" she asks.

"I do, Nana!" He runs to her, holding up his fish on a string.

"Oh my! What yummy fish you've caught!"

"I know!" He's so excited he's rocking on his heels. "Get in my tummy, fishies!" He giggles at himself, and Caden puts his hand over his mouth, laughing with him.

"Did all y'all catch fish?" Kathryn asks.

Mikey nods gravely. Caden toddles over and holds up his line.

"Nice catch, Caden!" she exclaims.

"Nana, wanna see what we're working on?" Drew asks, not looking up from his task. While she inspects their cars, I tell the boys to wash the paint off their hands in the bathroom sink. I take their fish, promising to take good care of them.

I survey the family room, debating where to hang them.

"Aha!" I say no one. Amanda chuckles at me as I sprint up the stairs. I tie the first string around one of the loft railings and drop the line over the edge so the fish dangle over the chair Amanda sits in.

As I start the third line, Kelly's door cracks open. When she sees me, she goes to close it but then stops, looks down, and sighs before emerging. Her makeup is smudged, and her eyes are puffy from crying, but she still looks beautiful. Licking her lips, she nods and offers a tight-lipped smile. I nod back and continue with my task. She slides silently past me and goes into the bathroom. She turns on the water. There's a clink of the toilet seat going up, and then I hear retching.

By the time I descend the stairs, three little boys are bouncing around, arms upstretched, pointing at their fish.

I reach Caden first and pick him up, swinging him high over my head. He throws his head back in laughter. I let him slide down into my arms, and I kiss all over his neck, tickling him as his giggling grows louder. When I set him down, Jacob stands, arms akimbo, looking like he's ready to punch me.

I give him my biggest smile. "Your turn!"

He hesitates, narrowing his eyes at me. I crouch down, arms outstretched and hands shaped into claws, and stomp toward him. "Monster mommy needs little boy neck! Monster mommy hungry!"

He caves and throws his arms up, face beaming. Before I let him go, I whisper in his ear, "You'll always be my first, forever and always."

His little arms get tighter around my neck. "I love you, Mama."

"I love you so much more, my beautiful boy."

He giggles. "That's Daddy's song."

And on cue, Travis and Chris come back inside, sweaty and red faced. I set Jacob down, and he runs for his daddy. Mikey stands quietly, looking up. At their fish? Or waiting for his mother?

I squat down next to him. "Do you want your turn, Mikey?"

He looks at me, his large, serious eyes glistening.

"Mikey?"

"Is my mommy okay?"

"Yes, buddy. I think she's not feeling so great, but I'm sure she's okay."

"Will you help me take care of her?"

I see my mother's face.

"Please?" His chin quivers.

"Yes."

"Promise?"

I take a deep breath. I can't promise this.

"Promise," I whisper.

If Jacob had overheard, he'd inform him it doesn't count without the pinkie shake.

I'm in the kitchen making tiny burger patties when Kelly joins everyone in the great room. I sigh with relief that Kathryn is on the back porch, sitting in an Adirondack chair, her grandmother's quilt tucked around her legs.

Lauren, who'd been reading with her mother, comes back inside just as Kelly approaches the kitchen.

"What ya making for supper, Miss Jenna?" Lauren asks.

"Mini burgers."

"Mm, yum." She sits on a stool, draping one long arm over the back. "Need any help?"

"Nope."

"I was hoping you'd say that."

I look at Kelly as she draws nearer. She looks less pale and has added a glittery, rosy shimmer across her cheeks. My jaw clenches. I force myself to breathe.

"Where are the boys?" she asks.

"Watching a movie downstairs," I tell her.

She nods and looks away from us. Gazing toward the lake, she drums her fingertips on the countertop. Is she looking at Kathryn? Is she planning her apology?

"What are we having with the burgers?" Lauren asks, though her eyes remain on Kelly, staring her down.

"French fries, baked beans, chips, and applesauce."

Nathan pipes up from his chair. "Is that breaking rations, Jenna?"

I startle. "No, sir."

"I didn't mean to be stern. Just want to make sure we're being careful, is all."

"We're only doing two cans of beans tonight. Plenty for another few dinners. And we'll still have three bags of fries left. Just figured since it's the only night we'll have buns for burgers, we might as well have a memorable burger night."

"Ah, sensible as always, Jenna," he says.

Kelly moves away from the counter and toward the back door. She pulls cigarettes out of her sweater pocket, slides one out, and holds it between her fingers. As I put the burger patties in the fridge, Everett shrieks.

"I think this lil' man is ready for his mama," Nathan says as he shuffles toward me. "And this papa is ready for a nap."

"Thank you for entertaining him."

"My pleasure," he says, kissing Everett's temple before passing him to me.

"Does that mean you need help now?" Lauren asks as I grab my nursing blanket and settle in Nathan's still warm chair.

"Nope."

"You sure?" Lauren swings her long legs toward us.

"I've got the fryer set up and ready, the patties made, the beans on the stove."

"Have I told you you're the best little sister—ahem, I mean sister-in-law—in the world?"

I ignore the "little sister" part. "Don't say that too loud," I tell her. "Amanda might fight me for the title."

"I'd like to see you in a fight, Jenna. That'd be a sight. No offense, but I think you'd get your butt kicked."

I laugh. "You're probably right."

Kelly moves in my periphery; I turn to find her staring out the window, still holding her cigarette up in the air.

I look back at Lauren, who, following my gaze, flips pretend hair over her shoulder and rolls her eyes.

"How much longer on that movie, you think?" Kelly asks, approaching us. "Think I have time for a short walk?"

"Sure. We've got the boys," Lauren says smugly.

"It's no problem." I nod.

"Thank you. Just need a little fresh air."

When she gets to the front door, Lauren calls, "Watch out for coyotes!"

While I miss my own home and space, having sisters to lend a hand is such a blessing. I hum and rub Everett's back. After he drifts off to sleep, I lay him down and cover him with his plush yellow blanket.

When I come out of the bedroom, the great room is empty, so I sneak into the bathroom to freshen myself up before supper.

Kelly has left her toiletry kit on the counter, along with various bottles of hair products and perfumes. I pull my hair out of its ponytail and pick a bottle that promises high-octane sheen, spraying liberally. I flip my hair over and spray some utopian uplift. Then I rummage through her makeup. She has the kind of products I eye at the store but can never bring myself to buy. As I'm marveling over how smoothly her expensive eyeliner glides along my lash line, I hear my mother's voice: *Would you look at her.*

And Jed's: *She's as ugly as a hog, that one.*

Yes, and poison. Trying on Mama's lipstick. Poison trying to pretend otherwise.

"Well, don't you look pretty!" Amanda says as I descend the stairs.

The urge to scrub my face brings heat to my cheeks and makes the back of my neck burn.

I count in my head: one, two, three, four, five, six, seven.

"How were the boys? I thought I heard a fuss," I say at the bottom of the stairs, looking around and spotting the boys running around on the porch, no jackets. Kathryn still sits in her chair, but Henry has joined her. Good-natured Henry, no doubt delivering his best stories.

"Oh, nothing." Amanda waves her hand in the air, then continues her knitting.

Travis strolls over to me, and I point at the boys, asking, "No jackets?"

"It's actually warmed up a bit. Dad's thermometer reads fifty-five degrees."

"Really? Maybe I should get some sunshine today too, then."

He puts his arm around my waist. "Your hair looks great. What'd you do different?" He nuzzles his face against my neck and inhales deeply. "Smells great too."

I stiffen.

"What's wrong? You seem tense." He trails his fingers down my back.

"Just tired."

"You must need that sunshine. Maybe we'll get some in the woods tomorrow," he says, winking.

CHAPTER SEVENTEEN
KELLY

I have no idea where I'm going. I just have to get away from all these judgmental stares. I doubt Kathryn will give me a chance now. She was barely hiding her disdain before I broke her precious family heirloom. Seriously, who gets that upset over a fucking dish? It's not like it was crystal or porcelain, for fuck's sake.

I head down the gravel drive, pause to consider direction, and choose left. Going right leads back to the main road and what remains of civilization. I took half an oxycodone after breaking Nannie's dish—and then treated myself to another half—so I feel like I'm floating down the road while the gravel crunches beneath my feet.

The road slants gently downward and then curves right and back up again. At the top of the hill, I stop to look back at the cabin on its perch overlooking the lake. The view of the mountains beyond is even more breathtaking from here.

I light another cigarette, inhale deeply. I see no other houses, not in this direction at least. But behind me, in the distance, another log home sits farther down the road, nestled into the side of the mountain. I wonder if the owners are there. I decide to find out.

I walk on, hoping to find it empty, hoping for what beyond that, I'm not sure. Maybe the boys and I could move to this cabin. Lie to the Super Baptists and tell them we're trying our luck making it to South Carolina to be with family. Maybe I really should try to get there. Surely the Baptists would give me gas if it meant I'd no longer be a nuisance to them. Mother would be thrilled to see me. It's been over two years.

I'm surprised by a sob that erupts from nowhere.

"I miss you, Mama," I say out loud, even though I've never called her by that title—only whispered it to myself in weak moments when I wanted her but would never dare go to her. Mother has no patience for vulnerability. Besides my late grandmother, she's the strongest, most resilient woman I know. I don't believe I've ever seen her shaken.

The road slants upward again, and I stop to catch my breath. I could turn around, go back to the cabin, parcel out small amounts of vodka to help along my pill and its lovely blurring of the edges of my reason. The problem is, I'm almost out. I'm on my last bottle, unless I can find the ones Jenna stashed somewhere. The thought pushes me forward. If the house ahead is empty, maybe they have a liquor cabinet.

I go off the gravel lane as I get close and walk in the tall grass beside it. If there are people home, I don't want them hearing me approaching. A branch breaks to my right, and I pause, listening. I peer into the shadows of the trees, hearing Lauren's bitchy comment as I walked out the door: "Watch out for coyotes." I'm sure she'd just love that, me eaten alive by a wild dog. Jenna, too, I'm sure, would love to find my remains out here, maybe a telltale long blond hair, some fragments of clothing, some bones. I can see them standing over the site of my demise with heads bowed toward one another, giggling behind their praying hands.

No further sounds come from the forest, so I continue, slower, and listening. The house sits tucked into the hillside, not perched on top like the Baptists', but the layout looks similar, with the high, long deck running the entire back end of the house. I crouch in the tall grass and watch the windows. After several minutes, I stand and go around the right side of the house, where the gravel drive curves around to the front porch and garage. They have a small concrete pad outside the garage door just like at the Baptists' cabin, but there are no cars parked there.

Moving as silently as I can, I cross the small front yard and tiptoe up the steps to the front door. There are windows on either side, and I look through the one on the left. The house is dark. No lights, no movement. I take a deep breath and try the door. It's locked, as expected. I leave the porch, go to the garage, and peek inside. No cars.

I continue past the garage and around the other side, where there's access to the back deck. Going carefully around the corner, I peek inside the first window. This must be their second home, just like the Covingtons'. I try the first set of double doors, then the next, and finally, the last set. All locked. The glass is too thick to break.

I light another cigarette and consider my options. I passed the kitchen window getting to the back deck, and I could probably break it and sneak in that way. Or I could go down below the deck and try the glass doors that lead to the basement. But they'll be locked too, I'm sure, with glass just as thick.

I walk around the perimeter of the house to be sure the kitchen window is the only viable option. There are no other ground-level windows I can reach, so it will have to be the one. I find a large rock and hurl it at the window. The shattering sound is so loud that I instinctively drop into a crouch and hold my breath.

I wait until my knees ache. Then I wait a little longer. Squirrels chatter, playing in the leaves behind me. A light breeze comes from the mountains, rustling the leaves like a chorus for the squirrels.

No one is coming.

I grab a large magnolia leaf from the many at my feet. I rise slowly. I wrap it around my fingers and break the last shards of glass.

This is not a stage or a pageant. This is not getting my husband back, or even getting revenge. This is certainly not taking care of my children. But this is getting what I need.

I nearly bust face crawling through the window, and I almost laugh as I thud onto the kitchen floor. But then I remember why I'm here.

Leaning against the cupboards, I take in the fading light and shadows, the dust dancing in the air.

Just give me a minute. I'll figure this out. If I figure this out, will you come back? To me and the boys?

Fuck you. You aren't welcome here. I'll fucking figure this out without you.

And there's Caden, his image dancing before me like the dust. Caden clinging to Mikey, that beautiful, soft, golden hair and blue eyes just like mine.

I shake my head, come back to the present.

I have no idea what I'm doing. Who am I kidding? Not myself, certainly. I spread my hands out on the hardwood floor, which is nicer than Kathryn and Nathan's. Real wood, not laminate. Shards of glass dig in, and I welcome how they pierce, knowing I'm too numb to really feel it.

I want to cry, but I know it will do no good. It will only wreak havoc on my face. So I sit up, letting the glass dig in further, and push up to my feet. It's silent and growing darker. I need something. Now. I shake my hands, and a soft raining sound follows.

Cupboards first. One after the other. Dishware, pots and pans, coffee mugs, vases. Not what I'm looking for.

I cross the floor, go around the island, and there it is—it must be. An antique dresser against the wall. I'm on my knees and spreading open the doors, and yes, here it is. More whiskey than vodka, yes, but relief is in sight.

CHAPTER EIGHTEEN

JENNA

Thankfully, the boys don't ask where their mother is. They don't seem to think of her while they sit at the children's table, passing ketchup and mustard and all of them talking at once.

The burgers are so good that no one speaks. The lights are dimmed—a habit we never engaged in before but now do so religiously—and fire shadows dance along the high walls of the room. The fresh venison is juicy, cooked perfectly. Chris's most redeeming feature is his mastery of the grill. I chew the bun slowly, knowing it might be my last for a very long time. I wonder if we can find a bread maker on a trip to town so we can start making our own.

On a trip to town? What am I, crazy? I look at Travis, and he looks back and winks before returning to his food.

"We need to get more meat like this tonight, brother," Chris says, wiping his mouth.

"They're really good. Y'all did good," Kathryn says, popping a fry in her mouth and sitting back.

"We need to find more bread!" Henry pipes up from across the room.

"It'd be covered in mold by now," Amanda tells him.

"All of it?"

"Most likely, sadly."

Travis says to me, "Wish I woulda gotten you that bread maker you asked for for Christmas," as he stands with his plate and kisses the top of my head. "Sun's going down; we gotta get stinky."

Chris puts a handful of fries in his mouth as he's rising, grabs his beer, and chugs it. As he's turning away, he says to Amanda, "You've got my plate, right, baby?"

"Oh, you!" She swats his butt as he walks away.

I join Travis at the kitchen sink.

"I guess you'll have to keep an eye out for our house-guest, unfortunately," I say.

"Nah, I saw the direction she headed off to. She went left on the gravel road, opposite direction of our trail. And she's a damn idiot if she went off the road. Can't save stupid."

"What do I tell the boys if she doesn't come back?"

I look in their direction. Henry and Ava are no longer at the table, but the little ones are still working on the last of their fries, chattering happily. It's early for supper. What will I do with them after this? I hadn't even thought about it.

In my periphery, I see Amanda pulling Everett out of his high chair. I look back to Travis, who says, "I bet she'll be back before long. She doesn't look suited for long hikes."

I inwardly smile. I might be chubby, but I can keep up with Travis on the trail.

"Gotta get out there. Chris'll be bitching any minute." He gives me a quick kiss.

"Be careful." I lean in, one more kiss, *please*. He obliges.

"Always am," he says as he heads out.

"I love you!" I call after him.

CHAPTER NINETEEN
KELLY

After sitting awhile, leaning against the cabinet, nursing my first painful sips, I decide to poke around the kitchen. The owners must not visit as often as their neighbors down the hill; they have a small supply of canned goods, perishable goods, and in the freezer, one pint of double-chocolate ice cream. I take a small tin of cashews. The rest I leave untouched, in case the boys and I need to hide out here or raid this place when we head out.

I find a book bag and head back to the liquor cabinet, load two bottles of Ketel One, a bottle of Jameson, and another of Jack Daniels. I squeeze six cans of Coke in between, then run to the bathroom for hand towels, which I shove between the bottles to keep them from clanging when I walk back. I open the side doors and find a flask, which I fill with vodka and slip into my back pocket.

In the bathroom, I find a handful of Vicodin, and I grab some high-end hair products and stuff them in a side pocket. I take a pocketknife from the bedside table and turn on the small flashlight that sat beside it. It works, but I'm losing light. I can come back another day. I leave the upstairs level unsearched and let myself quietly out the front door. No need to lock it.

The sun is fading faster than I anticipated. Long shadows stretch out from the woods on either side of the gravel drive.

"Fuck," I mutter, then stop, standing in the tall grass beside the house. I take a drag from the flask. It's silver, monogramed with, "WTC, Jr."

There's an owl hooting to my left, and I hear rustling in the leaves, loud enough to echo, behind me. Squirrels. Very large, cute squirrels. One more sip for courage, then I hurry to the gravel.

I know coyotes, at least, will be scared of the noise I'm making. I train my eyes on the distance ahead. If any of the Super Baptists are coming, I need to drop my bag before they see it. Another reason for the towels. Keep my babies safe.

I stash the bottles in the woods a few hundred feet from the house. The men never go this direction. Their hunting path starts on the other side, goes down the hill, and then winds to the right toward the lake. I go to the very edge of the hill, hold on to a small tree to slide down a few feet, and hang the bag on a low branch on the next tree down. Then I grab some leaves and pine straw and cover it as best I can, without losing hold.

The scramble back up leaves me breathless.

They're cleaning up supper. I stand in the shadows, leaning into the corner of the deck, watching. I light a cigarette. They look like they're doing a choreographed ballet—one turning this way, another turning that way, looks and words tossed around easily, like dancers and thoughts. My boys are part of it, not skipping a beat.

The silver flask feels so smooth against my fingers as I bring it to my lips.

CHAPTER TWENTY

JENNA

Where the heck is she?

With Everett on my hip, I herd the children toward the sink, having asked them to carry their plates. I catch Jacob's lopsided plate just in time to watch Caden's last few fries fall to the floor in slow motion. Mikey overcorrects, grabbing Caden's plate and flinging ketchup in the opposite direction. It lands with a splat on the wooden column separating the kitchen from the family room.

Mikey turns to me with his chin already quivering, leading Caden to ask plaintively, "Mikey?"

"Ketchup! Ketchup! Mom, Mikey got ketchup on the wall!" Jacob yells loudly, pointing at the offending splatter.

Mikey's face collapses, tears suddenly where there had been none, and he runs from the room and up the stairs, leaving Caden, who looks at me and holds his arms straight up, crying along with his brother.

Setting the plate back on the table, I scoop Caden up with my free arm and whisper in his ear, "It's okay, bud. It's okay."

"But Mom! Ketchup on the wall!"

"Jacob, I see it. It's okay. Just put your plate in the sink, please."

He looks at me incredulously.

"It was an accident. Plate, please."

He nods but also huffs as he goes around the island. Caden has his face pressed into my neck, his tears seeping into the crevices of my skin.

Amanda comes back through the mudroom, talking as she enters. "Those boys are just begging their dad and uncle to let them go hunting. I've got to say, the men seem like they're bending." Then she notices me. "Uh-oh, hands full."

She comes around the island with her arms extended. Everett perks up and slaps my chest with his hand before reaching his whole upper body toward his aunt. I cling to his chunky little thigh. Aunt Amanda retrieves him just in time.

"How about you pick a movie?" I ask Jacob as I shift Caden to both arms.

"I don't want to watch another movie." Closing his eyes and throwing his head back, he sighs loudly. "I'm so tired of movies."

"I was thinking we should have a family prayer night, all of us, this evening," Kathryn says, joining us.

"That means we get to talk to Jesus, right Nana?"

"Yes, Jacob. Jesus loves to hear from His children."

I look up toward the loft, listening for Mikey, knowing I won't be able to hear him from here.

"But first, how about a bath in Nana's big bathtub!" She leans over, smiling at Jacob.

"Yes!" Jacob jumps up and down. "Can Caden and Mikey play too?"

"Of course. There's plenty of room. Why don't you help me get it started?" Kathryn reaches out her hand, and Jacob hops twice before he takes it.

"I'm off to get Mikey," I say.

Amanda just nods as she talks to Everett, walking toward the fire.

"Sorry for ketchup, Miss Jenna," Caden says quietly, pronouncing the *J* as a *CH* sound. *Chenna.*

"It's okay, buddy. And you can just call me 'Jenna,' remember?"

"Can I call Miss Kathryn 'Nana?' Or Mr. Nathan 'Papa'?"

I've reached the top of the stairs as he says this. I stop and lean back a little, so I can see his face. His eyes are so startlingly blue. So like Travis's eyes. When I dream of our second loss, his eyes are this blue.

"I'll have to talk to Jacob first ..." I start, not sure what to say. Would Kathryn and Nathan allow it? If I asked them first, before Travis, they might agree. Just while the boys are here. What can it hurt?

Caden nods, considering this. He asks, "No sharing?"

"But Jacob is sharing. His nana and papa, his toys."

Caden nods again. "Sharing is hard."

"You're the sweetest little boy on the planet." I kiss his forehead, breathing him in. "Let's get Mikey. It's bubble bath time!" I tickle his side gently, and he erupts with laughter.

Their bedroom door cracks open, and there's Mikey, peeking up at us. I smile back at him. The door inches open a little farther.

"Are you ready for a bubble bath in Nana's big tub?"

"But ..."

"Accidents happen. No big deal, kiddo."

His slow-spreading smile lights up his face.

"Let's grab pj's." I push open the door, and the smell of urine greets me in return. Clothes and toys litter the floor. Her black bag is on its side, with beauty products falling out in a pile beside her bed. Surveying, I spot the source of the urine smell—a trash bag of dirty diapers sits in the corner. Only a few, but more than enough for this small room.

The dresser between her bed and the boys', which usually has one lamp and a photograph of Henry and Drew, is now covered with a random assortment of items: stand-up lighted mirror, Arctic cup, two prescription pill bottles, aspirin, face lotion, toy soldiers, makeup wipes, pack of cigarettes, and a different photograph. I get closer and lean over.

"That's Daddy," Caden says, pointing.

It's a picture of Kelly with her husband, and Mikey and Caden. They're bundled up, with snowcapped mountains behind them. Kelly looks radiant—and five years younger.

"When was this taken, Mikey?"

I turn to see him holding a diaper and pajamas tightly against his chest. He shrugs.

My chest expands watching them. Such sweetness. I reach for my phone to capture it—Caden talking to the pirate in his hand while Mikey and Jacob race boats, diving through soap suds—then remember I no longer carry it everywhere. How do I make sure I hold on to this?

This moment that's just right, the boys playing happily, their innocent and excited babble filling the room, bouncing off the walls like light.

CHAPTER TWENTY-ONE

KELLY

The sight of Jenna carrying Caden while holding Mikey's hand, leading them into Kathryn's bedroom, makes me light one more cigarette before going in. The men have gone off to hunt. I heard them jibing each other and breaking branches as they started along the trail. I wish I could go with them. I wish I could be free. Like Patrick. Just deciding one day that his wishes mean more than ours and walking away.

One more sip, then I must go in. One long, last inhale. One more sip.

Only the uptight, bitchy one sits in the family room as I slip in the door. She's got Jenna's baby in her lap, and she's making ridiculous faces.

"Long walk," she says, without looking at me.

"The boys okay?"

Fuck her. Fuck what she thinks. My hands are cold. Crossing the room, keeping opposite to where she sits, her perpetual basket of yarn at her feet, I hold my hands up to the fire.

"They're in the bath. Can't you hear them?" she says.

It's the loudest sound in the room, their happy voices traveling through the open bedroom door.

They're happy here.

The fire blurs before my eyes. Taking a deep breath, I turn and sit on the hearth. My boys are warm and fed. They're giggling in a tub of warm, soapy water, with all the toys they could want. I have help caring for them, until I find my way back.

"I'm sorry. I got turned around." I can do this. A few more days. "Thank you for being so kind this morning."

She barely glances in my direction, holding her hand toward me, to silence me. "I did what I did for my family. You better learn how to respect hospitality that you haven't earned."

CHAPTER TWENTY-TWO
JENNA

Oh, to catch their slippery eel bodies with a towel, while they giggle and squeal; it's like catching tangible joy.

Kathryn kneels on the floor with me, laughing as the boys run around, silly, smiling.

This might have been. All these boys, mine. Not taken, claimed by God, for some reason I still do not understand. After our second loss at seventeen weeks, I stopped talking to God. Outwardly, I made the motions. At church on Sunday and at family suppers, I bowed my head. I promised I'd pray again when Everett was conceived. If he came to life, I would surrender and know I was deserving of my losses. That I must repent.

But this. Now. Could they be mine? Did I need such loss to feel this—my knees on the tile, my arms opened wide—this bittersweet joy. This immediate joy.

~

She's passed out in her bed when I sneak the boys in, kissing them, wrapping blankets around them. The bedroom smells better since I removed the trash. I try not to stare at her as I leave the room. She's cleaned up though. The toys are neatly put away and stacked in the corner. The dirty clothes are in a pile, so I collect them.

I look back at the boys as I close the door. Mikey pins me with his eyes. I return his gaze. I hope he reads, "I'll always love you if you let me." I blow him a kiss, and the corners of his mouth turn up just enough for my heart to dance.

CHAPTER TWENTY-THREE
KELLY

I wake in the dark and stay as still as possible, trying to remember what's happened, trying to calm my rapid breath.

I was helpful. I unloaded the basket of washed dishes. I remember being so careful, after the morning's mishap. Amanda had gone downstairs, with Jenna and the boys, while I hid in the closet, a coward. They're happy here. They're happy here, so I put away the dishes, quietly, carefully.

I remember that. And I went to our room and picked it up. Toy soldiers, Legos, cars—put into containers so they can be taken out again. Reconfigured. Made better.

And we'll do that—make it better. *Believe me, boys. Watch Mama.* We're going to come out swinging. Fuck this shit. If the power isn't up in a few days, we're ditching these Super Baptists. I'll figure it out.

I breathe in the darkness, the silence. So silent now, with the power out. As my eyes adjust, I can make out the shape of the boys across the way. Holding my breath, I can hear theirs—Caden's gentle puff of air, Mikey's throaty exhale, not quite a snore. I try to think of other ways we could survive, besides here, if this continues. If it goes on and on. But sleep pulls at my eyelids, and I drift off, still searching for an image of another place, an alternative refuge.

CHAPTER TWENTY-FOUR
JENNA

I get out of the shower and hear Travis and Chris downstairs. I hurry through my process of lotions and hair detangling. I tiptoe out of the bathroom and stand at the railing, listening, towel wrapped tightly around me.

"We have to start catching deer every trip out," Chris says. "And if not, some kind of meat—turkey, hog. Something."

"We've still got some stock in the garage," Travis replies.

"That's not a long-term solution." Chris paces, takes his ball cap off.

"Who's saying we need that?"

"Who's saying we don't?"

"Look, Chris, this thing can't last much longer."

"You have absolutely no evidence that that's the case. And we only have three weeks' worth of meat. Four weeks, if we stretch it."

"We'll get a deer tomorrow." Travis goes to the sink and

washes his hands. "Plus, we have a shit ton of canned food. Soup, tuna, vegetables."

Chris gets a beer from the fridge. "And how happy are the kids gonna be if we feed them canned food for weeks?"

The fire is dying out, and I start to shiver in my towel. I cross the landing silently on bare feet and close our bedroom door. I'm not sure I want to hear the rest.

But when I come back out, they're still talking, and others have joined in. I lean over the railing. Chris and Amanda have taken Kathryn's and Nathan's chairs, and Brent and Lauren are nestled in their usual spot. Travis stands in front of the fire, bouncing back and forth on his feet.

I head to the bathroom, hurriedly adding some gel to my curls. I'd planned on doing a face mask and straightening my hair, but my curiosity takes me downstairs.

"In a couple of months, it'll be warm enough to start planting. We can go ahead and plant cold weather veggies now, like cabbage and kale," Brent is saying as I get to the bottom of the stairs.

"Just kill me now if it's going to last that long," Amanda says. "And you think our kids are going to eat cabbage or kale?"

"Where's Kelly?" Lauren asks as I come into the room.

"Passed out in her bed."

"Whoop, whoop!" Lauren hollers.

"The babies, Lauren!" Brent says, glaring at her.

She puts her hand over her mouth, giggling.

"Seriously?" he says.

"I'm sorry. It's just so heavy in here. Are we really talking about building garden beds? I think it's all silly." She starts untangling herself from the blanket she shares with

Brent. "Well, if our lovely houseguest has decided to have an early night, I'll retrieve the wine I've hidden."

"Ooh! You have some too! Should I get mine?" Amanda asks.

"Let's see how long mine lasts," Lauren says over her shoulder as she heads to her room.

"Hey, baby," Travis says quietly in my ear as he puts his arm around me. "Boys go to bed okay?"

"I had my hands full for a minute, but they all took a bath in your mom's tub and had so much fun."

"Yeah?"

"Yeah. It was a nice night." I look up into his eyes. "The boys are really bonding."

"Jenna." He pulls away. "You know they aren't family, right? They won't be a part of our lives forever."

I look away before I answer. "I know." My voice falters.

I can't cry in front of the Covingtons. I can't, and I won't. I turn away from Travis before my eyes tear up against my will. I head toward the kitchen, where Lauren has her back to me, opening a bottle. Four wineglasses are lined up on the counter. I dab at the center of my eyes with my fingertips, forcing myself to take slow, deep breaths. Sometimes the grief hits like this, still. Out of nowhere.

I steel my shoulders and go to the mudroom to change the laundry. Someone has taken my load out and left it wet in a laundry basket on the floor. I ball my fists and close my eyes, forcing the darn deep breaths, again. I want to punch something. I really, really want to punch something. I still have several more loads to do in this tiny darn washing machine, and someone had the audacity—

"Psst."

I startle, my eyes fly open. Lauren stands to my right, extending a glass of white wine.

"I'm so sorry about the laundry," she says. "I'm the asshole. I'll do your next two loads, promise."

My shoulders drop inches. I take the glass.

"Kait literally has no clean clothes. Like, none. Not even a onesie. Apparently, I underpacked. I also promised Brent I'd take care of the laundry when he was having a moment today."

"Having a moment?"

"Oh, you don't know what a diva my husband is behind closed doors. That man is positively distraught at the lack of a system around here."

"A system?"

"For responsibilities, like cutting up firewood and filling the bins, cooking and cleaning up dinner, but especially laundry rotation, like who can do laundry when. Instead of this free-for-all." She laughs. "He's really kind of cute though. I can see why he's such an efficient manager at work."

"He might be right though. It would be easier if we all had assigned times and tasks."

"Oh my God, of course the teacher in you would agree with him. What was I thinking?" She laughs and turns, gesturing with her hand that I should follow her into the kitchen.

She picks up another glass and hands it to me, nodding and saying, "For Amanda," before turning back to the counter to grab the last two glasses.

I tentatively sip my wine. The last time we drank, Kelly got in Mikey's face.

She's asleep. She's asleep, but she could wake up any minute. I resist the urge to tiptoe.

Chris takes a chug of his beer and goes back to needling Travis. "Back to what we were talking about."

"I don't think we should do too much planning for the future without more information. That's all I'm saying," Travis says, staring at the fire instead of his brother.

"When is preparation ever a bad thing?"

"When is paranoia ever a good thing?"

Chris removes his hand from the mantel, squares his body to Travis.

"Chris," Amanda says, quietly but firmly.

He waves his hand dismissively at her, still glaring at Travis. "It's not paranoia when it's actually happening. Right now. Right now, we're in the longest blackout we've ever seen. Right now, we have no idea what's really happening. We have no idea how long it will last. Hell, how do we know there aren't armed men out there?" He waves his arm toward the windows. "Right now, about to knock on our door?"

"Bro, I love you, but you've watched way too much TV, just like my wife."

"Wake up, Travis!" Chris grabs his shoulders and shakes him.

Amanda stands up, her knitting falling to the floor.

Chris releases his grip, holding his hands up, palms forward. Travis takes a step back, but I can see the tension in his shoulders.

"I'm sorry, but you're wrong," Chris says. "It's not paranoia. We need to prepare in every way we can for the worst possible scenario."

Travis bows his head, stroking his beard and studying the ground. He looks back up. "Then maybe we should go back to the shelter, talk to the National Guard guy I met my last time out. See if they have more info. I didn't think to ask too many questions. Maybe they can tell us a timetable or something, about what to expect, about how long this will last."

Chris turns and paces the length of the room, slapping his cap against his thigh. After a few laps, he stops and says, "But we need to be hunting, getting food, not wasting a day in town."

Travis throws his hands up. "It's not wasted if we get valuable information!"

"And seeds," Brent says. Everyone looks at him. "If the soldiers tell you we need to prepare for the long term, your next step should be looting for seeds."

"And medical supplies."

We startle at the sound of Kathryn's voice. She's standing just outside her bedroom door, in her bathrobe. "I don't think it's too early for long-term preparations." She goes to turn, stops, and looks back at us. "God provides, but He also taught us to build an ark."

CHAPTER TWENTY-FIVE
JENNA

It's one of those nights when I'm awake more than I'm asleep. I startle when I feel Travis rustling around and getting up, hear him slipping on his pants. I feel an uncomfortable mixture of exhausted and anxious: my eyes don't want to open, yet I can't lie still. I get up with him.

It's so dark, and silent. Everett sighs in his sleep. Travis motions for me to go back to bed. I ignore him.

He makes more silent gestures at me as I approach him in the dark. He won't dissuade me; I need to know their plan. I slip on my robe and follow him out the door.

Downstairs, Chris is busy, with very bright lights on above the kitchen island. He's compiled snacks, fresh deer jerky, and bottled water. He wears his pistol in a holster on his hip.

"You see the totes still packed and ready from my last trip to town?" Travis asks.

"Yeah, they're already loaded in my truck."

"Oh, we're taking your truck?"

"Yes, little bro, we are."

"You grab the extra ammo?"

"Why don't you go look and take your own inventory."

I turn to follow on Travis's heel, but Chris says, "Jenna," and I stop. Travis continues without me into the mudroom, then the garage beyond. I nod and look toward the mountains, shrouded in a dark-gray fog. Why do I feel I have to listen to him?

Chris leans toward me, resting his elbows on the counter. "We'll be safe."

Nodding some more and attempting a smile, I slip my cold hands into my bathrobe pockets.

"Don't you worry, little sissy, not at all." He stands straight again, holding eye contact while he takes a sip of his coffee. I maintain his gaze despite the intense urge to roll my eyes, and they water for their effort.

I hear a door opening behind me and turn around to see Brent coming out of his bedroom, fully dressed and in hiking boots.

"Going for an early-morning hike, bro-tato?" Chris asks.

"No," Brent says, scratching the back of his neck while he approaches. "Any coffee left?"

"Yeah, there's another cup or two."

Brent helps himself, then turns and leans against the counter, taking a slow sip.

"You're not thinking you're going with us, are you?" Chris asks him, tilting his head slightly and narrowing his eyes.

"Yeah, actually, I was."

"There's no need for that."

"I'm a gardener. I can help. I know what seeds to look for, and fertilizers, soil, et cetera."

"Write us a list," Chris says, crossing his arms against his chest.

"I'd really like to get out of the house. I'm going a little stir-crazy."

"Have you ever fired a gun?" Chris asks.

"Why does that matter?"

Chris stares at the floor for a few minutes, then looks back up at Brent. "Look, man, at first I thought Lauren was crazy, falling for a city boy who's never hunted or fished a day in his life."

I watch Brent for signs of tension, but he shows none; he rests easily against the counter, sipping his coffee and listening.

Chris continues. "But over time, you won me over. You're great to my sister. You treat her like a queen, which is exactly why you're not coming with us. If something happened to you, my sister would kill me, because unlike you, she can shoot a gun. And she's a good shot too."

Brent chuckles. "She's told me many times how great a shot she is. And I know both you and Travis are as well, which is why I'll be perfectly safe. Besides, there aren't zombies out there."

"She didn't actually say yes to this, did she?" I ask.

Travis enters from the mudroom. "Everything looks good. You ready?" Then, "What's up, Brent? Why you up so early?"

"I'm going with you."

Travis's eyebrows shoot up. "Is that so?"

"Yes, it is. I can be of use."

"I'll grab an extra pistol then," Travis says and goes to the gun safe.

"So, you're fine with him going with us?" Chris asks, his tone seething.

"He's a grown-ass man. He can make up his own mind

about what he does and doesn't do," Travis says as he punches the code on the safe.

Chris throws his hands up. "Let's go then. I want to be back before dusk so I can get back to the woods with my rifle." He storms out to the garage.

Brent looks at me and shrugs, giving me a guilty grin.

"Please be careful, Brent. Don't take any unnecessary risks. And please, please, help my husband do the same!" I give him a hug. "I'm serious!"

"Yes, ma'am."

Travis holds a pistol toward Brent. "Loaded, safety on. Have you held one before?"

"Yes." He takes the gun. "Lauren has taught me."

"Then why didn't you say anything to Chris?" I ask.

"And ruin his perception of me?"

As Brent leaves us, Travis turns to me and reaches out his arms. I gladly go to him, resting my head on his chest as his arms encircle me. He kisses the top of my head. I hear Brent letting himself out to the garage, and then the house is quiet.

"Please be careful, Travis." I look up at him, and he kisses me deeply, with longing. I feel my body responding to him. He pulls away, chuckling. "No time for any of that," he says as he kisses my nose.

"I love you," I say.

"I love ya too, babe."

He strolls away from me, confident and self-assured. I bite my lip, hard.

Please, Mother Mary, keep my husband safe.

I believe in God, the Father Almighty, Creator of Heaven

and Earth; and in Jesus Christ, His only Son, Our Lord, Who was conceived by the Holy Ghost, born of the Virgin Mary ...

~

I slip back under the covers, in the dark quiet.

Please God, Mother Mary, keep him safe. Please bring him home to me. Please.

And then I curl into a ball.

I try to hear Travis's measured voice in my ear as I count. One, two, three, four, five, six, seven. When will he be home? When will we be home?

His measured voice couldn't keep our babies safe. I clutch my necklace. My gift from Travis. The ashes of our second loss, our baby boy.

Hail, Holy Queen, Mother of Mercy: our life, our sweetness, and our hope. To thee do we cry, poor banished children of Eve.

~

Everett wakes me with his shrieking.

"My beautiful boy," I say, as I reach for him.

He lets out a blaring scream. I check his head for fever. None. I grab him and hold him close, but he resists, bending backward, screaming louder.

It's deafening.

I bounce, trying for a brisk pace in our small room.

He throws his head back again with his mouth open, and I see it—the tiny white corner peeking through.

I'm halfway down the stairs while Everett screams before I consider the time, the crowded house, or that I'm not alone.

I pause on the landing, turn back around. His

screeching echoes against wood echoing against more wood. I want to cover my ears like a child. My lip is sweating.

"Shh."

I bounce as I continue downstairs, hurrying to the freezer, teething rings, and relief.

CHAPTER TWENTY-SIX
KELLY

I wake earlier than normal. Beams of sunlight hit the crack between wall and ceiling, blinding.

Whispering, then giggling, then shushing each other. They're keeping each other's secrets safe. I squeeze my eyes against the sunlight and wonder which hurts worse—the light, or being excluded. Who will keep my secrets safe now?

I remember yesterday—sitting in a stranger's house, raiding their liquor cabinet, watching dust.

More giggling, followed by, "Shh."

I roll toward the wall, away from them, make a snoring sound.

They have no idea how tenuous our situation is.

They continue whispering, and I strain to hear them. Their voices are too muffled, too indistinct. Patrick was my secret keeper. Yearning, sudden and intense, makes my skin tingle as if he were lying right next to me, as if I could feel the heat of him. Tears roll down my cheeks. Turns out I wasn't his secret keeper, though I thought I was. Turns out Daddy set him up in the family business because Patrick's family—one of the few old-money families left—was bankrupt.

No one told me I came with a dowry.

I wake again, and they're gone. I feel the absence in the room as soon as I'm awake. I bolt upright.

Legos and soldiers spill across their bed and the floor surrounding it. I rub my eyes, run my fingers through my hair. My temples are throbbing. Maybe it's time to go home.

Home.

I can see the slant of sunlight across my room. I can see Mother breezing in, halfway through her sentence as she enters, because what she has to say is that important. I should listen before she even arrives.

I should go now, before Jenna gets her claws any further into my boys. I was desperate when I let them pick me up. I thought this would only last a matter of days. I never foresaw this—living with them, day in and day out, relying on their kindness indefinitely.

I also didn't realize I was moving in with a Baptist preschool teacher.

I take a small sip of water, squeeze down a low-dose Valium. So few remain. I lie back down, suddenly queasy, and roll onto my side. Put my hand against the wall. What am I doing? Why don't we leave? Get the hell out of here?

My upper lip is sweating. I look at my Fitbit to check my pulse. I've forgotten to charge it. I take it off and fling it across the room.

I hear my mother's commanding voice: *Snap to it. Now. Chin up. Stiff upper lip. Powder and more powder if necessary.*

Cradling my head, I force myself up, my feet thudding on the cold wooden floor.

CHAPTER TWENTY-SEVEN

JENNA

How do I get through this day? I'm so tired. I've always loved this cabin, but it's so loud now. All these voices, all these angles where the sounds bounce and come back. And why do all the boys get cranky at once?

We've grown too used to gourmet breakfasts. That's part of it. Mikey didn't join in, but as soon as Jacob asked, "Where's my biscuits?" banging on the table like a caveman, Caden chanted alongside him.

Henry sulked to the table, saying, "Bread is a thing of the past," grabbed a granola bar, and retreated.

Nathan was nowhere to be found.

Kelly didn't join us. For that, at least, I should be grateful.

As soon as breakfast was cleaned up, I dragged a tote of railroad toys to the family room and put in a *Thomas the Tank Engine* DVD, crossing my fingers they'd take the bait if I didn't suggest a thing. Thankfully, Caden squealed as soon as he heard the music, and then again when he saw the treasure of railroad pieces to build with. Cue Jacob being bossy and Mikey taking interest.

I sigh.

At least one boy isn't grouchy. I look down at Everett, drinking away sleepily. I've copied Kathryn and decided a few minutes on the porch with a blanket is a good thing.

He looks up me, holding my eyes, even though his are droopy. This love, it aches. I will not look away.

~

The railroad tracks don't last nearly long enough.

I've caved and broken out my giant drawing pads, earlier than expected.

"You first," Mikey says, grinning and pointing at Jacob.

Jacob squeals and yells, "Splat!" as he falls backward.

Jacob has picked green for his outline color, for the Hulk. We take turns tracing his arms, legs, fingers. One by one, each boy is traced, outlined. Jacob adds muscles to his biceps, half-circles really, swirling his marker around and around to fill them in. Caden decides on purple pants and gives himself lopsided, googly eyes.

Mikey makes his hair blond and his eyes blue.

"Your turn, Mommy!" Jacob shouts.

"Yes, Ms. Chenna, yes!" Caden climbs into my lap and grabs my cheeks, nodding my head up and down for me.

~

Mikey is in a fit of giggles, holding the marker above my head. He's giving me some crazy hairdo before I'm allowed to get up.

"Almost done," he says as I hear the marker glide past my ear.

Jacob sits on the other side of me, watching the progress and covering his mouth with one hand. He's given himself the hiccups with laughter.

"Mommy!" Caden exclaims.

I glance over to see her coming into the room.

"Mommy! Look!" Caden jumps up and down and points. "It's me!"

Go away! You aren't needed here! Go away!

Mikey's hand drops to his side, the open end of the marker resting against the sole of his shoe. I wait and watch his face, hoping he'll meet my eyes. He keeps his glued on her.

"It is you! In purple pants! I love them!" She kneels next to Caden, circles his waist with her slender hand.

I sit up slowly, running a hand over my hair.

"Your turn!" Caden says to her, pointing at the paper.

"I can't right now, baby. Maybe later."

He doesn't argue. Just curls further into her embrace, resting his head against her shoulder. She kisses the top of his head.

"Thanks for entertaining them," she says, smiling and looking up at me. "Is the washer available?"

I notice her black leather bag, unzipped and full of her clothing. I've been washing the boys' clothes. How I wish I'd been lazy and not changed the laundry while the boys ate lunch. But it's already folded neatly in baskets at the bottom of the stairs, waiting to be distributed.

"You're in luck. It is." I wonder if she's had training in real pageants, a course on how to smile on command, brilliantly, charmingly. I look at her teeth for signs of Vaseline.

"Thank you," she says. Then she turns to Caden, buries

her face in his hair once more. When she looks up, her expression has changed. She stares past us, tears in her eyes. "My lovebug," she whispers as she kisses his cheek, then stands.

As she walks away, I turn to Mikey, who sits silently next to me, one hand on my knee.

Whispering, I ask, "Can I turn around now? Can I see my hairdo?"

He nods, slowly raises his dark eyes to meet mine.

"Mommy, look at your hair!" Jacob calls out.

I wink at Mikey and take his hand before turning around.

"It's your crown," he whispers in my ear.

He's drawn a rainbow over my head, like a halo.

I stand at the kitchen counter, looking at our meat, debating how much to cook for supper when Kathryn comes up beside me.

"Cook more than enough," she says.

I turn to look at her, meet her bright-blue eyes. She puts her hand on mine, squeezes.

"God will bring them home to us, and He will provide."

I nod and look away so she can't see my fear.

He will be safe. *Mother Mary, please keep him safe.* They'll come home with supplies and good news, and before I know it, this will be over. He'll come back to me, and we'll go home.

Supper at home, our home. Travis talking about his day while I bring dishes to the table with my heart gladly serving, watching as Travis pulls Jacob's seat closer, tickling him before tucking the napkin neatly into his shirt. Just us.

Everett in my lap, a luxury. Before, when we only had Jacob and nothing had been lost, Travis insisted on certain things. Like Jacob eating on his own in his high chair. No bassinet in the bedroom. Insisting Jacob shouldn't be strapped to me in his sling, all day, every day.

"A simple, filling meal," she says once she sees my ingredients: Salisbury steaks, instant mashed potatoes, gravy, canned vegetables. She squeezes my hand again. "You've done well."

She goes to the pantry, moves some things around. Nathan has gone through the house, turning off unnecessary lights, and now bends over the fire, poking and prodding the wood to catch. He's turned the heat down low, and I feel a chill even as I move around the kitchen. He seems increasingly worried about the propane level.

Kelly has left for a walk, alone. She put her laundry in, grabbed herself a snack, and came back to the family room, focused on Caden. She all but ignored Mikey. She asked them to walk with her though. Mikey didn't answer. He looked at the floor, at the fireplace, and finally out the window, head tilted toward the sky. Caden waited, watching his brother. Just when I thought Mikey would break, Kelly did instead.

"That's okay. I know it's cold. I'm just going to get a little fresh air. If that's alright with you, of course," she said, looking at me.

"Of course." I tried to meet her eyes, but I found myself looking anywhere else—at her perfectly styled hair, or her overly powdered forehead, or her long, bony hands as they fidgeted.

She blew Caden and, I suppose, Mikey a big air kiss before slipping out the door.

~

Amanda shuffles in in slippers, her eyes puffy from a nap. Pulling her sweater closer around her, she opens the fridge.

"How's it going in here?" she asks.

I finish forming the patties and go to wash my hands as Nathan says, "You trying to cool down the house?"

"Sorry," she says and closes it. "I'm really craving brownies. Or cake. Or ..."

"We've got ice cream," Nathan offers.

"Ice cream!" Jacob shouts from his spot on the floor, sitting cross-legged. Mikey lies on his belly next to him, head resting in his hands, intensely focused on their movie.

"Shh." Mikey puts his finger to his lips.

Jacob leans his head then his whole body sideways, staring Mikey down, but Mikey doesn't even notice.

"Jacob!" Amanda says, in a better teacher voice than I can ever muster. He snaps up, reconsidering whatever move he was thinking of making.

Poor Mikey startles so completely he leaps to a seated position. "Sorry," he says, looking down.

"It's okay," I say over the roar of racing cars in the background. "Finish the movie, boys. Then we'll have supper and dessert."

As the boys' attention goes back to the TV, Amanda comes and stands beside me at the sink. "I'm sorry I scared him. I keep forgetting how timid he is," she whispers.

"He shouldn't be that timid to a teacher tone." I look at the boys' heads, all lined up. They should all be mine.

"I wonder what the poor things have really been through," she says.

I nod.

"Oh, sweetie."

I keep my eyes on the boys.

"I didn't think," she says.

"It's okay, really." I turn and look into her gorgeous green eyes. "Really."

"I bet you want to give her a good beating."

I chuckle. Nod again. Wonder if she means my mother or our houseguest. "If I was the violent type." I look down, wipe the counter again, though it's not dirty, trying to clear my mother's face from my mind.

"All we can do is pray for her, and for them." She removes her hand from mine. "Should we get these steaks in the oven?"

I come back to the present, smell the fire, feel the chill, and look up toward the high ceiling, shrouded in shadows. "Yes."

She opens the oven door for me as I slide the deer meat in.

As soon as I straighten, I whisper, "I've got boxed brownie mix."

Amanda's eyebrows shoot up. "But we're out of eggs."

"We have applesauce."

"You can substitute applesauce for eggs?"

"Yes."

"And that's why you're skinnier than me." She puts her hand on her hip. "And don't go arguing with me again that you aren't." She smiles at me. "I love having a sister-in-law who can cook. Between you in here and my husband on the grill, I'm never going to see a size 8 again." She shrugs. "So, brownies for dessert?"

I look toward the counter, where my packets of instant potatoes and line of canned vegetables sit, waiting to be warmed. Brownies will stretch the meal.

I nod. "The men will be pleasantly surprised when they

get home, won't they?" I say as I go to the garage to retrieve the brownie mix. It's hidden along with various "luxury" food items, in a tote I tucked back in the corner, behind coolers and miscellaneous garage clutter.

When I return, Amanda has gotten out the applesauce, oil, and a large mixing bowl.

Lauren comes strolling in with Kaitlyn in her arms. "The men aren't back yet?" she asks, rubbing sleep from her eyes.

Seems everyone's gotten a nap but me.

"Not yet," Amanda says.

"Are we worried?" Lauren asks, looking from Amanda to me.

"I've been wondering why they've been gone so long," Amanda admits. "Chris really wanted to make it back before dusk so he could hunt for a couple hours. Although I'm starting to suspect his whole insistence on needing more meat is just an excuse to spend as much time in the woods as he can."

Lauren walks toward the pack 'n' play to change Kaitlyn's diaper. By the time she returns to the kitchen, I'm mixing up the brownie batter and Amanda is spraying the pan. Amanda puts her finger to her lips as Lauren takes in what we're making.

"Ooh, brownies?" Lauren whispers, looking toward the family room. "I guess the kids don't know?"

"Trying to keep them engrossed in the movie till the very end," Amanda says quietly. She motions toward me. "This one has three times the patience I had when mine were little."

"I'll second that," Henry says as he ambles in, picking up a fake apple from the decorative bowl of pretend fruit on the counter. He mimics taking a bite out of it. "Could we please, please put this away somewhere, out of sight? You do realize the cruelty of it, right? No fresh fruit to be had, but we get to pass by its imitation several times a day."

Amanda glares at her son as he stands with one hand on his hip, the apple still in the other. He glares back at her with her same intense green eyes.

"Maybe Jenna's sons are sweeter than you were when you were little," Amanda says, putting her hand on her hip to echo her son.

"Well, if I was less sweet, was it nature or nurture? Hmm? Either way, it's still your fault."

"Henry!" Kathryn says, coming into the kitchen with Everett.

"I'm just messing with her, Nana. She likes to spar with me." Henry winks at his mother and gives his grandmother a kiss on her cheek.

Amanda huffs and goes to the second oven. "Temperature, Jenna?"

I glance at the box. "Four hundred degrees."

CHAPTER TWENTY-EIGHT
KELLY

After doing my laundry, I escape for a walk. I feel like I'm suffocating in the house, with Jenna fawning over my boys and entertaining them with all her fabulous art projects.

I slip out the front door and light a cigarette. The clouds create dancing shadows on the lawn as I step off the porch. Birds chatter, and a chill breeze rustles the leaves, but the sky is clear enough that the late-afternoon sun warms my shoulders as I cross the clearing beside the house.

Sliding down to my stash, I rest against a tree as I fill my flask, then my water bottle. Once the bag is tied back in place, I scramble sideways along the incline, making my way to the opposite end of the clearing. I emerge from the woods when I can no longer see the kitchen window and pick my way through brambles until I reach the gravel drive.

Turning left, I go off the road and follow a small trail that cuts through dead switchgrass, sipping whiskey and trailing my hand along the brittle stalks. The barren trees, with their black finger-branch silhouettes against the turquoise sky, deepen my loneliness. I stop and crouch to examine a dainty purple wildflower, wanting to clear Patrick's face from my mind, but failing.

How could you? Why did you?

Plucking the flower and pinning it behind my ear, I continue, dabbing at my tears before they can ruin my eyeliner.

There's no telling how long I've been wandering, watching birds and squirrels, and even spotting a bunny and an owl. Collecting wildflowers and ferns in a bouquet as I meander back toward the cabin, contemplating my next step. Craving home. Charleston in spring—cascading lavender wisteria and clusters of white star jasmine trailing along old brick walls. Magnificent old oaks, Spanish moss drooping from their dark, gnarled branches, lining the streets. And Mother and Father. How are they surviving in that big old house? Has their help stayed or abandoned them?

A five- to six-hour drive. Do the Baptists have enough gas to get me that far? Lighting another cigarette, I realize with dismay that I only have thirteen left.

Fuck.

The men are pulling up in Chris's big red truck as I approach the house. His camo-netted hat sits slightly askew on his head, and his dirty-blond hair sticks out on either side.

Brent climbs out first, from the back seat, and goes

immediately to the truck bed to retrieve a large box. A huge smile plastered on his face, he heads toward me and the open land beside the cabin.

"Good afternoon, Kelly!" he calls.

"Good afternoon." I smile but hurry past him, desperate to hear news.

I reach the driveway as Travis opens the tailgate, then takes his hat off to wipe the sweat from his brow. He startles when he sees me.

"How was town?" I ask.

"Um, well, worse than I expected, to be honest." Putting his cap back on, he looks me over discreetly before settling into eye contact. "I see you've been collecting wildflowers."

Smiling, I hold my handful of colors toward him. "Do they smell good?"

CHAPTER TWENTY-NINE
JENNA

Beauty lets out a muffled bark before rising. She listens another count and then howls, nails clattering across the hardwood floor.

Wiping my hands on my apron and turning the gravy off, I turn toward the mudroom, but I'm stopped by Amanda, holding Everett toward me.

"Henry, Drew, Ava ... Daddy's home!" she shouts and heads to the garage.

"Daddy!" Jacob screeches. Then he zigzags around the adults and runs outside, barefoot, before I can stop him. Kaitlyn wails in protest at the noise, which startles Everett, so he grabs my shirt and joins in the screaming.

"Shh, bubby, it's okay," I say, rubbing his back.

"Miss Chenna?" Caden tugs at my leg. "Miss Chenna?"

"Yes, sweetheart?"

His face is terror-stricken. I crouch down and put my arm around him as Everett continues to whimper in my ear.

"What's happening?" Caden says as he snuggles close and puts his thumb in his mouth, breathing erratically.

"It's okay, my love, it's okay. Mr. Travis and his brothers have come home. That's all."

Peeking over his head, I spot Mikey standing forlornly by the family room column, watching us.

I beckon him, and he comes eagerly. As he gets to me, Caden puts his arm out to his brother. "Come, hug," he says.

Mikey grins and steps into our group hug. The noise of the house—everyone rushing to get outside—fades as I hold my boys in my arms.

I pass through to the garage with Everett in my arm and holding Mikey's hand, the boys trailing behind me. Drew and Henry unload totes while Ava asks her dad if he found any chocolate, and Brent gushes to Kathryn and Lauren about all his garden finds.

And then I spot them.

She leans against the truck holding a bouquet, with purple wildflowers tucked behind one ear. Travis holds Jacob with one arm, his back to me.

Mikey pulls at my hand, makes me realize I've been squeezing his, hard. I swallow. Loosen my grip. Look at his sweet face looking up at me.

"Sorry," I whisper.

"Mommy!" Caden yells, releasing Mikey's hand.

Travis turns around with a smirk on his face. I feel like I've been punched in the stomach.

"Miss Jenna?" Mikey says.

Kelly sidesteps Travis, says something to him, and hands him the bouquet. Then she turns toward Caden, opening both arms extra wide, her face beaming. "My lovebug!"

He jumps into her arms, and she swings him up and holds him close, his legs wrapping around her.

"Miss Jenna?" More urgently this time. I look down into Mikey's dark, serious eyes.

I want to run. Past the noise and all the voices around me, from the look I saw on both their faces, even from the plaintive little boy beside me. I feel like I'm shrinking, folding in on myself; my gut, my lungs, my heart, squeezing smaller and smaller. I'm struggling to breathe, but still I squat down to face my boy and release his sweaty hand, the sweat mine or his, I don't know.

"Can we still stay here?" The way his mouth quivers as he looks at me—with the eyes of an old soul, not a little boy—snaps something. The tiniest crack.

"Of course you can. You can stay with me as long as you want. You can stay with me forever."

"Really?"

"Really."

"Mommy too?"

"Supper's getting cold, y'all!" Kathryn shouts above the din. "Let's get inside and eat. Finish unloading later."

Travis's hand appears beside me, and he helps me to my feet. "Hey, baby," he says, leaning in for a quick kiss. "Miss me?"

I rush around delivering platters to the table as they all file in and take their seats. As soon as we've prayed, Ava calls out to the quiet room, "Y'all find out when the dang power is coming back on and I can go home?"

"Ava Grace!"

"Mom! It's the end of the world, and I'm not allowed to say *dang*?"

"She's got a point, Ma," Henry says.

Amanda rolls her eyes and mutters under her breath, "Lord, give me strength."

"The power isn't coming back anytime soon," Chris says, then turns to me. "Great steak, little sissy, and gravy too."

"Does that mean another week? Two weeks? A month?" Ava asks.

"Would you let me eat my supper in peace?" Chris turns halfway around to look at her at the children's table.

"Please, Daddy. Just tell me what you found out. *Please.* I miss my friends."

Chris sighs. "I wish I had an answer, baby, but I don't. The soldiers don't know. They don't have any more information than we do."

Everyone is silent. Everett slaps his tray and babbles, "Da-da! Mama da-da ba!"

"So, we have no idea," Henry says quietly, bowing his head. Ava puts her face in her hands, her slender shoulders giving away her struggle not to cry.

"Should we be scared?" Drew asks, sounding younger than his eleven years.

"No, we should not be scared," Kathryn says, her voice firm but reassuring. "We're luckier than most families right now. We're safe. We have food and power and plenty of deer in them woods and fish in that lake. We have each other, and we have God."

"Yes, we do," Nathan says. "That's all we need."

"And guns," Chris says.

"Chris." Amanda jabs him.

"What do we need guns for?" Drew asks, and Amanda gives Chris a look.

"For shooting deer. Duh," Chris says and helps himself to another steak.

Kathryn continues. "Have y'all thought about what it's like for folks stuck in cities and apartment buildings? Or the families that've had to go to shelters and sleep on cots next to strangers? There's no need to be afraid. But we should all, all of us, be grateful right now for what we have, 'cause there's a whole lot of folks going without."

The room once more grows silent. Travis's knee bops up and down beside me. As the sun slides past the mountains, the final slants of sunlight slice across the room.

We bribe the older kids with babysitting money and an extra dessert serving so the adults can hold a meeting on the back deck. Amanda makes herself a large bowl of brownies and ice cream before anyone else can get to the sweets.

I run around picking up choking hazards and dangerous everyday items while Kathryn and Ava help the little ones dish up and Nathan lights the firepit, then fiddles with the chairs—making sure they're in a perfect circle.

"Listen to your cousins, or you're going to bed early," Travis says as he passes the boys on his way to the porch.

"Yes, sir!" Jacob salutes before returning to his mound of sugar.

I settle the babies in, Kaitlyn in her swing and Everett in his exersaucer, guarded by Beauty. After throwing one more log on the fire, I give Ava a quick hug. "Thanks for watching the little ones."

"Thanks for all the art supplies," she whispers and hugs me back in a rare moment of Ava sweetness. It feels like sunshine after days of rain, and I hug her tighter.

"Anything for my budding artist." I kiss her cheek lightly before she can pull away.

By the time I reach the deck, I find Kelly has once again seated herself beside my husband.

Lauren rises from the seat on the other side of him, winking at me, and says, "Warming your seat for ya, little sis."

"Is she younger than you?" Kelly asks. She faces the house, with darkness behind her, and the mountains, the wilderness. The light from the house makes her face look pale, almost ghostly, next to Travis's year-round woodsman tan. She looks at me. "Not that you look older. I just assumed you were, since she's the baby of the family." She gives me a small, tight smile.

I feel a flush starting on my cheeks, resist the urge to run my hand over my messy bun.

"I call her that because she's so tiny, obviously," Lauren says.

"Remember that time you threw Jenna across the room?" Brent asks, laughing.

"I remember that night! I caught her!" Travis says, laughing along with him.

"What? Y'all tossed Jenna around?" Kathryn asks, looking back and forth from Travis to Lauren.

"Y'all, c'mon on," Chris says and motions behind him, at the house and the kids. "We may have paid them to give us some time, but that doesn't guarantee it."

"Well, then, out with it, Mr. Antsy Pants," Lauren says, widening her eyes and tilting her head, giving him her full sarcastic attention.

"It's bad," he starts, waiting, looking around the circle to see if he has everyone's attention.

I can feel Travis tensing beside me. I put my hand on his knee, but he starts bouncing it again, and I take it back.

"Like, bad." Chris turns his head slowly, looking at each of us, one by one. He takes his hat off, roughs up his hair, places it back on his head. "The soldiers are clueless."

"I wouldn't say clueless. Seriously?" Travis crosses his arms.

Chris spits on the deck. "Clueless babies."

"Chris," Kathryn says.

"They were young," Brent admits.

"There were several older guys, older than us," Travis interjects.

"Oh yeah, all three of them." Chris rolls his eyes.

"This isn't helping," Kathryn says, and silence ensues, except for the hissing of the propane firepit and the occasional breaking twig in the woods behind us.

Brent clears his throat. "It does seem like we should prepare for a long stay."

"How long?" Lauren asks.

"No one knows," Brent replies.

"The soldiers didn't have *any* answers?" Amanda asks.

Chris stands and goes to the railing. Looking into the darkness, he says, "They were all scared shitless. Half of 'em have abandoned their posts and gone home. The ones that are there, well, that's 'cause their families are there." He walks the length of the deck and, on his return, continues. "Said they'd shoot looters on sight, but there ain't enough of them to guard the shelter and hospital, let alone all the stores in town."

"The hospital is still up and running?" Kathryn sits up, absentmindedly smoothing her blanket over her knee.

“Yes. Well, one wing. And they’re struggling with a flu outbreak,” Brent answers.

“People from the shelter?” she asks.

Brent nods.

“Bad time of year for people to be gathered in close quarters,” she says.

“Yes, it is,” Brent replies.

“Guess y’all took your chances with looting, with all the totes you brought back,” Nathan says quietly.

“We had to.” Chris slaps his cap against his thigh. “Things are bad out there, Dad. Those boy soldiers know nothing. And if the army doesn’t have a clue ...”

“What’d you get?” Lauren asks, looking at Brent.

“Well, I already told you about the gardening supplies,” he replies. “We’re set for cabbage, kale, lettuce, tomatoes, beans, herbs, peppers—”

“And?” Lauren throws up her hands.

“We didn’t get nearly enough,” Chris says, sitting back down. “We went out of the way to the old Piggly Wiggly’s and got some canned goods and toilet paper there, a pack of paper towels. A few odds ’n’ ends from the pharmacy.”

“But you did bring Ava three bags of chocolate,” Amanda says, taking Chris’s hand.

“We tried to hit Walmart, but there were some rough-looking men stationed out front, with plenty of firepower,” Travis says.

I shiver. Pull my shawl tighter around my shoulders.

“How scary,” Kelly says and puts her hand on Travis’s arm. “So glad y’all made it back safely.”

How can she not see me glaring at her?

“It’s scary out there. We’re lucky we made it back,” Chris says, leaning forward and staring at her hand, which still rests on Travis’s bicep. She slips it back into her lap as he continues. “The army is shooting looters on sight because they themselves have no supplies. The government hasn’t sent ’em shit. Not a single MRE, no fuel, nothing. Their orders are to loot surrounding areas for supplies while recruiting anyone willing to help.”

“You’re so dramatic,” Travis says, huffing and standing, then turning away from us to pace the porch.

Chris throws up his hands. “Well, little brother, this is a dramatic situation.”

“Enough,” Kathryn says. She turns to Brent. “Will you please relay how it went? From start to finish?”

CHAPTER THIRTY
KELLY

She's constantly stealing glances, like I won't notice. Poor thing. I really don't understand a woman who doesn't keep herself up. Does she think her husband wants to see her in that messy bun with no makeup? Poor, deluded thing.

As soon as Travis starts pacing, I rise to join him, lighting a cigarette as an excuse. He's right. Chris is a dramatic baboon.

The whiskey was a good choice. It's given me a whole different glow.

Brent starts speaking, and I suppose I should listen. But Travis keeps pacing, and as he heads back in my direction, I raise an eyebrow at him. He smirks and rolls his eyes.

"Soldiers said they're running low on fuel already." Brent clears his throat, "Can't figure out how to get the pumps running at any of the stations in town. Heck, they don't even know who owns 'em. They're no longer running the lights, only the heat. The women are having to walk down the street to the Cartecay River to do their laundry. They're bringing back gallons of it for cooking and bathing, although we definitely saw a few moms washing their kids in the river.

"They've separated the healthy from the sick. The sick ones have been moved to the gym. The hospital wing that's still up only has four beds left, and they're already making hard choices."

Travis sits back down, and I notice Nathan taking Kathryn's hand. Shit. This is getting serious. I take another swig, close my eyes for a second to appreciate the Percocet as it kicks in. I could float right over the mountains.

"Can we help?" Jenna asks in her nauseatingly mousy voice.

"Just like your husband, aren't you!" Chris exclaims, jumping up again. "Offering Mom to the soldiers!"

"Whoa, I can't *offer* Mom, and I didn't," Travis says.

"You asked if they needed nurses!"

"I asked how many had stayed to help! And how many doctors there were!" Travis throws his hands up.

"Exactly!"

"I wanted to know if we'd be able to get help if we needed it!"

"Boys," Nathan says, louder than I've ever heard him speak.

"Don't make your father stand up," Kathryn adds.

Jenna is pulling at her shawl, drawing it tighter and tighter, like an insect spinning a cocoon. She reminds me of a caged animal.

"Chris, sit down," Nathan says, quieter, but with more authority than I expected from him.

"Brent," Kathryn says, turning toward him, where he sits just beyond Nathan. "How badly do they need my help?"

Nathan takes her chin in his hand, saying quietly, "Katie."

She shakes her head free.

"Are we not Christians? Are we not required to minister?" she asks. Turning to Amanda on her other side and taking her hand, she closes her eyes and says, "We're hard pressed on every side, but not crushed. Perplexed, but not in despair. Persecuted, but not abandoned. Struck down, but not destroyed."

CHAPTER THIRTY-ONE

JENNA

I bite the inside of my cheek until I taste blood. How could I suggest we help?

When Kathryn quotes from the Bible, it feels as though I've been dunked in ice-cold water. Chris stays silent, but as soon as she's finished speaking, he storms off the porch and around the side of the house.

Ava comes outside and asks quietly, "Is everything okay?"

"Yes, sweetheart, it is," Kathryn says. "Nothing to worry about. The boys behaving?"

"Yes, ma'am."

"We'll be in soon."

Ava nods and goes back inside.

Amanda makes no sign of going after Chris. Kelly still stands away from the group, leaning against the railing.

"What are you saying exactly, Mom?" Lauren asks in a tone only she can get away with.

"That we're being tested. That God is asking hard things of us. Sacrifices even. What would Jesus want me to do, Lauren, do you think? Did He give me the healing gifts of a nurse if He didn't intend that I use them?"

Lauren closes her eyes and sighs. Licking her lips and looking up at the sky, she crosses her arms and turns back to her mother. "I just want my family, the people I love, to be safe. I'm sorry that I don't care about my neighbor the way a Christian should."

"And if it was Brent, or your father, sick and in need of medical care right now, how would you feel if not a single doctor or nurse stepped up to care for him?"

Silence.

Brent takes Lauren's hand. She turns to him and says, "Is this what you want too? You want to be the family that helps?"

"Yes, I do," he says quietly.

Lauren nods. Sighs loudly. Then stands. "I want wine. And a lot of it."

"Lauren," Kathryn says. "Is that necessary?"

"Yes, Mom, it is."

"Lauren ..." Brent's hand lingers in the air, ignored.

"When did my daughter turn to drink?" Nathan mutters.

"Y'all need to relax," Travis says, standing again. "Everybody's coping in their own way."

"I'll take a glass too, please," Amanda says. "And you should grab a beer for my husband."

Brent puts his head in his hands, staring at the wood slats of the deck, as Nathan stands and puts his hand on Kathryn's shoulder.

"Perhaps you should lead us in prayer, Mama," he says.

"I'm all for prayer, Dad, but we need to be planning, hunting, fishing, and looting. Leave the prayer to the women," Chris says as he comes around the corner and rejoins the circle.

"I agree that a prayer is called for." Kathryn puts her hand over Nathan's. "To set our hearts right with God. Our plans are guided by His hand. We must remember that."

Once we're in the quiet of our own room, Travis comes up behind me and hugs me, resting his chin on my shoulder.

"This is starting to feel like a bad dream. Something we need to wake up from. But how?" he whispers in my ear, and chills race through my body.

"I wish we could go home," I say.

"I'm getting pretty sick of my brother."

I bite my lip so I won't speak of the houseguest. I don't want to start a fight.

He kisses my bare shoulder, then my neck. "Here, let me help you with that," he whispers as he unlatches my bra.

"Fudge!"

"What?"

"I forgot to pump and dump."

He sighs loudly and drops his arms. "So much for getting laid." He strips off his pants and gets into bed.

"I'm sorry."

"You need to tell Lauren no next time she hands you wine. You don't even like it that much anyways."

I keep my back turned so he can't see my tears. "I know. You're right."

Once the machine is plugged in and I'm settled in with a suction cup on each breast, Travis mutters, "Not to mention, the waste of milk." Then he turns off his lamp and rolls away from me.

CHAPTER THIRTY-TWO
KELLY

My boys have once again disappeared. I sigh and sit up, my stomach grumbling. Reaching into my black bag, I pull out pill bottles and Kind bars. I only have three protein bars left. While chewing, I lay out my bottles, debating which to take.

The Super Baptists gave me a list of responsibilities. After the arguing, there came the prayers—calling upon the mighty divine hand of God to direct their Christian and charitable course. And then the fuckers outlined job titles and designated me housemaid.

At first, when they started discussing an apocalyptic home school, I thought they were joking. I crept back to my corner and lit a cigarette to keep myself from laughing. Of course, they bestowed the title of head huntsman to Chris, who responded by strutting up and down the porch like a bird showing off his feathers.

I pick up my list of chores, then get up and pace the room as I read it:

. . .

Kelly's Responsibilities

Mondays/Wednesdays/Fridays:

Vacuum hardwoods on main floor and top floor

Tuesdays/Thursdays/Saturdays:

Vacuum carpeting in basement

Mondays:

Sanitize all handles, doorknobs, and light switches

Help Jenna with any school week preparations

Help Amanda with any weekly meal preparations

Tuesdays:

Empty all household trash cans

Sweep the front and back porch

Wednesdays:

Strip sheets, wash and remake beds, 8 total + two cribs

Wash all bathroom and kitchen towels, fold and replace

(Wednesday: all personal laundry prohibited)

After vacuuming hardwoods, mop main and top floors, taking extra care in kitchen and dining area

That bitch Amanda. "Taking extra care." You can tell she hasn't been laid in eons.

Thursdays:

Scour bathrooms, including toilets, sinks, and baths, 4 total

And probably too fat to lean over a tub and clean it herself.

Fridays:

Deep kitchen clean: scour stove, microwave, sinks, counters
Empty all household trash cans
Sanitize all handles, doorknobs, and light switches
Saturdays:
Dust all surfaces, on all 3 levels
Polish wood surfaces with wood cleaner

Are you fucking kidding me? Do they realize how much wood is in this house?

Sundays:
The Sabbath—Bible study after supper

I stand in the center of our tiny bedroom and let the list fall from my hand. Maybe I should have expected this. I've been here ... How long have I been here?

I start pacing again, trying to count the days on my hand. What have I done since I got here? The days are a blur. Maybe I should start a journal to keep track of these monotonous, never-ending days.

Reaching down, I pick up the list, recheck my Wednesday duties. Today is one of my heaviest workloads. They've decided to get their worth out of me, in case this ends tomorrow or the next day. Sneaky assholes, taking advantage of me when I was too intoxicated to pay attention. What would they do if I don't concede? If I flat out refuse their ridiculous list?

An image comes back to me, of pacing the garage while the boys stayed warm in the running car, me pleading with a God I don't believe in to rescue us and redeem me.

I shudder and reach under my pillow, feel my flask. Cold, hard metal. It's still half full of whiskey. I decide on hydrocodone. Wash it down with whiskey. I'll float happily along, dusting and scrubbing like Cinderella, awaiting my Prince Charming.

CHAPTER THIRTY-THREE

JENNA

I reach for Travis as I awaken, but he's not here. Everett babbles in his crib, grabbing his chunky feet with his even chunkier hands.

Once I finish breastfeeding, I peek outside our room. Kelly's door is still closed. A few voices float up from the kitchen—Kathryn's, Nathan's, and Jacob's.

Leaning over the railing, I call, "Good morning!"

Jacob looks up. "Mommy! Good morning!"

"Volume, baby."

"Sorry, Mommy. Daddy went hunting really, really early. I wasn't even awake yet."

"He's going to get us a deer, I just know it!" I smile at him, and he smiles back. Everett slaps my chest and calls out, "Achoo, Achoo!"

Jacob giggles.

"Kathryn, do you mind if I take a shower?"

"Not at all, dear, go ahead," she says from her chair, where she's reading her morning Scriptures.

"Bring me that little guy," Nathan says. "Take a few

moments for yourself. You have a lot to do today to get our little school up and running."

Brent takes a break from building his greenhouse to carry in my totes from the garage. Kathryn tells me to use the kitchen table for home school planning, and before long, papers and plans are strewn across its wooden surface.

Ava approaches and stands beside me, silently watching, her arms dangling instead of on her hips in her usual stance.

"Do you want to help?" I ask.

"Oh, could I? I'm so bored."

"Absolutely."

We spend hours creating poster boards, copying worksheets by hand, and planning our first week of school. Ava hints that she wants to teach art, Drew asks if he can show the little ones how to make fishing lures, and Henry avoids the endeavor altogether.

At one point, I turn to her and say, "Ava, it's like a light has come on in your eyes. You're a natural."

She smiles at me, "Right back at ya, Aunt Jenna."

Kelly trudges by several times, carrying dirty linens to the mudroom, her hair pulled into a ponytail, her face red and splotchy from work.

For lunch, Lauren sets up the long arts-and-crafts table

on the back deck. She takes the boys on a scavenger hunt to collect decorations for our centerpiece. We all sit down to a tablecloth adorned with rocks, pine cones, and a bouquet of greenery with the first few wildflowers of February. While we eat dinner, Kelly sweeps and mops the kitchen.

After lunch, we ask the children to decide on a name for their school.

"Slimy!" Caden shouts. "Slimy School!"

"Silly school," Henry says as he heads inside.

"Pointless? Is that what you meant?" Drew asks his brother, who isn't listening.

"Covington Christian Academy," Ava says.

Henry stops halfway through the door, turns toward his siblings. "Perfect. We rule the world."

"We rule the world!" Jacob shouts. Hopping out of his chair, he asks, "Can we make a sign for our school? A big one? A really big one?"

We're painting our final touches when Beauty rises, growls, then barks.

"Are they back?" Lauren asks.

I pause my paintbrush and look beyond the boys as Brent rounds the corner.

"They got a buck!" he calls out.

Chaos ensues, but of a good kind. Drew and Henry help Travis and Chris skin and clean the deer, which Chris says will feed us for a month, while Nathan and Brent finish building the frame for the greenhouse. Ava and I hang our school banner and clean up our supplies. Kathryn decides to bathe the boys early. Amanda sings to herself in the kitchen as she cooks supper, and Kelly—looking bedraggled, with wisps of hair sticking to her face with sweat—runs back and forth carrying clean linens to bedrooms, rushing to get the beds made.

Everyone retires early after a satisfying meal of fresh venison, rice, canned vegetables, and homemade corn bread. The freezer is fully stocked with meat, and even the fridge too. I give Everett his nightcap early while Travis showers. I've barely seen him all day. At supper, everyone excitedly talked about the buck, the greenhouse, and our Covington Christian Academy mascot. Travis never even glanced in my direction.

When he comes into the room—in pajama pants and bare-chested, a towel around his neck—I'm waiting for him. I've draped a scarf over the one lamp I've left on and lie propped up against the pillows. I'm wearing the one sexy thing I packed—a blue silk baby doll nightie with dainty flowers etched into the neckline.

Travis's eyebrows shoot up the minute he takes me in.

"Oh yeah?" he says, tossing the towel onto the chair and slipping off his pants.

"I wanted to make it up to you. For last night."

"I'm down for that," he says, flinging the covers back and sliding in beside me.

"Let me show you just how much."

CHAPTER THIRTY-FOUR
KELLY

They're still sleeping, Caden with his head against Mikey's shoulder, his golden hair falling over his face. I lie still, watching their faces, the sunlight illuminating the particles in the air. Mikey's eyelids flutter as he dreams, and Caden snuggles in closer to his brother. They're so beautiful, it aches.

I never cuddled with my sister. We never even shared the same bed. I was her enemy the minute I entered the family, which I never understood. She was better than me at everything we did—tennis lessons, piano practice, etiquette school. She was president of nearly every club she joined, her shelves were lined with trophies and medals, and it all came so easily. She never broke a sweat, never got nervous or shaky, and walked into every room like she owned it—just like Mother. Because my sister was so successful and busy, Mother didn't make her do the beauty pageants she made me do.

I couldn't compete with my sister. So instead, I did everything Mother asked of me. Competed in every pageant without complaint—in a bikini and high heels before I'd even sprouted breasts. And before any of Mother's social events, from a simple dinner party to a formal ball, I made index cards of all the important names and their accomplishments so I could entertain and compliment all of Mother's guests. But unless I'd recently won a crown, the topic of conversation at these events were always my sister. Mother, her arm draped over Kimberly, would say, "Guess what my amazing daughter just accomplished."

Mikey snores, throws his arm over Caden. I roll onto my back. Stare at the ceiling, the light-brown pine boards. Stretch my feet, which ache from yesterday's work, and then my arms overhead. I feel refreshed. I did barely drink yesterday, with how much running around I did. Maybe today is the day—no pills, no alcohol. A fresh start. Spend some time with my boys, some actual quality time. Pull out those claws Jenna has in them—one by one.

CHAPTER THIRTY-FIVE

JENNA

Excited for our first day of school, I wake early to shower and set up my supplies. But by the time I exit the bathroom, Kelly's door is open and her room is empty.

Ours is as well.

"Fudgesicles," I mutter under my breath as I hurry down the stairs.

Last night, we rearranged furniture and moved Everett's pack 'n' play to the foyer so we could create a permanent spot for the scrapbooking table, which is now the school table. My totes are stored neatly in the corner.

As I get to the great room, I find Kathryn feeding Everett a bottle of breast milk while Brent and Travis are in the kitchen, packing a cooler with lunch and drinks.

"Wanted a little bonding time with this little one before we go to town," she says, smiling at me. "Good morning."

"Good morning. Where's Jacob?"

I look out toward the deck, and there's Kelly—cuddled up on the wicker love seat with Caden and Mikey, a blanket draped over them.

"He's helping Papa with the greenhouse. First thing he said when he woke up, that he wanted to get some work in before school started!" Kathryn laughs. "It was so precious." Then, following my eyes, she says, "Yes, unusual sight, isn't it?"

"Is she reading them a story?" I ask as I take in the book she's holding.

Lauren strolls over to me, Kaitlyn held against her shoulder as she burps her. "It does appear that way, yes."

Lauren and I stand in the driveway, our babies in our arms, as our husbands and Kathryn pull out of the driveway.

"I absolutely hate this," Lauren says, shaking her head.

"I hate seeing them go, but it does seem like the right thing to do. You really don't think so?"

"Well, of course I know it's the Christian thing to do, to help your neighbor and all that, but I guess I'm an isolationist." She winks at me and turns to head inside.

Following her, I say, "You're the most social person I know, besides Travis."

Lauren laughs at me. "Politics, Jenna. Like an isolationist nation that doesn't get involved in— Oh, never mind. I don't care about my neighbor. I'm sorry if that's selfish. All I care about is my family. Don't get me wrong. I commend those who serve. I just don't want my husband and mother to be the ones doing it."

"I understand. I don't want them going either. I want to help, but I'd be terrified to even drive into town right now."

"I love you, Jenna, but you're scared of your own shadow!"

Engrossed in our first day of school, I forget three of our members are missing. The children are engaged, curious, and respectful toward one another, assuaging my worries about handling such a wide age range. Except for a few eye rolls from Henry—which he tries, but fails, to conceal—and one brief tiff between Jacob and Caden over the green glitter glue marker, the day goes better than I could have dreamed.

Kelly's job for the day is cleaning bathrooms. She doesn't complete her work though. She starts with Kathryn and Nathan's bathroom, demurely asking Amanda where the cleaning supplies are, her hair pulled into a fashionably messy bun. I don't know how she gets it to look that good, that effortless. Even when she emerges nearly two hours later, her cheeks pink and her face glistening, she's gorgeous. After only twenty minutes in the half bath, she skips Lauren's bathroom and heads upstairs to the one we share.

Chris creates his dry rub for the venison steaks first thing after breakfast, filling the great room with an array of scents—onion, garlic, rosemary, thyme, basil. After lunch, he puts them in a marinade, and the scent again fills the room. Then school takes an unexpected break for snack time. And as the sun's descent signals evening approaching, he and Amanda work side by side in the kitchen, whispering to one another and flirting, like they once did, years ago.

Nathan continues building the greenhouse, lumbering in every so often for a glass of iced tea. After recess, he tells the children about the greenhouse, how it works, and what vegetables and herbs we'll be growing inside. Jacob gets his first show-and-tell, pointing out the seven nails Nathan let him hammer into the frame.

Kelly claims a migraine after she finishes our bathroom and retreats to her room. She's faking, but I let it pass. I'm the one who reads the stories to the children. I cuddle the boys. Fingers crossed she stays hidden all night.

CHAPTER THIRTY-SIX
KELLY

As I was scrubbing the yellow-pink sludge of Nathan's piss off the base of his toilet, it occurred to me: this new plan of helping in town takes the gas I could use to get home. Did they consider that in their planning? They'll use up our gas helping strangers at a redneck shelter, and then what? We'll all be stranded here?

After shaking out rugs and washing them, sweeping and mopping, and scouring the shower and giant bathtub, I skip the mirror and smoke a cigarette, only my second for the day. Three left. In my frustration, I chug nearly half my whiskey.

In Kathryn's closet, I find a row of dusty flasks. Consider stealing one. Decide against it.

Skipping both bitches' bathrooms, I clean ours, finishing off the last bit of whiskey. Now I'm out. After sitting against the wall, debating with myself, knees pulled to my chest, I choose a fake headache and sleeping the day away. A walk to my stash is too much effort.

~

Despite wishing that sleep would carry me through the night and into another miserable day, my stomach wakes me with grumbling. Barely any light comes through the window. The bedroom is shrouded in gray. Voices carry up from the great room.

Travis is home.

CHAPTER THIRTY-SEVEN
JENNA

They come home laughing and beaming, and with fresh supplies—water glassed eggs and unpasteurized milk from a nearby farm, flour, two giant packs of toilet paper, and a stack of books for the kids. The fresh ingredients are put to good use for freshly baked biscuits. Kathryn bustles around the kitchen, baking and chatting about their day.

"The hospital is making hard choices, like Brent said, but it's not quite as dire as the boys made it sound."

"That's good," Amanda says as she slides the green bean casserole into the oven.

"One doctor moved himself, his wife, and his children into his office at the hospital, made a makeshift home of it. His youngest child—such a darling girl—has cerebral palsy. Pretty severe, in fact. So moving into the hospital made the most sense for his family."

"Gosh, I can't imagine having a sickly child during this," I say as I take a seat at the high counter, next to Lauren. Everett slaps at a toy on his exersaucer and lets out a shriek when the plastic flower lights up and dances to a little tune.

The boys have taken the men out to the greenhouse to show off the progress, and Chris stands at the grill with a beer in his hand.

"Thank God my children are healthy," I add.

Lauren leans over and nudges me with her elbow. "Sister. You just made the sign of the cross."

"I did?"

"You did."

"Old habits." I shrug, but a flash of heat spreads across my cheeks.

In my periphery, I see Jacob and Mikey come zooming around the side of the house, running all the way down the deck and back again, chasing each other. Just as Travis, Brent, and Nathan come through the double doors, Travis talking loudly, "Gonna have a whole dang produce department out there," Kelly descends the stairs.

Of course. Perfect timing, our lovely little house maid.

"The farm down the way that gave us the milk and eggs said they'd give us a few chicks once their hens start laying again," Brent says as he approaches us. "Apparently, hens need a certain amount of daylight to maintain egg production. Who knew? But the farm doesn't have enough generator juice to run the lamps they usually do in the winter to keep the ladies laying." He stands behind Lauren and puts his arms around her, then kisses the top of her head.

"Why are they being so generous?" Lauren asks him, leaning into his embrace.

"The farmer asked the doctors to make a house call for his ailing mother, but they've been too overwhelmed at the hospital and shelter to get to her. Miss Kathryn here paid them a visit and tended to his mama."

Kelly reaches the bottom of the stairs as Brent says this, stalling and looking uncertain. As she takes her first tentative steps toward us, Travis strides across the room, reaching into his pocket.

"Heard you got a headache from all the hard labor these ladies are making you do," he says as he gets to her. Then he holds up a pack of cigarettes. "I believe this is your brand."

Her eyes widen in surprise as she looks up at him. She's maintained the perfect messy-bun look and still sports her workout gear: light-gray leggings paired with a low-cut tank top.

I glance at Amanda, who's standing across from me at the kitchen counter. She mouths, "What the fuck?" Alarm and dismay written across her face, she marches outside and directly to Chris.

My heart is racing. Sweat already beads on my upper lip. I squeeze my hands between my knees, a sorry attempt to stop their shaking. He knows her brand?

Brent, clearly as clueless as my dear husband, says, "Travis went on a solo scavenging trip after dropping us off at the hospital." He turns toward Kelly, who's smiling up at Travis and saying something I can't hear. "You got lucky. He found several cartons of cigarettes."

Lauren swivels, looking up at him, her eyebrows higher than I've ever seen them. "Seriously?" she whispers to him.

"What?" he whispers back, confused.

"Thank you again," Kelly says as she prances toward the doors with a delighted grin plastered on her face.

A few seconds later, Kathryn emerges from her bedroom holding her house slippers, takes one look at us and says, "What's happened now?"

CHAPTER THIRTY-EIGHT
KELLY

The look on Jenna's face just now makes this whole stupid apocalypse worth it. Likewise, the evident anger emoting from Chris and Amanda as I pass them only adds to my glee. Gloating and leaning against the railing, I inhale deeply.

Chris and Amanda scurry into the house, Chris carrying his precious platter of steaks.

They gather in the kitchen. Kathryn points toward the basement stairs; the children march down them in a single-file line. Mikey, the last one in the group, pauses at the top of the stairs, staring at Jenna with a concerned look on his face.

Traitor.

Lauren and Jenna still sit on their stools, while Lauren rubs Jenna's back and whispers something in her ear. Such a crybaby.

Kathryn joins Nathan in the center of the kitchen, near where Chris and Amanda stand, both with their arms crossed. Travis paces from the double doors and back, occasionally jerking his head to look at them and say something. Nathan looks back and forth between his sons, stroking his newly grown beard with a worry wrinkle creasing his brow. Chris suddenly slams the counter with his hand, leaning forward and shouting. Travis turns to face him and throws up his arms, yelling back. Kathryn steps forward and holds up her hands. Her sons freeze.

Jenna is now hunched over, her shoulders bopping up and down.

Brent takes a few steps toward Travis, puts his arm around his brother-in-law's shoulders. The family stands silently and listens to whatever defense he's presenting.

Brave man.

As soon as Brent's mouth closes, Chris starts pacing and shouting again. Travis hollers something at him and storms through the mudroom, slamming the door so violently that I feel the vibration where I stand.

I use the chaos that has ensued—over a fucking pack of cigarettes—to sneak through Kathryn's double-glass doors into her bedroom. Tiptoeing into her closet, I retrieve two of the seven flasks in her collection. All initialed with "JMF, III." Apparently, Kathryn's father or grandfather was a drinker. Is that why she married soft-spoken, teetotaling Nathan?

After filling them at my stash, I amble back to the house, using the light from my cellphone flashlight, taking long slugs. Enjoying my fresh pack of cigarettes. Turns out the side pockets on leggings fit a flask perfectly.

And what to make of the night's tension? If Travis bringing me cigarettes was an innocent act of Christian generosity, then why the insane family drama? Don't they know he'd know my brand because he's a former smoker? Because he smoked my brand himself. Maybe darling Kathryn and Nathan never knew he smoked. I could see that. What would they say if they saw the fancy silver Zippo he also slipped me?

His blue eyes were so intense when he looked at me, his fingers brushing mine as we made the exchange. Heat sprang up on the back of my neck; I knew everyone was watching us. And then I thought of Patrick. And for a moment, I felt crushed with guilt. Until I remembered. So, I smiled up at Travis with all the charm and seduction my mama taught me and walked away while he was still interested.

I truly didn't expect the explosions that happened after.

One thing is certain. The Super Baptists are fraying at the edges. I wonder how strong their carefully crafted family really is.

I thought mine was airtight.

CHAPTER THIRTY-NINE
JENNA

The bedroom is dark when I wake, groggy and disoriented. The night-light casts a yellow circle on the floor, though I don't remember turning it on. What do I remember?

He brought her cigarettes. He knew her brand.

Chris screamed at him. Oh, how he screamed. How Travis hollered back, so defensive. Why so defensive?

My mouth feels dry. I reach for my cup, find that my hand is shaking, my arm is weak.

As I lie back against the pillow, my eyes land on Everett and his tiny chest, rising and falling in the shadows.

Surely he didn't go out of his way for her. He just happened upon them. He was out searching for supplies. That was his job. Why didn't I defend my husband?

A Bible verse comes to me as I close my eyes and drift back to sleep.

Who can find a virtuous wife?

For her worth is far above rubies.
The heart of her husband safely trusts her;
So he will have no lack of gain.
She does him good and not evil
All the days of her life.

When I wake up again, my mother-in-law sits on the edge of the bed.

"I had to, dear. You were beside yourself," she says.

Confused, I try to sit up, but I'm still weak.

"I gave you the lowest dose I had. I didn't know it would knock you out so bad." She sighs, puts her hand over mine. "Everyone responds to medication differently."

"Travis?"

"Not to worry, dear. He'll only be gone a couple of days, I'm sure."

Gone, gone because of you.

"Where is he?"

"Just a little solo hunting trip. He needs some time away from Chris. They've always had a volatile relationship. You know that."

Everett shrieks, then giggles and grabs the crib rail with his chubby hands, pulling himself up.

Kathryn stands. "Good morning, sweet boy," she says as she picks him up. Turning to me, she says, "I'll feed him a bottle from your supply in the fridge. You need to pump and dump. Get that benzodiazepine fully out of your system."

At the door, she stops and says, "Take your time. Your legs might still be wobbly."

She's right. They shake when I stand and hobble to the closet.

With Travis gone, I go for comfort—my worn-out sweatpants from college.

Sitting down in the window seat, I look out at the treetops while detangling my curls. Travis does need a certain amount of time to himself. He loves being around people, but it drains him. Sometimes, after weeks of working on a client's account—endless dinners and meetings and "schmoozing," as he likes to call it—he goes cold. Needs time to recharge. Those are times I'm supposed to give him space. And even though my mama appears more during those times, like a shadow waiting behind the pantry door when I'm getting out the boys' oatmeal, I know it's because she thinks she's won. She thinks he's really gone this time.

And every time he comes back, I want to wink at a shadow, because I know she's in one of them.

Kathryn insists on returning to town, which reignites Chris's wrath. I whisper to Ava, asking her to take the children downstairs for a game. Henry stalls, lingering at the top of the stairs, watching his father.

"You shouldn't go without Travis to protect you." Chris stands arms akimbo, glaring down at her.

"I do not need a bodyguard."

"I'm still going," Brent says quietly, sipping his coffee.

Chris waves his arm at him in dismissal. "We need you here, Mom. And who knows where the hell Travis is or when he'll come home, the hothead."

"I'm not listening to any more of this," she says. "I gave my word at the hospital, and I'm keeping it."

She grabs her lunch box and thermos, nods at Brent, and heads to the mudroom. Brent throws back the last of his coffee, then gives Kaitlyn a kiss on her nose. Lauren rolls her eyes at him, still annoyed. He kisses the top of her head and follows Kathryn out the door.

CHAPTER FORTY
KELLY

I wake, and the boys are gone—doing school with precious Miss Jenna, no doubt. Let her be Miss Schoolteacher. I'll be Travis's vixen.

I smirk. Slowly sit up, reach for my pills.

My chore list sits on the bedside table, the stark white paper glaring in the sunlight. Today is kitchen, and trash bins. I sigh. At least two flasks are full.

I hope Travis doesn't stay in the woods too long. At some point—I guess while he was packing his things for his hunting trip—he slipped two cartons into my room. They were waiting for me, sitting on the floor. Another present.

As I'm slipping my shirt on, someone knocks on the door. It's Amanda, holding a tray of food.

Without a smile, she thrusts the tray in my direction. "We've decided that cleaning the kitchen in the middle of the school day will be distracting to the children."

With the tray in my hands, I nod dumbly.

"And we don't need you going to look for Travis in the woods either. No walks today."

I nod again, feel the heat rising in my cheeks. She takes a step forward, and I step back.

"Good. Then we're understood," she says as she pulls my door closed, leaving behind the faintest whiff of bitter apples.

CHAPTER FORTY-ONE
JENNA

The minute Kathryn walks through the door, I know something is wrong. Amanda sees it too and sends the children to the basement. As Lauren emerges from her bedroom, where she was putting Kaitlyn down for a nap, Kathryn closes her eyes and mouths something to herself, her chin quivering.

"Where's Brent?" Lauren asks, looking from me to her mother.

Kathryn hurries to her, shaking her head. "Oh, my daughter, I'm so sorry."

"Where's Brent?" She's demanding now, her voice shaking.

"There was an accident."

"An accident? You left him at the hospital?"

"Lauren." She takes her hands. "Baby, he didn't make it."

"What do you mean he didn't make it?"

"Let's sit down, sweetheart." Kathryn tries to pull her toward the couch.

"I don't want to sit down."

"Oh, sweetheart, he was shot. He's ... He's dead."

Then came screaming like I've never heard. I'll never unhear it.

As Lauren collapses to the floor, we rush to her, throwing our arms around her, around Kathryn. It can't be so. My knees shake as I try to hold on. This can't be. Brent is about to walk through that door, with that smile of his that lights up his whole face. He's going to go straight to Lauren and put his arms around her, as he always does. This can't be. My vision is mottled as the tears stream down my face.

Lauren's wailing sends waves through her body and into mine, her shudders wracking my bones. This can't be. It just can't.

The screaming wakes Kaitlyn. She's expecting her daddy. She takes her bottle from me but soon grows fussy, then wails. Her face is red and pinched, and she waves her tiny fists around in anger, punching at the air. I try singing, but my voice comes out cracked and harsh, which only makes her cry harder.

Lauren paces, demanding answers.

When Kathryn tries to speak, Lauren talks over her, then holds her hands over her ears, screaming again. "No!"

Amanda comes to the top of the stairs. "The children are scared." She turns and hurries back to the basement.

"Lauren, sweetheart, you have to calm down." Kathryn reaches for Lauren, but she whirls around, arm raised. Kathryn backs up; Lauren punches the wall.

"Fuck!" she screams, holding her hand.

Nathan comes rushing in from outside.

Kathryn, her face wet with tears, says, “My medicine bag. Now.”

Nathan brings it to her.

“Restrain her,” she says.

Nathan, confused, shakes his head.

“Please, Nathan.”

Lauren continues her back-and-forth—crying, then talking to herself, then cussing at the ceiling—still clutching her hand.

Nathan approaches her slowly, holding out his arms. She rushes into them.

Kathryn gives her a Xanax, brushing the hair from her daughter’s face as she rests it on her father’s chest.

Kathryn and Nathan hold their daughter between them and take her to her room.

I’m left with Kaitlyn, still whimpering in my arms.

I pace and bounce, wondering where the hell Travis is.

Why Brent? The most generous of us. What do we do now?

CHAPTER FORTY-TWO
KELLY

They've made me a fucking prisoner. Thank God I have two full flasks. When I grow bored with the games on my phone, I paint my fingernails, then my toes. As the whiskey settles into my blood, I announce, "Fuck it," to my empty room, open the window, and light a cigarette with my shiny new Zippo. Practice blowing smoke rings through the screen. Watch a pair of squirrels chasing each other. Think of Travis.

By three, I'm pacing and chugging. At four, I empty my pill bottles, count them, swallow a Percocet, then hide them under my mattress. So few left. Can't risk Jenna or Amanda finding them.

I'm flipping through an old magazine I found at the bottom of my bag when someone screams. And keeps screaming.

I creep to the door and crack it—the full force of the sound rushes in.

Someone is dead.

Tiptoeing to the railing, I spot them. Lauren hunched

over and wailing, with Kathryn, Amanda, and Jenna creating a circle of arms around her.

CHAPTER FORTY-THREE

JENNA

Kathryn was with Brent when it happened. He was helping her in the emergency room when a man, distraught, came charging through the waiting room and into the main corridor, shouting and waving a gun. Brent calmed the man down and eventually learned that the man's child was gravely injured and that he'd run out of gas trying to get to the hospital. He'd run the rest of the way, leaving his wife and child on the side of the road.

Brent, in the process of gaining the man's trust and talking him down, asked for the gun. The father, sobbing, was about to hand it over when a young soldier rounded the corner, panicked, and began firing. Brent got caught in the crossfire. The man died; the soldier survived. Brent passed in Kathryn's arms before they could even get him up on a gurney. He died begging Kathryn to take care of his girls.

~

The boys don't ask questions when we call them up for supper. I wonder how long that will last. Maybe they think Uncle Brent joined Travis on his hunt.

Amanda told her children, taking them into her bedroom, one by one. Drew keeps his head down as he takes his seat at the table. Ava's shoulders curl forward, and she keeps wiping her nose on the sleeve of her shirt. Henry doesn't come to supper at all.

Kathryn prays, and we eat in silence. Four empty chairs glare at me. Lauren remains in bed, Kelly remains a prisoner, Travis has abandoned us, and Brent—

As night approaches and the darkness deepens, we meet on the deck for a family discussion. Stand huddled in a circle—shoulders slumped, arms crossed, heads bent.

Brent's body is still at the hospital. The local funeral home doesn't have the energy or resources for cremations or cosmetics, but they are offering simple services, a burial, a prayer.

"I don't want him in a strange cemetery, no family or friends near him," Kathryn says, swiping at a tear.

"We can bury him on our land, Katie," Nathan says, putting his arm around her.

"Maybe the chaplain at the hospital will come back with us if we offer him a homecooked meal. Fresh-made biscuits. Maybe even some supplies. A bottle of wine ..." Kathryn trails off.

"We should plant a tree by his grave. And a small garden. He loved to ..." I can't finish. I cover my face with my hands. I wish Travis were here.

"I'll carve him a cross with his name," Nathan says.

"I'm going to town—by myself—to collect his body," Chris says, holding up one hand. "No arguments. We're done with town. Done."

Kathryn looks up at him. “There’ll be a lot of folks in need at the hospital—”

“Mom!” Chris bends forward, looks her in the eye. “They aren’t family.”

“I agree, son,” Nathan says, looking at Kathryn. “We tried to help. We paid a steep price. It’s time to take care of our own.”

CHAPTER FORTY-FOUR

JENNA

I can't sleep. I keep reaching out and feeling the emptiness that's Travis's spot. Keep getting pierced by Lauren's new reality, and my own selfishness.

When I close my eyes, I see Brent's face—the kindness in his eyes, his contagious smile. When the sun fills my room, I roll over to watch Everett.

I want to go home.

I'm surprised to find Kelly awake when I open her door without knocking.

"What the?" she says, sitting on the edge of her bed. She rolls her eyes. "Guess I'll be locking the door from now on." She wears silky blue pajamas that make her eyes sparkle in the morning light.

Caden sits at her feet, playing with toy soldiers. Mikey is still in bed, his back against the wall, holding a book up with his knees. He gives me a tiny grin. His hair is messy and extra curly today, with adorable little ringlets framing his eyes.

"I'm sorry," I said. "I thought you'd be asleep."

She doesn't look at me.

"Keeping the door locked all the time isn't safe, though."

Now she looks at me. Stares me down but doesn't speak.

"Time for school?" Caden asks, hopping to his feet and toddling toward me, his parrot tucked under his arm.

"No school today, bud. It's Saturday."

"Saturday? Really?" Mikey says as he lays down his book and scoots off the bed. "I wanted to do school." He glances at Kelly, then ducks his head, takes a few sideways steps to the left.

"Well, we aren't having school, but we are going for a hike. We're searching for pine cones and cool rocks and stones. You boys ready to get dressed?" I hold my hand out to Caden.

"I'll dress them today." She stands and opens a drawer, her back to me.

Mikey looks at me, waiting.

"We figured it would be easier for you to clean the kitchen if we all cleared out of the house for a while."

Kelly turns and sneers. "Of course y'all did." Holding a T-shirt toward Mikey, she adds, "Everything okay? I heard a lot of crying yesterday."

I look at Mikey, who's carefully watching me.

"Everything's going to be fine. We do have some adult things to discuss this evening though." I smile and wink at Mikey. "We've left the cleaning supplies on the counter. Shouldn't take more than a few hours."

I give her a tight smile and leave.

CHAPTER FORTY-FIVE
KELLY

Mikey watches me, leaning against the bed with his arms crossed, while I sit on the floor, tying Caden's shoes.

"You don't have to go on the hike with Miss Jenna. You could stay with me today."

Caden takes his thumb out of his mouth.

"We want to go," Mikey says.

"Come with, Mommy," Caden says and smiles.

"I have to clean the kitchen, unfortunately."

"Why?" Caden asks, holding up his parrot and tilting its head to the side, and then his own, mimicking.

I know what I should say: because we're their guests, and we're repaying their generosity.

"Miss Jenna doesn't like me."

Caden's head tilts another inch as his eyebrows scrunch. "But why?"

"Miss Jenna likes everyone," Mikey says quietly, looking down.

A brief knock, and in barges Amanda.

"You boys ready?" she asks.

Caden puts his thumb back in his mouth, pulls his parrot under the crook of his arm, and watches my face. Mikey kicks at the rug with the toe of his shoe.

I want to keep them home. I want to ruin Miss Jenna's little picnic. I also want them to love me.

"You boys go and have fun. I'm going to have fun too. I'm going to listen to music, dance, and sing while I mop the floor, just like Snow White. Maybe I'll get a visit from a talking squirrel!"

I pull Caden close, burying my face in his hair, then pull back to look at his beautiful face. "Bird wants to go flying in the woods today. He told me."

"He did?"

"He did. So you better let him fly, and bring me back a flower for my hair."

He rushes back into my arms.

CHAPTER FORTY-SIX
JENNA

We're cleaning up after a tense breakfast—thankfully, Kelly had the sense to stay in her room—when Chris comes in from the garage and announces, "I'm packed and ready. I'm leaving now."

He goes to Ava first, and as she rests her head on his chest, she wipes away a tear. "Please be careful, Daddy."

He takes her face into his hands, kisses her forehead, and then each cheek. "Always."

He hugs her one more time before turning to Drew.

"Do you have to go?" Drew's voice cracks and skips an octave, betraying him. He looks down, his face turning red, and shoves his fists into his pockets. Chris grabs him in a bear hug, holding him with so much might and love that we feel we should look away, but can't.

"You know I have to." His voice gruff, he looks down at his son, gently pulls Drew's face up so he can look him in the eye. "A man takes care of his family."

"Then let me go with you," Henry says, standing. "Let me help."

"Absolutely not." Amanda's voice rings out across the

great room. “No.”

“Mom, Dad needs me.”

“You’re not a man, yet,” she answers.

“I appreciate it, son, I really do. But it’s too dangerous,” Chris says, putting his hand on Henry’s shoulder while Drew still holds onto his dad with both arms.

“Mommy?” Jacob says, tugging on my sweater. “What’s wrong? Where’s Daddy? And Uncle Brent?”

I kneel down to look into his eyes.

“Oh, bud, everything’s going to be okay. Uncle Chris just has to go into town, but he’ll be very safe, and he’ll be back really soon.”

He juts out his chin and squints, considering this. I glance over at Chris, who’s now huddled with his sons, their discussion hushed and yet filling the room.

“And Daddy?” Jacob asks.

“This is bullshit!” Henry yells, breaking from their circle with tears streaming down his face. Halfway across the room, he stops and raises his fists, looks up at the ceiling and screams, “Bullshit!”

As he thunders down the stairs, Amanda takes a few steps forward, but Chris says, “Let him be.”

The kids are streaming out the doors, Beauty bounding alongside them, Amanda leading the way. As I turn to pull the door closed, Nathan and Lauren come out of her room. She leans heavily on his arm. My capable sister, my amazon warrior, shuffles in slippers with vacant eyes and disheveled hair.

She curls up in Brent’s spot like a cat, soaking up the last of his warmth.

CHAPTER FORTY-SEVEN
KELLY

I watch through the window as Jenna and Amanda lead the children around the side of the house and into the woods. I've been left with a broom and a mop, a bucket of cleaning supplies, and a snoring widow curled up on the couch.

Kathryn and Nathan have retreated to their bedroom with their miserable, squealing grandbaby.

After washing the dishes, I walk to the glass doors and look over the lake.

Fuck it.

I slip into the garage, begin searching for the two bottles of vodka Jenna and I put in my cooler when we were packing. I'm jolted back to that memory—looking into her soft brown eyes while I sniveled and begged for help. I wish I'd never followed her here.

Before finding my vodka tucked under the workbench, I discover Jenna's stash of luxury food items and half a joint wrapped in an aging *Playboy* magazine.

With ice clinking in cheap orange juice, I pop in my earbuds and get to work.

I've scoured the stove and both sinks. Cleaned the counters and even the backsplash. Got every crumb. Scrubbed the specks of food dried like concrete inside the microwave.

Make another vodka, finish off the orange juice.

Lauren stirs and sits up, looks around, disoriented. Pats at her hair like she doesn't know where she is, or who she is.

I hold my breath.

Her eyes are unfocused. She grabs a throw pillow and holds it to her mouth. Rocking, she groans, her voice growing deeper, her rocking more violent.

"Shh." I go to her, sit beside her. "Shh." I stroke her hair. "I know, I know."

A door cracks open. Nathan comes around the corner.

I look up at his kind, lined face and the tears welling in the corners of his eyes.

"Thank you," he whispers as he bends and lifts his daughter by the arm, soothing her with something whispered in her ear.

As Nathan gets Lauren settled back into bed, Kathryn reemerges and straps Kaitlyn into a stroller.

"We're taking the baby for a walk. Just a short one," Kathryn says, straightening and grabbing a straw hat off a hook near the mudroom door. "Remember that Henry stayed back, so don't be alarmed if you hear noises from the basement."

I nod, start sweeping. After they leave, I make a third drink—this one with fruit punch. Then I turn up my music and start mopping. I'm halfway through the dining area—mop in one hand and drink in the other, swaying my hips to the music—when I bump into someone. Startled, I whirl around and find myself face to face with Travis.

He mouths, “Sorry,” and I pop out my earbuds.

“No worries.”

He smirks. “Nice dance moves.”

“You like those?” I swivel my hips, peering up at him. He smells of pine trees and sweat.

He reaches out one hand, places it gently on my waist. “Yeah, I like the way you move.”

I smile back at him.

“Uncle Travis! What the hell?”

We startle. Travis’s hand falls back to his side.

Henry stands at the top of the stairs, his hands balled into fists and his face bright red. “Uncle Brent is dead.”

He turns and storms back down the stairs.

CHAPTER FORTY-EIGHT
JENNA

We plan on telling the little ones the news after we gather our flowers and finery and have our picnic lunch. We've brought a blanket to spread in the clearing near Travis's deer stand. Drew is in the lead, followed by Ava, her long hair plaited in a French braid. I bring up the rear, my boys in front of me, Mikey holding Caden's hand, while Jacob chatters, looking back at them every so often to make sure they're listening.

Uncle Brent isn't coming home. My heart is racing. How do I do this? *He's never coming home.* Or maybe I should lead with, *Uncle Brent is with Jesus.* But then that initial information—that terrible knowledge—in a sentence so tied with the Lord's son and our savior. Will they be angry with Him? Immediately? *Only you got mad at God when He took from you. Only you, poisonous thing.*

I stumble over a root, catch myself before my ankle turns.

"I see it!" Drew announces, pointing up at a tree. He stops, holds a branch of brambles aside for his sister. She passes him, slipping her backpack off one shoulder.

I feel like I can't breathe. Everett gurgles behind me, in his BabyBjörn.

"Can I climb Daddy's stand?" Jacob asks, running toward it. Caden rushes after Jacob.

"Absolutely not," Amanda answers for me.

Mikey looks up at me, and I reach for his hand. He smiles.

"I love you, sweet boy."

His smile widens, but then he looks down. Tilting his head, he gives me a sidelong glance.

"You say that a lot, Miss Jenna." He looks back down, kicks at a leaf with his red shoe.

"Because I feel it a lot."

He lets go of my hand and grabs my legs, both arms thrown around me, burying his face in my thigh and sighing.

We've gathered a large bouquet and filled a basket with forest treasures: pine cones, rocks, chestnuts, and a handful of feathers. The children finish lunch—a hodgepodge trail mix of chopped granola bars (our last), dry cereal, raisins, and nuts—in record time. They've each been given one cookie. Drew shoved the whole thing in his mouth and closed his eyes to savor it, while Ava still works on hers, taking tiny nibbles.

"Is this the last cookie?" she asks, holding her final morsel.

"No. We have the ingredients to make one more batch," Amanda says, pulling her hood over her head. A brisk wind has started, coming up from the lake. She looks at me, speaking to me without words.

It's time.

My heartbeat starts thumping in my ears again. I take a breath, hold Everett a little closer.

Ava grumbles. "At least I'll be skinny when the world goes back to normal."

"You're already skinny," Drew says, rolling his eyes. "What if it never goes back to normal?" he asks, looking at his mother.

"Then, Jesus, kill me now." Ava crosses her arms.

"Not funny, Ava," Amanda and Drew say in unison.

Recognition flickers on Ava's face, and her eyes fill with tears. "I didn't mean ... I didn't think ..." Her voice trails off.

"Mommy?" Jacob says. "What's going on?"

Here it is. No escaping it.

I take another deep breath, look from his sweet face to Mikey's. Caden is snuggled up on the blanket with his cheek on Mikey's knee and his thumb in his mouth. I reach my hand out to Jacob. He takes it, his bright-blue eyes searching my face.

"There was an accident," I start.

"Daddy?" He lets go of my hand and stands, ready to run and find him.

"No, baby, Daddy's fine." I bite my cheek, but the tears are here. There' no stopping them.

"Baby, Uncle Brent is with Jesus." I try to reach for his hand again, but he pulls away.

"What? Where?"

"In Heaven, baby. Uncle Brent is in Heaven with Jesus."

"He's dead?" Jacob asks, his voice breaking and tears slipping down his cheeks.

"Yes," Drew says, sobbing. He reaches his arm out to Jacob. "I hate it."

Jacob erupts, groaning in anguish, and goes to his

cousin, curling up in his lap.

"What's that?" Caden asks, sitting up.

Mikey, staring stonily ahead, says, "Remember our hamster, Oreo? Remember what happened to him?"

Caden looks from Mikey to me, then back to Mikey. "Oh no." He crawls to me, snuggles in next to Everett, burying his face in my chest.

Drew scoots sideways, awkwardly putting one arm around Mikey's shoulders while still holding Jacob with his other.

"It sucks. It really sucks," Drew says, trying to catch his breath.

Ava puts her head on her mother's shoulder. "I didn't mean it, Mama."

"I know," Amanda says, stroking Ava's hair.

The wind picks up again, rustling the few lonely leaves still holding on. Caden slurps his thumb under my chin, while Jacob's sobs begin to quiet. My face is wet with tears.

Jacob turns to me. "How?" He hiccups. "Why?" He looks at Drew, then up to the sky. His beautiful eyes find mine once more, "Why, Mommy?"

I feel my face betraying me. "I don't know why."

I want to scream. I want to dig my hands into the earth and wail. Send my despair up to Heaven. Let Brent hear how much he's loved.

"We should pray," Amanda says, opening her Bible.

Jacob continues crying, wiping his nose with the sleeve of his shirt before burying his face in his cousin's chest once more.

"We must remember what Jesus said," Amanda starts, then waits until she has everyone's attention. "For God so loved the world that He gave His only Son, so that everyone who believes in Him may not perish but have eternal life."

CHAPTER FORTY-NINE
JENNA

When we get home, Travis is on the wicker couch with Lauren, her head resting on his shoulder. Like Kathryn, she's always loved him most.

I try to set Caden down, but he resists, his thighs clamping around my waist. Everett is still latched onto my back.

Jacob runs ahead of us, shouting, "Daddy!"

Dinner is tense. I haven't had a moment alone with Travis. When he came in, he pecked my lips like I was his mother. Avoided my eyes. Got pulled away by Chris to discuss something, while my hands were busy shaping another batch of venison meatballs, these seasoned with cumin, coriander, and ginger, for something different. No saffron in Kathryn's spice cupboard.

Everyone is so quiet it's unnerving. Lauren doesn't come to dinner. Nathan is barely eating. Even the children are quiet, and Henry keeps glaring at Travis like it's his fault somehow. Kelly has a vodka on ice with something pinkish red in it—not hiding it anymore in her metal Arctic cup.

The children's juice. She's drinking their fruit punch with her vodka.

Goddamn you.

I startle when Everett slams his palm down on his tray, declaring, "Mama!"

He signs that he's hungry. His tray is empty. I give him the last of my French fries.

I read a story to the children by the fire. No radio tonight. The world has already invaded our home too much for us to bear.

Kelly sits in a wingback chair, drinking and not listening to the story. She looks out toward the mountains, but her eyes are unfocused. The other adults retreated to the porch to discuss funeral plans. Ava and Henry finish dishes and join us in the family room, sitting across from Kelly. Caden yawns and lies down, resting his cheek on his brother's knee.

I keep reading. "Paul asked his father, 'How do you know?'"

I pause and look up as I turn the page. Henry leans forward, his elbows on his knees, staring at Kelly. When I turn to look at her, she wakes from her trance. Looks at me first, then Henry. She shakes the ice in her glass and takes a swig, holding his gaze.

"Aunt Jenna," Henry says, turning to me.

"I'm off to bed," Kelly says, standing. "Do you mind

bringing the boys up when the story is over? I'm suddenly so tired."

I nod, glancing at her and back to Henry. He sits back in his chair, crossing his arms.

"Mommy," Jacob says. "The story?"

My body feels assaulted by pins and needles by the time Travis and I are alone. He comes in as I'm changing and sits on the edge of the bed, stares at the wall.

"I should've been there." He slumps forward, resting his forehead in his hands.

I go to him, and he wraps his arms around me, buries his face in my breasts. Lets out an anguished cry as his arms tighten across my back.

"Shh," I coo, running my hand through his hair.

I watch Everett's chest rising and falling through the slats of his crib. His white noise machine hums in the corner.

You should have been there, but you wouldn't have been, either way. You'd be out scavenging, finding her cigarettes. Picking up a shiny Zippo for her, which she now props on her nightstand like a trophy.

"I should have protected them," he says, his voice thick, muddled.

"You wouldn't have been there to save him. You would have been out looking for supplies ..."

I picture my fortress walls. Feel the weight of stone, thicker than the width of my body, the metal-gray gleam, smooth and cool beneath my hand.

"Like your last trip to town," I finish, pulling back and looking down at him.

"My last trip to town?"

"When you were out looking for presents for our houseguest."

He shakes his head, dumbfounded. Throws up his hands. "What?" he asks.

"You wouldn't have been there. Either way."

He stands, and I stumble backward.

"Seriously?" He lunges forward, his face so close I can feel his breath. I back against the wall, feel the smooth grain against my shaking palms.

"Brent is dead, and you're worried about cigarettes?"

He's seething. Turning, he swings open the door and walks out.

Leaves me standing in the doorway, in a T-shirt and underwear.

CHAPTER FIFTY

JENNA

I wake expecting an empty bed, but Travis snores beside me.

"Ma ma," Everett says.

I can't bring myself to look at him. Not yet. I stare at the wall. Feel the warm tears sliding down, hear them landing on my pillow.

Today is the day we bury Brent. The men will dig a hole, and we'll lower his body into the ground. We'll face him toward the lake and the view.

The chaplain refused to come. It's just us and our houseguest.

"Ma ma ma ma ma."

Travis stirs.

I don't want him to watch me breastfeed.

Sitting up quietly and slipping from bed, I grab Everett, whisper in his ear, "Good morning, bubby." Stroke his fine hair with my thumb. A wind gust howls through the trees, startling us both.

"Shh."

I kneel on the window seat and point.

"Wind. Just wind."

The trees bend against the gray-white sky.

We bury Brent today.

Travis moans, and I look back as he rolls over, reaches his hand toward my pillow, and sighs. He's so beautiful, it aches.

"I need to see him!" Lauren cries, pacing in the kitchen.

The hole is being dug. The coffin rests in the garage, waiting.

The children are downstairs, making picture collages of Uncle Brent.

"The funeral home sealed the wood ..." Nathan says, scratching his head and looking at Kathryn.

Lauren stops, facing the mountains, which are barely visible through the fog.

Kathryn walks toward her with hands extended, like she can touch her before she gets there. "But he hasn't been embalmed, Lauren. He's not in good shape."

She whirls and screams, "I don't care!" Then covers her face. "I'm sorry, Mama, I'm sorry."

Kathryn rushes to her, encircles her. Nathan is close behind, holding them both.

I stand rooted, unsure what to do.

"Daddy, please," Lauren cries.

Nathan turns to go unseal the pine coffin. Lauren strides to the garage like the woman I know. Moments later, she returns with her parents propping her up.

Chris heads outside, carrying a chair to the burial site.

The garage door is open as we assemble. The wind is

brisk, unrelenting. We make way for the pallbearers, including Ava, who insisted.

We follow in silence. Amanda holds Kaitlyn while Kathryn holds Lauren. Jacob holds my hand, tightly.

I try to focus as Kathryn leads us in prayer, but her words slip by my ear unheard. I watch dark birds gathering in the distance. Feel Jacob's hand grasping my thigh, his bony shoulder bopping up and down as he cries. Everett is in the cabin napping. His monitor buzzes against my hand, tucked in my jacket pocket.

The houseguest stands across from me. She holds Caden, and I realize it's only the second time I've seen her hold one of her sons. Mikey stands several feet away from her, his eyes trained on the hole before him. Travis is next to me, but not. I can't feel his presence. The walls are too thick.

Kathryn starts singing, "Just a Closer Walk with Thee," in her strong soprano voice.

CHAPTER FIFTY-ONE

KELLY

There's nothing worse than a family that grieves without alcohol. They barely speak. They pray and sing, but those are someone else's words. They aren't saying any of their own.

Lunch is so quiet I can hear a woodpecker outside, knock, knock, knocking.

Lauren stares beyond us, her hands tucked in her lap. She picks up her fork, moves her food around, puts it down again.

How is this honoring Brent? Where are the stories?

He'd come alive again, even if for a moment, in a memory, a retelling. Then Lauren would hear how much he was loved. Then she'd see him through their eyes. She'd get to be near him, for a little while.

Instead, she excuses herself and goes back to bed.

The boys keep following Jenna around like puppies. When she picks Mikey up like he's a toddler, letting him wrap his legs around her waist, I go to my room for my jacket and pilfered book bag.

Time for a hike.

I don't ask if she minds this time. I blow the boys a kiss and slip out the door.

I head back to the cabin I raided a few days ago. A lifetime ago.

There are still no signs of people. Letting myself in the front door, which I left unlocked, I go straight for the liquor cabinet. Choose a beautiful whiskey glass from the many. Pull my Arctic cup from my bag—prepacked with ice—and relish the clink against glass as I drop a cube in.

An empty house—quiet, and without death.

Wandering into the master bedroom, I take a long swig before placing my drink on the mantel. Then I spread my arms and plop on the king bed, plush with a pile of throw pillows.

We should come here. Ditch the Super Baptists.

A large TV hangs above the fireplace. For a moment, I imagine lounging in this bed, watching TV for days, curled up in the crook of Patrick's arm. He'd twirl the end of my hair around his finger without realizing it, without knowing how safe it'd make me feel.

I push up from the bed, grab my drink. Linger by the glass doors, sipping, sipping. Sipping. Meander to the closet. Pull out my flashlight instead of turning on the light, safer that way. Finger through a handful of blouses and tops. Jenna's size, not mine. A bright blue shines in the corner. I find a basket of scarves with a gorgeous silk shawl that I wrap around my shoulders.

After a refill, I head upstairs. Stop at the landing to assess the sunlight. There's still a few hours left. The upstairs bedrooms are plain and spare—guest rooms. Bed, nightstand, extra bedding. But the boys could have their own rooms, and I could have my own space.

I could wake in the morning and call up to them, "Good morning, boys!" They'd come rushing down the stairs to see me. Me. No syrup-laden preschool teachers here.

I find a four-pack of toilet paper in the upstairs bathroom and stuff it in my backpack. The Covingtons' supply will run out soon enough. I'll have my own secret stash.

Time for a smoke. I head out to the identical deck and lean against the railing. I wonder what they're doing down the hill. Then I decide to not care.

After rummaging through the garage, I find the outdoor cushions and set up the rattan couch. I make my third drink. Then I drag the comforter off the master bed and settle in.

I regret coming back to the Covington cabin. Everyone is congregating for supper with morose faces. Jenna runs around directing children—my boys—handing out plates, silverware, and linen napkins. No more paper ones.

They don't even notice me come in. Travis stands by the fire with his arm raised and resting on the mantel, nursing a beer. His gaze focuses on the flames; he doesn't see me either.

I approach the table, and Caden calls out, "Mommy!" Drops his pile of napkins and rushes to me. Mikey keeps laying down forks.

"Nice hike?" Amanda says, sitting down. "Must be nice

not having to worry about cooking and food rations." She spreads her napkin across her lap and turns to Jenna, who's carrying in a platter. "Must be nice, right?"

Jenna just nods, sets down the canned vegetables, and walks back to the kitchen.

I wish I'd filled my Arctic cup with a fresh drink for this meal. And taken a Percocet.

I see my grandmother, standing by the kitchen island, hand on her slender waist, large emerald ring glinting, shaking her head at me. *You should save some whiskey for him, darling, after this day.*

Kathryn approaches the table carrying her Bible. Fuck. She smooths her hair with her hand before sitting, then looks around expectantly as everyone gets to their seats.

She cracks it open and clears her throat. "God said, let light shine out of darkness. He gave us that light, made His light shine in our hearts so that we may see the glory that is God. We also carry the death of Jesus within our bodies, so that the life of Jesus may also be revealed in us."

She pauses, takes a drink of water. Looks toward the children's table, making sure they're listening.

"I want us all to remember Brent but not lose heart, for our momentary troubles are achieving for us an eternal glory that far outweighs them all. We must fix our eyes not on what is seen, but what is unseen. Since what is seen is temporary, and what is unseen is eternal. And remember too, what Corinthians teaches us about death—our earthly bodies are planted in the ground when we die, but they will be raised to live forever. Our bodies are buried in brokenness, but they will be raised in glory. They are buried in weakness, but they will be raised in strength. They are buried as natural human bodies, but they will be raised as spiritual bodies. We must remember and hold on to the fact that Brent is with Jesus now and happy to be with Him."

She closes the book. The fire crackles, and someone's stomach gurgles.

"Henry," Kathryn continues. "Will you please lead us in Our Father?"

"Yes, Nana," Henry says.

The family takes hands. Nathan's large hand is clammy. Amanda refuses my outstretched palm as she bows her head to pray.

CHAPTER FIFTY-TWO
JENNA

Travis is acting like a caged animal, pacing, pulling and pulling at his hair, until I imagine chunks of it falling to the floor.

"Please talk to me," I say. I sit on the bed, cross-legged, holding my sides.

I'm sorry. I'm sorry about the cigarettes. I'll never speak of them again.

He sits on the edge of the window seat. Looks at me. Looks away.

Please. I'm so sorry.

Everett gurgles, and we both startle.

He starts pacing again.

"I need some air," he says.

He grabs my cheek roughly with one hand and kisses the top of my head. I hold my breath until the door clicks shut. Then I let out a moan, pillow jammed against my mouth.

Gone. Gone because of you.

I kneel beside the bed. Slip my rosary beads through my fingers, one by one, smooth and hard.

"Hail Mary, full of grace," I whisper. My throat catches. I take a deep breath. "The Lord is with thee ..."

The hardwood hurts, and I count that as my penance.

My rosary complete, I wobble as I stand with sore, aching knees. I make another sign of the cross, for good measure, and set my rosary back in its blue velvet pouch. Mary's favorite color. Then I tuck Everett's blanket closer around him, whispering another prayer, for his safety, for a long life. Try to picture him as a man with gray hair and wrinkles around his eyes.

After remaking the bed and fluffing the pillows, I find myself pacing and chewing on my nails. Where is he?

Gone, gone because of you.

Please, no. No escape to the woods. Not again. Please.

I get my rosary back out and put it around my neck, tucking it into my flannel pajamas.

I crack the door slowly. Listen. Hearing nothing, I venture to the railing. A small lamp on the narrow table behind the couch casts a small circle of light, no more. And then I notice the flames on the porch. Someone—no, two people—by the fire. I see an arm extend, a lighter spark. See the long hair as she leans forward.

Shaking, I fall to my knees, clutch the balusters. He leans back, lights his own cigarette.

Mother Mary, one two three four five six seven. Mother Mary. Breathe, one two, breathe, three four—

"Miss Jenna?" comes a voice, urgent and crying. "Miss Jenna?"

"Shh, I'm here," I say. "What's wrong, Mikey?" I stand, go to him, where he clings to their doorframe. I scoop him up, and he rests his head on my shoulder, wrapping his arms and legs around me.

He struggles to catch his breath. "Bad dream," he says,

burying his face further into my neck.

I step into their bedroom, close the door. Caden sleeps sideways on the bed, his feet dangling off the edge.

Sitting on Kelly's bed, I rub his back. "Want to tell me about it?"

He shakes his head, crying harder.

I start rocking. "It's okay, baby, let it out."

And he does. While his body shakes with the torrent of his releasing, I sing, "Kumbaya, my Lord," softly in his ear.

His breath slows, but his hands grasp tighter.

"I saw you." He shudders, takes a deep breath. "In the hole, not ... not Uncle Brent."

His sobs begin anew.

"Oh, baby, baby, it's okay. Let it out. Let it out," I say, rocking and rubbing his back. His top sticks to his sweaty back. "I'm here. I'm here. I'm not leaving you. Ever."

I'm not sure how long I've held him, but when his body relaxes against mine, I sing, "You Are My Sunshine," as I carry him to his own bed and tuck him in. Running my hands through his beautiful wavy hair, I kiss his forehead, then each cheek.

"I love you, Miss Jenna." His dark eyes intense, he takes my hand and holds it.

"Have I taught you the secret code?"

He shakes his head, and his hair falls over his left eye.

"Three squeezes means 'I love you.'" I press his hand. "So we can tell each other whenever we want, without anyone knowing." I wink.

He squeezes, and then I do too, but with four this time. "I love you forever," I whisper.

CHAPTER FIFTY-THREE

KELLY

There's no mistaking the need in his eyes when he finds me.

I've been sitting by the fire, enjoying the clear sky, riddled with stars. Hoping for company, but not expecting any.

"Using up all the propane?" he asks, teasing me as he takes a seat.

"The evil houseguest strikes again." I smile, twist my hair around my finger.

He chuckles. I pull out my flask and pass it to him. "Whiskey."

He takes a long pull, hands it back, asking, "More where this came from?"

I nod. Flip my hair. Take a long chug, holding eye contact as I do.

As I pass it back, I graze his fingers with mine.

"Cigarette?" I ask, holding one out.

"What the hell?" he says, taking it. "How's that Zippo working for ya?"

"I love it." I hand it to him.

He turns it in his palm. "She's a pretty one." He leans toward me, rolls the flint wheel. I inhale deeply as he turns and lights his own.

We sit in silence. Smoking, passing the whiskey, looking out into the night.

"What did you do? Before all this?" He waves his hand in the air, like the situation is right in front of us. I suppose it is, with all that darkness stretching before us.

"Real estate."

"Did you like it?"

"Loved it. Damn good at it too."

"I bet you were. Look at you."

I lean forward and put my hand on his wrist, raising one eyebrow.

"Not here," he says, this voice thick.

I nod.

We go around the side of the house.

His big hand clamped around my wrist, he pulls me, making me want him more.

He takes me to the last SUV in the driveway, releases me as he pushes me against the car. He looks me in the eyes for a few seconds, contemplating whether or not to kiss me, then goes for my neck instead. Travels along my collarbone while reaching into my low-cut sweater and finding my nipple, twisting it gently.

I moan.

He puts one hand over my mouth while his mouth finds my nipple, working it between his lips, his teeth. I unbutton my pants and yank them down. He swirls me around, and I bend over, ready for him.

CHAPTER FIFTY-FOUR
JENNA

They aren't on the deck when I pull Mikey's door closed behind me. I stand frozen, my feet cold on the hardwood floor. The propane fire is low, but still burning.

Where are they? Leaning over the railing, I hold my breath and listen.

Nothing.

Tiptoeing down the stairs, I'm halfway across the family room when I hear Everett whimpering.

"Fudge," I mumble as I hurry back upstairs.

By the time I reach our room, he's wailing. I snatch him up. His skin is on fire.

"Shit."

He felt warm earlier this evening, but I assumed it was a low-grade fever from teething. My Tylenol is downstairs.

"Shh, bubby," I murmur as I carry him down. "Shh."

In the kitchen, I take his temperature. It's 103.2 degrees. Bouncing him with one arm, I shove the syringe into the bottle. Where the hell is Travis? And the godforsaken houseguest? Are they taking a nighttime stroll in the pitch black?

It takes three attempts to fill the syringe with one hand. Everett screams in my ear. I bite my lip. I will not cry. I squirt the medicine in his mouth and grab a cloth, wetting it. Drape it over his head as I hurry back to our room.

I wake, disoriented. The shower is running. I've been dozing in bed with Everett, leaning against the headboard. What time is it? Groggy, I look around the room.

Is that Travis showering? Why is he showering? I look at the clock. It reads 12:35 a.m. I rub my eyes with my free hand.

Then it comes back to me—two dark figures leaning toward one another.

My heart seizes.

Not my Travis. Not my Travis. He's washing off the cigarette stink. Why, Travis?

I struggle to control my breath, to still my body, to stop the tears. Everett fidgets, his eyes flutter.

Why is he showering? Why was he with her?

Everett wakes, screaming. Deafening. Stops, then coughs, then spews vomit across me, the pillows, the headboard. It gets in my mouth as I'm still struggling to breathe. Warm, splattering, and never ending, and when he does stop, he resumes his screaming.

We're both covered in a pale-yellow sludge.

Crying along with him, I slowly rise and lay him at the end of the bed, the only dry section. He shrieks, angry, balled fists waving in the air. I strip off my wet top, drop it at my feet. Discover slimy peach chunks in my bra. I gag. The air is sickeningly sweet.

Grabbing baby wipes, I clean my face, my neck, my breasts. I don't want to know what's in my hair. I turn to Everett. My breath has steadied, but my hands haven't. He fights me, kicking and rolling side to side, as I undo his onesie. As I'm pulling the wet, sticky material off him, Travis comes into the room.

"What the—" he starts, until the smell reaches his nose and his hand flies up to cover his mouth.

"He has a high fever." My chin quivers as I speak. Damn you! I want to yell at him, scream like my mother, make him cower and beg.

I wipe Everett, cleaning the crevices in his neck, under his arms. He rolls and thrashes, with his eyes squeezed shut and his mouth wide open, blaring.

"Where were you?" I sound small, pathetic. My tears fall on Everett's face.

He goes to the dresser. Retrieves a clean onesie. He won't meet my eyes as he holds it toward me.

My hand visibly shakes as I take it from him. I search his face. Mama wasn't right, was she?

He looks at my mouth, not my eyes.

"Jenna, he's screaming."

Like I want to be. "Where were you?"

"Jenna, he's screaming!"

I turn back to my baby, slide the soft cotton over him. "Shh, bubby, shh."

Travis hands me a blanket from the crib. Wrapping Everett and gingerly picking him up, I hold him close to my sticky chest as I rub his head. "Shh." Staring at Travis.

Meet my eyes, you bastard. "Where were you?" I ask.

"Jenna, you're a mess. Look at you."

Crying harder now, I can't stop. I won't. "Where were you?"

He snarls, throwing up his hands. "In the garage!" he yells. "Working! Getting my mind off Brent, damn it!"

Everett's shrieking cranks up again, so loud my ears ring.

"Shh, bubby, shh."

"I can't believe you're grilling me when he's sick! Some mother you are!"

He grabs a T-shirt, yanks it over his head, and leaves me.

Despite his screaming, I have no choice but to put Everett in his crib. I strip the bed as quickly as possible, dropping the sheets outside the door. Once the bed is made, I change myself, wiping the now crusty vomit off my shoulders, my breasts. We keep crying, both of us, and my head is pounding.

Once we're settled back in bed, Everett finally quiets and falls asleep, hand curled around my finger. I close my eyes, but sleep won't come.

How many times has he lied to me? How many times have I forgiven him? Always white lies, or lies of omission, or lies to not hurt me. Going to the strip club with the guys instead of playing poker, like he said, the forgotten receipt left balled on his bedside table. Or saying he was working late when he was at the Braves game with a colleague. The wife of said colleague brought it up at the company picnic a week later. And I never said a word. Forgave him outright. These are the compromises we make for marriage, for love, for feeling safe.

Safe. Is that a feeling I really know?

Really?

~

Everett wakes himself and me again with his puking. Frantic, I rush downstairs for fresh linens and more medicine, leaving Everett in the center of the bed, surrounded by pillows.

The third time he wakes and vomits, we make do with a clean blanket and no sheets. Instead of leaning against the headboard, I keep him in the center of the bed, my hand on his belly. I fall asleep with my cheek pressed to his.

~

I'm woken by a gentle rapping at the door. As it opens, I blink. I'm startled to see Amanda looking down at me.

"Rough night?" she whispers.

I nod. My hand still rests on Everett's chest, with its gentle rise and fall.

"Chris abandoned me a few times when barfing was involved." She continues to whisper, her green eyes bright and concerned. "Just a stomach bug? Or do you think Kathryn brought the flu home with her after all?"

~

My sister-in-law is a godsend. She not only gave me a break so I could shower, she already disinfected the kitchen before she visited me, after she found the vomit-covered bedding and washed it. She gave Travis a good scolding, too, while cleaning the kitchen. What would she have said if she knew the whole story? But what is the whole story? A cigarette? Drinking and flirting? Something worse?

I'm so tired. I'm so tired my knees feel like rubber.

Pressing my hand against the tile wall, I rest my cheek against my hand.

He loves me. He loves our sons.

You! Gone because of you! You're poison! He left because of you! Judd, fatherless. Your fault. Yours!

Mommy standing over me with a belt, spitting on me as she whips me. Me, curled tightly in a ball, like a snake, like the poisonous thing that I am. Shielding my head with my arms and praying, "Mother Mary, one two three four five six seven ..." Waiting for her to answer.

I don't know how I ended up here, curled up and naked at the bottom of the tub. The water is cold.

Taking a deep breath, I clear the condensation from the bathroom mirror. Puffy, bloodshot eyes stare back at me.

Poison. Ugly.

In the bedroom, I stand before the closet, debating, tears landing on my bare chest. I envision Kelly, standing elegantly with one hand on her tiny waist. How do I confront the woman trying to steal my husband?

Weeping, I beat at my fat belly until it's red and angry like I am.

CHAPTER FIFTY-FIVE

KELLY

I wake up feeling satisfied.

I fucked someone else, Patrick! I fucked someone else, and I liked it!

Stretching and rolling over, I face an empty bed, again. Sighing, I close my eyes, see Travis last night, how he looked at me. I slide my hand into my panties. Imagine Travis slipping into my room, in nothing but a bath towel drooping low on his hips.

When I step out of my bedroom, I hear the boys giggling downstairs. Peeking over the railing, I spot Travis with Jacob, Mikey, and Caden, building a train track. No one else is in the great room.

Hustling to the bathroom, I find it warm and humid from someone else's shower. Decide to skip taking one. I don't want to wash off his smell anyway. Instead, I wash my face and brush my teeth, spruce up my hair with volumizer and shimmer spray. Put a dash of blush on my cheekbones and a bit of glimmer on my lips.

Seven minutes, and I'm ready.

Wearing leggings and an extra-clingy sweater, I leave my boots in my room and descend in socks, so I can surprise them. Their old lab, Beauty, gives me away as I round the landing.

"Mommy!" Caden shouts. "Come look!"

The track stretches from the fireplace to the red couch and around both wingback chairs.

"Wow, it's so big!" I exclaim.

I smirk at Travis.

"Look at all our bridges!" Caden says, hopping up and down, pointing.

Mikey stays seated near the hearth and the railroad station, holding a toy attendant.

Travis lounges on his side, head propped on his hand. "Good morning," he says, barely glancing at me.

"Morning." Jutting out my hip and resting my hand there, I ask, "Where is everyone?"

"Miss Amanda and Ava took the movie box," Caden says, shaking his head.

"The movie box?"

Travis laughs and sits up. I want to plop down in his lap, feel his arms wrap around me. He reaches out and tousles Caden's hair. "The DVD player. They're having a mother-daughter movie marathon in Amanda's room, and also taking care of Everett. Jenna needs a break."

"Fun," I say as I sit. Not too close. Between him and Mikey. But close enough. I want a cigarette, but I can't squander this moment. "What are we building next?"

CHAPTER FIFTY-SIX
JENNA

The first voice I hear as I exit my bedroom is Jacob's, bossy and irritated.

"The log cabins are on one road. They should all be right here, on railway pass seventy-five. In the mountains. Duh!"

"Fine, fine," Drew says.

"Can we make a neighborhood of red houses?" Caden asks. "Red Lego houses only!"

Standing against the wall outside my door, palms pressed flat, I focus on my breath. I can do this. I can. Those are my boys.

Already hating the too-tight skinny jeans, I head downstairs with my heart in my throat. At the landing, I see her. Sitting near Travis in a half-circle of sunlight, leaning toward him with glistening hair and laughing.

Kathryn comes out of her room as I get to the bottom of the stairs.

"Good morning, Jenna. I hear you had a terrible night."

"Where's Everett?"

"Downstairs with Amanda and Ava. They wanted to

give you some time for yourself. You still look rough, dear. Do you need to go back to a bed for a little while longer?"

No! I want our houseguest gone!

"I'm okay," I mumble, trying not to cry. "How's Lauren?"

Kathryn shakes her head. Squeezes my shoulder. "Keep praying."

"Nana! Nana! Look at our new train track!" Jacob says, coming over and grabbing her hand. "Good morning, Mommy," he says as an afterthought. I wave at Mikey, who waves but then looks at Kelly, who holds Caden in her lap.

Travis follows me into the kitchen. Comes up behind me as I'm pouring my coffee. Putting his arms around me, he whispers, "I'm sorry about last night. I didn't mean what I said."

One tear escapes, lands in my coffee. His grip around me tightens.

"You're the best mother. You know that."

I hear the back door open and close. Must be time for a cigarette break. I turn to face Travis.

"Why were you with her?"

He looks confused. Rubs his hands up and down my arms. "Just now? I couldn't exactly tell her she couldn't play with her own kids ..."

I close my eyes and sigh. Look back up at him. "Last night, Travis. Last night."

I don't know what to make of his expression. Terror? More confusion? But then, as he speaks, I see it—the twitch. The tiniest tremble at the left corner of his mouth, and I know he's lying.

"It was just one cigarette. Under the circumstances—"

"You promised."

Putting one hand on his chest, I push out of his embrace.

~

I watch Travis through the kitchen window. He's in the lot beside the house, where we dug for worms only two weeks ago. Yet it feels like months have passed. His face drips with sweat, but he hammers on, finishing Brent's greenhouse. A memorial? Or penance?

What happened last night with Kelly? Will I ever know? I want to scream in his face. I want to pummel his chest until he tells me the truth—all of it, every little piece, from each and every year that I ignored it.

But then, I watch as he shows Drew how to hold the drill, patiently helping him line it up just right. How he gives Henry a high five after he carries two bags of soil, one on each shoulder.

Kathryn approaches me, hands me a sweet tea.

I go reluctantly. I go willingly. I go hoping I imagined the twitch in his lips.

~

He's surprised. Shields his eyes from the sun. Takes a long drink, then grabs my chin, holds my eyes. "I'm sorry, baby."

Tears well. I look away.

Drew and Henry squabble over something, and birds of various song surround us. Brent's grave lies a few hundred yards from us.

"I mean it. Won't happen again."

~

As I round the porch in anger and confusion, the sight of Nathan and Lauren stops me short. My knees, rubbery again, threaten to give. They sit on the wicker sofa, her head resting on his shoulder, her face slack and pale.

The sunlight feels like an affront. The sky and the mountains and the beauty are taunting us. As I get closer, Lauren raises her head. Her red-ringed eyes find mine.

She nods at Nathan and he rises, one large hand on the arm of the sofa, groaning.

"Jenna," he says as he passes, taking my hand and squeezing it.

Sitting down next to my sister, I force myself to look into her eyes, see the sorrow there.

"Oh, Jenna," she says, her voice breaking. "I miss him so much." Her crying starts anew, and I wrap my arms around her, holding her to my breast and rocking her.

The sun is sinking behind the mountains as I pace, holding Everett. Lauren is back in bed. Ava and Amanda remain sequestered downstairs. Chris came home from the woods empty-handed. The boys are cleaning up their city and track, which has Caden in tears. School is supposed to start back tomorrow. I can't remember what I had planned.

The oven timer beeps. After removing the casseroles, I wrap my shawl around myself and the baby, then step onto the back deck. As I get to the corner, I catch a glimpse of Kelly's golden hair. She's walking toward Travis, who's packing up his tools. He says something to Drew and Henry, and they nod, head back toward the house.

Once she reaches him, she holds out her cigarette pack. He shakes his head. She shrugs, lights her own, then pulls something out of her pocket. As she's taking a drink, I realize it's a flask.

She offers it to him.

Not my Travis.

He takes it from her hand.

CHAPTER FIFTY-SEVEN
KELLY

Grief is an uncomfortable guest. Strange, how absence can have such a powerful presence—at the dinner table, at night as you slip into bed. I wish Patrick had died. It'd be easier. Instead, he chose to leave me with his gaping absence. This black hole in the center of my life.

Travis dismissed me at the greenhouse. Tricked me—taking the flask from my hand and knocking one back before saying, "Cheers to that never happening again. Ever."

Handing the whiskey back, he turned and walked into the greenhouse.

Left me standing there, humiliated.

I stormed away, down the gravel path, walking blindly.

I wanted to scream, but I wouldn't give him that satisfaction. Sinking down against a tree, on the opposite side of the house from my stash, I wanted to cry but refused to. And then it occurred to me.

This isn't his first time doing this to a woman.

It can't be.

I'm prepared for dinner—full makeup, push-up bra, low-cut shirt, diamond pendant resting on my cleavage. Got a flask in my side pocket, and my Arctic cup is full. I wash down a Percocet with a quarter Xanax before stepping out my door.

Dinner is tuna casserole, except we're out of crackers. Jenna used stale cereal instead, and it's barely edible. Travis keeps complimenting her though, his arm draped along the back of her chair.

No one looks at me. It's as if I'm invisible.

Miss Amanda has planned a movie in the basement for the children's big excitement. A change of scenery is something, I guess.

Once supper is cleared and Amanda has guided the children downstairs, Chris grabs the radio and begins cranking.

"Why bother?" Travis asks, sitting in his mother's recliner. She's gone to bed, with Nathan and Kaitlyn. Jenna sits at his feet with a pillow and drapes a blanket over her shoulder and Everett as he nurses.

No one wants to sit in Brent's spot.

Chris pauses, listens. Static. Winding the handle and pacing, he asks Travis, "You hunting with me tomorrow?"

"I was thinking maybe fishing. I think the boys could use some fresh air."

Chris nods.

A voice breaks through the static. "Shelter-in-place orders issued nationwide. Federal and state shelters are overwhelmed and beyond capacity. Repeat: shelter-in-place orders issued nationwide.

"Law enforcement continues to report officers abandoning their posts. FEMA is reporting they have two weeks of supplies left for existing shelters. Repeat: only two weeks of supplies remain in many shelters across the nation. Charitable organizations are struggling with logistics with down communication. The military is seizing warehouse goods and distributing them throughout the country. This will take three to six weeks. Help is on the way. Do not lose hope.

Repeat: shelter-in-place orders issued nationwide. It is not safe to leave your homes. Board windows and doors. Riots have been reported in Albuquerque, Atlanta, Baltimore, Boston, Chicago ..."

Static.

Chris moves to the center doors, holding up the radio. Clips of syllables, nothing more.

"It's only getting worse," Jenna says softly, chewing on a fingernail.

"And more violent," Chris says.

Fuck. I'm never getting home.

The whole family retires before nine thirty. After tucking the boys in, I wander back downstairs and make a whiskey on ice, wishing I had orange zest.

Standing at the mantel, I study a picture of Travis. He stands on a small fishing boat holding a giant catfish, the muscles in his forearm bulging and a huge smile on his face. Next up, Lauren spiking a volleyball, tall and lean, towering over the other girls. Then, Chris and his sons, in matching pink polos. I roll my eyes, put the photograph down.

I meander to the foyer mirror, take a good look. I've gained some weight back. I examine myself as I turn side to side. I lost fifteen pounds after Patrick left.

Patrick. You left me, and now I'm stuck with these supremely religious assholes who think they're perfect.

I take a long swig. Pick up the cross on the foyer table. Cheap porcelain. I carry it with me.

In the family room, I grab a book off the coffee table—biblical quotes for wives.

In the kitchen, I trail my hand along the granite countertops. Stop at a cupboard, take a glass from Kathryn's juice set. They're small and blue, with white flowers etched on the sides.

At the window above the sink, I pause. Among Kathryn's succulents sits an emerald stone. Nathan likes to stand here, looking out, holding it in his palm. I slip it in my pocket.

Out on the deck, the moon is bright and nearly full, but there's two of them. I squeeze one eye shut, and the moon stills, becomes one again.

I line my prizes up on the railing. Light a cigarette. Close my eyes. Hear an owl.

There was a time, once, when you would have searched the world to find me.

Tears stream down my face as I hold the rock, toss it up once, twice. Then I reach back and launch it across the dark trees. I grab the juice glass and hurl it toward the shadow of a tall pine, and there's the sound—crashing. Breaking into pieces like everything around me.

The book is next. I hold my cigarette to its pages. When it starts to catch, I toss it into the wind and watch the glowing embers streak against the black sky.

My final offering—the porcelain representation of our mighty savior. I kiss it right in the center before flinging it like a frisbee.

I grab my whiskey, toss it back. But I'm out. Lighting another cigarette, I head for my stash. At the edge of the deck, I pause. Listen.

Did I hear something? The owl hoots again. I continue on, distrusting myself and the sounds of the night. Weaving back and forth in the darkness, I stop at the greenhouse to rub my eyes, try to clear my sight.

Fuck you, Travis. Fuck you, Patrick.

I need a little more whiskey. Just a little more, and I can blot this night out entirely.

Once I pass the raised garden beds, the ground heaves uneven beneath me. Keeping one eye closed, I head for the drop-off. When I reach the edge of the woods, I grab a tree branch and slide down to the next tree. It's almost within reach.

An explosion of breaking branches pierces the silence. A child shrieks.

"Mommy!"

More crashing, breaking.

I let go of my branch and lunge forward, falling, screaming, "Mikey!"

"Mommy!"

I land with a thud against a tree, pain slamming into my lower back and racing down my legs.

"Mikey!"

Struggling to breathe and wiping the dirt from my stinging eyes, I pant, trying to catch my breath.

"Maa," he gasps from somewhere to my left.

Scrambling over, I cling to branches and roots, my feet sliding out from under me as I keep calling, "Mikey, I'm coming, baby, I'm coming!"

He lies unmoving, stopped by a tree, as I was. I reach my hands out and feel for him in the dark. He's on his back.

When I get to his chest, he winces and grabs my wrist, sucking in his breath with a weak, rattling sound. I lay my forehead, barely, against his little chest.

"Please, God," I say.

"Mommy," he whispers.

I cradle his face in my hands, kissing his forehead. "I'm getting help, baby."

"Don't leave me, Mommy, please ..." He starts to cry but stops, gasping for breath, turning his face into my palm.

"Shh, shh." I kiss his temple. "It's okay."

Can I get him up the hill? How do I get him up the hill? Oh God.

"Mommy, please." His voice is hoarse, barely there.

"Oh, baby, I'm sorry. I'm so sorry."

And then I scream.

The forest echoes my wail. I crouch beside my son and whisper in his ear, "I'm coming back, I promise."

CHAPTER FIFTY-EIGHT
JENNA

I'm jolted from sleep. Someone is screaming—terrified.

"What now?" Travis groans as he flips the covers off. I scramble after him.

Kelly stands in the center of the great room. "Help! Help me! My baby! Help!"

Her hair is disheveled, full of leaves and twigs. She hugs her midsection as if in pain. We rush downstairs as Nathan, Jacob, and Kathryn come out of their room. Chris comes up the stairs behind us, loading a magazine into his pistol.

"Mikey! My baby! Oh God, hurry, help!" She stumbles toward the open doors, frantically waving her arms and sobbing. Travis shoves his bare feet into his boots, and he and Chris follow her down the deck and around the house. As I reach the side railing, Amanda, Kathryn, and Jacob join me.

Jacob tugs at my pajamas. "Mommy? Mommy, what's happened?"

I put my hand on his head, but I don't know what to say.

Please, God. No.

"Mommy." He tugs again.

I can't see anything beyond the greenhouse, despite the bright moon illuminating its slanted roof.

"Mommy!"

I look down and he points.

Caden stands in the doorway, clutching his parrot.

"Oh, buddy, come here," I say as I go to him, holding out my arms.

"Mommy?" He hiccups. "Mikey?"

"I don't know, baby, I don't know." The words fall from my mouth as I lift him up, hold him close. He clings to my neck.

I return to the railing, feel the rough wood against my hand as I grasp it. We wait, searching the darkness. An image comes to me, unwanted, my rainbow baby in my arms, lifeless. So small, so perfect.

Three dark figures approach, and one carries a limp body, arms and legs dangling.

My vision goes dark.

Not again, God. Not again.

~

"Jenna! Jenna!"

Arms encircle me, holding me upright.

"Jenna!"

Amanda, holding Caden, holding me.

"He's alive, Jenna." Nathan's baritone voice, deep and soothing. He's holding me too.

"Mommy?"

"She's okay, Jacob. She's okay," Amanda says, and my vision focuses.

"Mikey!" Caden cries, reaching toward the house. "Mommy!"

He's near hysterics.

"You got her?" Amanda asks.

"Go," Nathan says, and Amanda is gone.

"Where?" I ask, trying to turn and look.

"There, there now," Nathan says soothingly. "They're taking care of him. You worry about you."

I nod, tears streaming down my face.

Please, Mother Mary. I beg you.

I strain to see, twisting in Nathan's arms.

"Are you steady?" he asks, loosening his grip.

I nod. He keeps one arm around me as we turn toward the house.

They've laid Mikey on the school table. Kathryn stands over him, her stethoscope on his chest, her hand on his wrist. Kelly kneels near the fireplace, howling, clawing at her hair.

"Get her out of here!" Kathryn shouts.

I can't see Amanda and the boys. She must have taken them to the basement. Chris yanks Kelly to her feet, drags her toward the stairs.

"I can't hear him!" Kathryn barks, and Chris changes direction, takes her to the garage.

Travis stands next to the table, one arm across his chest and his hand at his mouth.

Kathryn closes her eyes. I hold my breath as I go to them.

Mikey gasps for breath, tears sliding down his cheeks.

Kathryn looks at me. "I need you."

I swallow. Travis steps out of the way. I lean down, graze Mikey's temple with my lips, whispering, "I'm here. I'm here."

Kathryn leans down, puts her hand on Mikey's forehead.

"You're going to be okay, buddy. I'm going to fix you right up," she says, then looks at Travis. "Scissors." Turning back to me, she says, "Hold his hand."

Looking into his eyes, she says, "Mikey, I'm going to ask you some questions. Don't try to talk. I want you to squeeze Jenna's hand once if the answer is yes, and twice if it's no. Got it? Once for yes, and twice for no. Can you do that?"

He squeezes my hand weakly.

I nod at Kathryn.

"Good boy. You're so brave," Kathryn says.

Travis comes back with scissors. Kathryn cuts Mikey's shirt down the center.

I gasp. Dark blue and purple blooms dot his rib cage. I sway. Travis puts his arm around me.

"Jenna, I need you," Kathryn says again.

I can do this. Mother Mary, give me strength. Breathe, Jenna, breathe.

She shines a small light in his eyes, asks him to follow it. Checks around his temple and head for bleeding or bruises. "Does your head hurt?" she asks.

Two tugs on my hand.

She feels along his arms, his hands.

"Does it hurt here, or here?"

Two more.

After checking his legs, she returns to his chest.

"This is going to hurt, Mikey. I'm sorry, but I need to feel exactly where you got injured, okay?"

He nods, tries to take a deep breath. Stops, winces.

"Squeeze Jenna's hand if it gets too much, okay?" He nods again. "You're going to be okay, sweetheart." She kisses his forehead. "You ready?"

I can't breathe.

She runs her hands along his rib cage, pressing. His face crumples, but he doesn't squeeze my hand. Then she gets to the lower right side, and he shrieks, digging his nails into my palm.

"Oh, baby." I put my mouth against his cheek. "I'm here. It's okay. I'm here."

As I straighten, Kathryn says, "I know it hurts to breathe, Mikey. I want you to take little, small breaths, as much as you can, but slowly. Slow breaths, okay?" She looks at me. "He has a broken rib, maybe two."

"Shouldn't we go to the—"

She holds up her hand. "No. We shouldn't move him right now. We wait, and we watch. With any luck, it's only his ribs."

We've turned the house upside down. The men brought one of the twin beds to the family room, where Mikey now dozes before the fire. There's a small table set up with medical supplies. Amanda and Chris took all the children to the basement for the night, even Everett. Only Kaitlyn remains upstairs, with Nathan. Kelly has been put to bed.

I hold Mikey's hand, studying his face, learning every line.

"Jenna?"

I didn't notice Travis approaching, but here he is, kneeling before me.

"Are you okay?" he asks.

What does that even mean? Death is right there in the shadows, wanting another of my boys, and you ask if I'm okay?

I dream she's standing over him, hair loose and falling around her pale face. She's whispering. Whispering. The shadows dance around her as she bends to kiss him. The spot where she kisses burns bright red, then turns into a scar, growing, running down his face, along his body, turning black.

Dark birds rush in, gather around her shoulders. Whispering, cawing, swooshing. She takes his wrist, her fingers turning into talons. Black veins appear beneath his skin where she grasps him. They begin snaking up his arm.

I wake with a start, sweat dripping down my brow.

He's here. He's here. His hand's in mine. His hand's in mine, and he's mine. And he's going to be okay. I kiss his brow, softly. In my periphery, I spot a small red glow.

Kelly stands at the railing, smoking a cigarette.

How dare she.

She left the door open, just a few inches.

I pull my hand away from Mikey's, slowly. Watch him, make sure he doesn't feel my absence.

I go straight to the woodbin, find a log that's just the right size.

I tiptoe through the door. She's crying and mumbling to herself.

One hard whack, and she topples forward, over the railing. Lands on her back with a thud and a crack as her head hits the concrete.

I'd pictured the fall carrying her farther, into the trees and their soft branches.

Holding my breath and listening, I lean over, slowly. Her face is tilted to the left, her hair splayed and filling with blood—the red so stark against the blond.

Still clutching my weapon, I tiptoe back inside, place it gently in the fire. Mikey's eyelids flutter with a dream.

When he wakes, I'll tell him it's true.

I'm his mother now.

ABOUT THE AUTHOR

Jess Renae Sherer, Detroit native, grew up in the South, where her passion for hiking, gardening, and the rich history of southern Appalachia began. She earned her bachelor's degree in sociology and cultural diversity from Kennesaw State University, as well as her master's in creative writing.

She resides in Atlanta, Georgia, with her husband, three children, two cats, one dog, and four chickens.

You can follow her on Instagram @jessrenaesherer.

www.ingramcontent.com/pod-product-compliance
Lightning Source LLC
LaVergne TN
LVHW091249110826
845146LV00002BA/589

* 9 7 9 8 9 8 8 5 8 4 2 1 6 *